MATTHEW AND THE FRONT ROOM RAILWAY

STEPHEN P JEFFRIES

Publish & Print
www.publishandprint.co.uk

Book cover design: Martin Peart

Published by www.publishandprint.co.uk

To Nick, Charlie and Pearl

CHAPTER 1

WHERE IT ALL BEGAN

Matthew was a good student, he worked hard and achieved good grades but were you to ask him if he enjoyed school, he would probably say it was just ok. He was a tall boy at five feet seven inches by the time he was fourteen and with an athletic appearance, always wearing his blond hair cut short, what he really enjoyed was taking the school bus to his grandfather Alfred's. Whilst both Wendy and Lans, his parents worked, Alfred would look after his grandson until they collected him on their way home from work.

Matthew cherished these two or three hours every day which he would spend at the large oak kitchen table with one of Alfred's albums spread out before them. Alfred had spent more than forty years working for British Rail and for thirty of those years had worked on passenger trains. He had inherited an early Kodak camera from his father, doubtless another find from one of the east end markets he visited and he took it on every journey, taking pictures of rural stations, pastoral scenes and the towns and villages that lined the routes he travelled, as well as page after page of engines and rolling stock. All these found their way into the numerous albums, which he stored in the kitchen dresser, every photograph with a note of where and when it was taken and every album with the year neatly stencilled on the cover. Matthew recalled being struck by one early black and white photograph of an unusual looking man. Unusual in that he had no hair at all, no hair on his head and no eyebrows but with a grin that spread from ear to ear. His grandfather had seen Mathew's curious gaze when he spotted this picture and told him he was looking at the greatest locomotive engineer who had ever lived, one Yuri Ivanov. He also remembered his mother telling him that the time his grandfather spent with him, after school and telling him stories, was the only time he spent away from his front room railway. And ask as he may, neither his mother nor his grandfather would tell him anything about this railway.

Alfred Giles Munro had a hard and somewhat poverty stricken upbringing but despite that it was a happy childhood. He had been born in 1934 and lived his formative years at 34 Woodland Cottages in Camberwell, south London. It was a two bed terraced house where the front door opened on to the street and the back garden was five paces wide and ten paces long. He was the second of three Munro children, Stanley being the first by four years and Laura his junior by two. Despite his relative poverty, like his father Louis, he was always immaculately turned out, whether at work or home.

Matthew had learned little of the intimate details of people's lives during the Second World War but he could see that his grandpa's eyes became moist as he recounted his experiences during those torrid times. Alfred and his younger sister were parted for the first time when she was barely three years old, when the boys were evacuated and he lost his brother, just turned twenty, to a freak work placed accident when a girder on an overhead gantry fell on him and he was mortally injured. On 1st September 1939, Germany's aggression in Europe finally culminated in England announcing it was at war. A few weeks later Louis received his call up papers and was given forty-eight hours' notice to report. He wrote long letters whilst overseas to his wife Daphne and revealed a heart, more filled with love than she had known and it made her cry as she read and re-read his letters. He also wrote with pride that he was fighting under Field Marshall Montgomery and in Egypt, a country neither of them had known anything about but which was brought to life in his letters.

On 5th October 1939 the boys were evacuated, they had dressed in their school uniforms, Alfred had never worn his at school yet and they took a bus ride to Liverpool Street Station, their departure point. Laura was considered too young and stayed with her mother. The station was seething with hundreds of children, all with little suitcases and a government issued gas mask, on which was attached a label identifying the child and their school. Behind a barrier stood all the mothers, weeping as their children boarded their allotted carriages. Whilst it was expected they would be away for a year or less, lull's in the war were just that and all told they spent three years at Biggleswade farm, two miles south of Halstead in Essex. The boys had fond memories of their time on the farm where they were well fed and cared for. Alfred picked up a variety of farming skills that would serve him well in future years.

One day in the autumn of 1941 lived on in the boy's memories. Their mother and Laura had moved in with her sister, near Felixstowe on the east coast, an area deemed safer than London. They took the train, one rainy Sunday morning, to where the boys were staying. Alfred and his brother were overjoyed at seeing their mother and sister but quickly saw from the look on Daphne's face that she was going to give them bad news. She sat the boys down and broke the news that their father had been mortally injured in Egypt. They begged to go home with their mother but it was not to be, several houses, just three streets away had been bombed and that was why she and Laura had left London.

Matthew was deeply saddened to see his grandpa so visibly upset. He told the boy it was important he should learn about his family but the tears in the old man's eyes, showed how the loss of so many loved ones had scarred him deeply. It was either his father or mother who collected him and following a session with his grandpa, he would question his parents about their experiences or memories of their childhood.

From a young age Alfred had taken a liking to all things mechanical at school and when his time came to leave and find a job he settled on British Railways, soon to be called British Rail. Following a year of making tea and sweeping floors, his keen interest in the workings of steam and diesel locomotive engines was noticed and he was promoted. As an Express Maintenance Assistant, he relocated to a works besides Kings Cross Station wherein stood four gleaming locomotives on turntables, feverishly attended to by a team of engineers, cleaning, maintaining and ensuring they were in perfect running order. These engines were known as Principle Express Trains and reserved for transporting foreign dignitaries, members of the Royal family and high-ranking government officials, as well as for special occasions. It was here that Alfred first met Yuri Ivanov and they joined the same team allocated to one of the engines.

From their first meeting, Yuri and Alfred became firm friends and he learned more of his fascinating and somewhat mysterious past. He was born within walking distance of

Moscow Yaroslavsky train station, where the famous Trans-Siberian Railway begins a more than five thousand miles journey, terminating in Vladivostok in the far east of the country. He came from a large family with four brothers and three sisters and his father before him had spent a lifetime working on the railways. He was of an indeterminable age but Alfred discovered he was at least sixty but looked forty and was reputed to be the best locomotive engineer the company employed.

His mother was always impressed at Alfred's rapid rise through the ranks and equally appreciative at the swelling pay packets he brought home. With money to spare Alfred decided to learn to drive and on passing his test, learned all he could about the Ford Anglia. Whilst his mother knew of his desire to buy a car, months had passed and she had thought no more of it. One Saturday morning in July, Alfred walked into the kitchen with a beaming smile on his face and led his mother to the street. Here he presented his sky blue 1948 Ford Anglia, although four years old, apart from a little rust along the chrome side strip, which Alfred would repair within the next few days, the car looked immaculate. His mother was suitably impressed and they took a ride around the neighbourhood.

Change happened quickly at work for Alfred, as a post war boom had caused demand to escalate from a growing peacetime population wanting to travel. From the maintenance of static locomotives, Alfred moved rapidly upwards, first as an assistant guard on freight trains but then as a guard and conductor on passenger trains. By now his pay allowed him to consider the idea of moving home and he spoke to his mother about the prospect. Living in south London had not been kind to his mother's health, often suffering respiratory problems. In common with many, he realized that he could buy a nicer home for less money, in a healthier location, away from the city.

They travelled around the Home counties, looking at satellite towns and finally settled on a beautiful, nineteenth century house called The Spinney in Patchets Lane, Whiteash Green, less than three miles west of Halstead and not far from Biggleswade farm. Once the farmhouse for a sprawling dairy farm, the business had failed and the land sold off, however, The Spinney remained standing in the middle of an acre plot. It had four bedrooms, a large kitchen and scullery, a separate lounge and dining room with a small study attached. The views from front and rear, were over the Essex countryside and when he drove his mother there for a viewing, she was immediately smitten. A Virginia creeper had taken over the entire front of the property, even covering part of the downstairs windows but Alfred relished the opportunity of spending time in the garden, tending to the neglected plants.

7

This was where Matthew now sat gripped, as he was every weekday evening, as his grandfather recounted the tales of his interesting life. With all the changes that Alfred had made in his life, he never lost contact with Yuri. As the years passed he learned more of the man's past from his secretive and difficult journey from his Russian home to the UK. One memorable day when Alfred had just arrived from a day-long trip on the Bournemouth Bell to the south coast, Yuri appeared on the platform. Alfred climbed down from the cab and they greeted each other warmly, as good friends are prone to do and after catching up, Yuri turned serious and asked Alfred to come with him to his home. Now Alfred had been friends with Yuri for several years and whilst Yuri had been home with Alfred many times and even joined the family for their Sunday lunch, he had never been to Yuri's home. They took the short bus ride to his home in Shepherds Bush and on the way Yuri explained that he had some valuable possessions that had been entrusted to him long ago but that he had been reticent to allow anybody to know about. However, as he went on to tell Alfred, he had noticed in his young friend a kindred spirit, somebody who not only possessed an ability to know and love trains but somebody who he could trust and rely upon. Alfred was decidedly curious at the things Yuri was saying but decided to keep quiet until he saw where the conversation was leading.

They arrived at a neat looking semi-detached house, just off the High Road. Yuri lead Alfred up the front steps and into his sparsely furnished but clean home. It was dark, as the curtains were drawn and Yuri switched on some lights, rather than open the curtains. He invited Alfred into his sitting room, at the rear of the house, which overlooked a small and unkempt garden. He offered his guest vodka, which was declined and Yuri busied himself fixing a drink. Meanwhile, Alfred looked around the room, a large, highly polished brass samovar stood on a small carved wooden table, elsewhere there were ornately embroidered throws casually draped over the furniture and the walls were covered with numerous prints and sepia photographs. He was drawn to a large framed photograph above the mantelpiece, like the others it was in fading sepia but he could distinguish what looked like a younger Yuri who was standing next to a miniature railway engine. What stood out in the picture was an older man standing with him, who had a striking resemblance to his friend. The Russian returned with his drink and stood next to Alfred looking at the picture. He told him that it was indeed of him as a younger man and his father, who was nearly a hundred when that photograph was taken. His father had died not long after but not before entrusting Yuri with the miniature engine in the photograph, which had been in his possession his entire life. All Yuri knew of the origin of the engine, was that it was presented to Czar Alexander the second, during the latter half of the nineteenth century. He knew this as his father had shown him an early photograph of the Czar with the engine. Yuri added that in that photograph, was another man, smaller than Yuri's father with a magnificent coiffured white moustache, waxed and twisted at the ends and which pointed to the ground. He was dressed in the garb of a Cossack, a wide sleeved shirt tied at the waist with a sash, billowing trousers tucked into leather boots and what could be an animal pelt, circular hat. He never learned who the Cossack was but suspected he may have been the original owner of the engine. His father did not tell him how this item had come into his possession, only that he had been hounded all his life by sinister people wanting to find this unique and priceless piece.

Matthew could hardly contain himself, bursting as he was with questions and a burning desire to see his grandfather's railway. He had known, from his mother, that his grandfather had spent decades locked away in his front room, 'playing' his grandmother had said, with his trains but Matthew was about to learn that grandpa's train was no mere child's toy. Yuri had told Alfred how a photograph of the Czar his father had shown him had disappeared and so did the Cossack and Yuri's father but not before packing Yuri onto a train with a solid wooden chest, secured with metal straps and padlocks, containing the miniature engine. At the time of the engine's disappearance, it was rumoured that the Czar was franticly searching for anybody who had knowledge of the whereabouts of it or anybody connected with its disappearance. Their fate was a foregone conclusion. The hunt had continued through the many decades that followed but Yuri's escape from Russia was planned with masterly cunning. With the assassination of the Czar the hunt for the engine had died down. He assured Alfred that in the more than half a century that the engine had been in his father's possession and then his, they had never been troubled by any suspicious enquiries but he took no chances and this was the first time he had told anybody this strange yarn. He did so, he said, as he was aging and with no heirs, he was determined to find a good and trustworthy home for it and he hoped that Alfred would provide that home. Alfred was both overwhelmed and more than a little mystified by Yuri's tale but kept his probing questions to himself until he had seen the engine. Yuri finished his drink and led Alfred to a small door, under the stairs. He opened the door and switched a light on and Alfred could see a narrow wooden staircase going steeply down into the basement. He ducked his head and made his way tentatively behind Yuri, down the creaking stairs. Once at the bottom Yuri switched on a bright overhead lamp, which illuminated an amazing model locomotive sitting on a track that ran around the perimeter of the basement. It was amazing because to Alfred's trained eye what confronted him was less a model and more a miniature of a life size engine. What Alfred could not fathom, was that whilst this was a wonderful piece of engineering, was it really worth all the death and intrigue that Yuri had attached to it. When he told Yuri of his thoughts, Yuri said he would very shortly show him what had been worth so much pain, caused by the engine that stood passively on the tracks before them.

In a serious tone, Alfred told his grandson that in time he too would learn the mysteries of the train but that time had not yet arrived and he must be patient. However, patience is not an easily accepted concept, especially by an excited fourteen year old. Alfred always deftly steered Matthew away from too many probing questions by changing the subject. As he turned a page of the large album on the table before them, they were looking at a photograph of the Elizabethan, British Rail's most prestigious train at that time. Alfred's, career took another leap forward when he was selected to work on the Elizabethan which was the first non-stop, London to Edinburgh locomotive passenger train to make the journey in six and a half hours.

Alfred spent many happy hours wandering through the Museum of Edinburgh that featured a history of the railway through the ages and it was here he met his future wife. On that memorable occasion, Cynthia De Beauvoir, as a schoolteacher, was escorting a number of children around the museum. After engaging her in conversation, he arranged to meet her and her charges, on the return trip to London. By the time the train was reaching the outskirts of the capital, Alfred had learned that Cynthia's parents had moved from France to the UK many years ago and that she was born in Barts Hospital, close to where the family home was, in Islington.

Since then, her parents had returned to France to take over the family wine business. Whist the environment had been her first love, remunerative work in that field was in short supply and she had diverted into teaching English at a French school in London. Their instant fondness for each other led to some serious dating and finally an introduction to his mother where she gained hearty approval.

Following a six-month courtship Alfred proposed and they were duly married at the Holy Trinity Church in town, a mid-19th century Gothic Revival church, complete with spire and an abundance of stained glass. Most of the village was in attendance and the local choir put on a sterling performance. They moved in to The Spinney, delaying their honeymoon for later in the year. After Cynthia spoke to her parents, they decided that their honeymoon would be a stay at the family home in Bordeaux. Her parents had not been able to come to the wedding as Cynthia's father had suffered a minor heart attack and was told not to travel. The newlyweds decided that as they both loved everything about The Spinney, they could quite happily live there. Alfred had no concerns about his wife and mother-in-law living under the same roof, as the two had bonded from their first meeting.

Alfred had desperately wanted his oldest friend Yuri to join them in celebrating their marriage and he had looked for him at the yard to deliver a personal invitation. Being busy courting, when he finally sought his friend, he was both dismayed and shocked to learn that he had left the company. Yuri had resisted installing a telephone and Alfred, in seeking his friend, was forced to visit his home. The mystery deepened when he arrived on his doorstep he discovered that a new owner had taken possession of the property. The young woman who opened the door informed him that she had bought the house through an agent and never knew or met the previous owner.

Through the selling agents, Alfred tracked the conveyancing solicitors Everard, Simpson & Partners, to the third floor of an old office block in Holloway. On arriving at their offices Mr. Everard invited him into his office, which was filled with files, spilling from his desk onto the floor and stacked on all but one of five chairs. To Alfred it appeared like something out of the pages of a Dickens novel. He was offered tea and sat and waited whilst Mr. Everard ferreted around his files, looking for something. His tea arrived with a plate on which sat two plain digestive biscuits. Finally, Mr. Everard opened a filing cabinet drawer, extracted a buff folder and withdrew an envelope which he handed to Alfred. On the front were written the words, 'Private and Confidential for the Strict Attention of Alfred Munro ONLY'. He thanked Mr. Everard but waited until reaching his home and sitting in his armchair by the back window before he opened the letter from his friend. Yuri wrote that he was truly sorry he had not been able to say goodbye nor join him in celebrating is marriage but the time had come for him to leave. Their friendship had meant so much to Yuri but he was very tired and was sure the nature of his departure would become known to his friend. It was a mysterious letter and the last time Alfred was ever to hear from his old friend.

The household arrangements suited all concerned; as Cynthia had continued to work in London she could not have been happier than to have a home cooked meal awaiting her when she returned from work. And whilst Alfred did not spend more than a few nights away in the course of a year, he was pleased that his wife had company when he was away. The living arrangements proved even more advantageous when within a few months of being married, Cynthia announced she was pregnant. With little pomp or fanfare, Wendy Delores Munro, Matthew's mother, screamed her arrival on a wet April afternoon. On this occasion Cynthia's parents were in good enough health to make the trip and were at her bedside when the baby arrived, together with Daphne, at the University College Hospital.

As has happened occasionally, his grandfather would recount stories of his early years rather than leafing through albums from his railway days and this was such an occasion. He told Matthew of his courtship and early married years past the birth of his mother and her childhood. Matthew was duly collected by his mother and the old man sat alone and reminisced of his first encounter with his old friend. He recalled his first ride and the moment Yuri had directed him to the couch, which was along one wall of the basement, behind an operating console. He had switched off the basement lights and only a dim glow remained from the console.

His friend had sat next to him and told him not to be concerned, which of course did the exact opposite and Alfred wondered what was about to happen that he should not be concerned about. He was assured no harm would come to him, in fact, quite the opposite. He was instructed to close his eyes,

16

relax and listen for some pleasant sounds. Sure enough he presently heard the faint sound of beautiful harmonic vibes. The sound grew louder, together with changing tones. He then perceived what at first he thought was a slow drum beat but which was in fact the sound of an engine. This sound so startled Alfred with its reality that he was forced to open his eyes, which he immediately closed again. His brain told him that what he had seen in that fleeting moment was impossible but his sight, hearing and sense of smell told him otherwise. He slowly opened his eyes again and drew a deep breath. He felt his heart pounding in his chest and fought against the urge to panic. Before him was not a miniature engine but a full size one, roaring with life and with white smoke billowing from its chimney.

Yuri was nowhere to be seen and Alfred was no longer sitting in an armchair but on a wooden bench on a railway platform. He remained seated, thinking that if he stood he would be as likely as not to fall over. His knuckles turned white as he gripped the sides of the bench and he slowly looked around attempting to make sense of a scene that made no sense at all. Yuri suddenly appeared from the cab window of the locomotive and casually beckoned Alfred to join him. He slowly walked towards the engine, still giddy with the experience and gripped a rail as he climbed aboard, at which point Yuri proceeded to answer Alfred's hitherto unasked questions, all but one – how could this be possible? To that question Yuri simply offered that it was not something possible within our realm of thinking. This hardly satisfied Alfred's practical and logical thought process but of course, what he was experiencing did not fit into any practical or logical category. Yuri grabbed what Alfred knew was the whistle handle and a shrill blast was followed by the now familiar sound of the engine's pistons, driving the wheel arms and the wheels beginning to turn over the track. Whatever Alfred was feeling at this moment, his only recollection was of an adrenaline rush of pure excitement. As the engine began to gather pace, heading towards a forest of giant pine trees, Yuri began to unpack the mysteries of the railway. The truth was that Yuri had no idea what hidden powers were at work only that it was not malignant and would appear to those whose thoughts were in harmony with the engine. The origin of the engine and who built it was the subject of wild speculation, of little doubt was that highly advanced minds had combined to build it but that malign forces had been harnessed to find and possess it. Since Yuri had become the keeper there had been no sign of unwanted or prying eyes. Certainly, Yuri said with a smile, people thought him strange, even rather odd but put that down to his Russian heritage and age. He went to great lengths to ensure Alfred knew exactly what care and protection the engine needed. As Yuri talked on, Alfred paid careful attention but he could not help but be fascinated by the sights and sounds of the passing landscape and changing vistas. They had entered a forest, where clouds of the locomotive white smoke rose up through the pine covered branches above and the whistle echoed as Yuri tugged the leaver. As they left the forest, there now appeared before them a breath-taking range of mountains and Alfred could see the track ahead, snaking in endless curves and switchbacks, as it rose towards a high pass and disappeared out of sight.

Alfred learned that Yuri had spent many, many years imagining and designing the landscape they now travelled across. The unfathomable, supernatural and mystical powers of the railway transformed those designs and imaginings into the reality they were now experiencing. As they travelled on, each new scene evoked another story from Yuri, how he built this village or that farm; how he had searched high and low for just the right type of tree or the right kind of church. Thoughts raced through Alfred's head at a hundred miles per hour, each thought only served to confuse him more, until he reached a point at which he considered, for the sake of his sanity, to just let the whole experience wash over him. They had pulled into a siding and stopped, Yuri beckoned Alfred to climb down and follow him. The siding had a line of tall trees close to the rail lines and Yuri picked a path that led through the trees. A gravel lane on the other side ran down hill to a small hamlet of no more than six or seven buildings. As they neared, Alfred could determine that one of the buildings that had a gently swaying sign affixed above the door was an inn. Yuri was obviously familiar with the place and entered the low doorway, which Alfred had to duck in order to pass through. Yuri was greeted by a barman as a regular and introduced Alfred as a visitor and friend.

One could not help but be affected by the warm welcome; there was a roaring fire on one side and the bar along another. Four men sat at a table playing some sort of card game and each looked as though they belonged on the land, all unshaven and dressed in rural garb of baggy shirts covered by grubby dungarees. Each had a tankard that a young man continuously refilled from a large jug and raucous laughter could be heard as one finished telling a yarn. Yuri began a conversation with the barman, a ruddy faced man who looked as though he enjoyed sampling his own stock. Alfred was not asked what drink he wanted but shortly two glasses of ale were put in front of them. Yuri explained that this was Old Shire, the traditional ale of the area, mainly due to the fact that the hops and barley needed for the brew, were grown all around the area and brewed not far from where they stood, all providing work for many of the local inhabitants.

Their pleasant stop lasted for less than an hour, after which their journey continued. They climbed higher and higher, around the switch backs Alfred had seen from a distant. He breathed in the cold air of the altitude and was light headed and invigorated, laughing and patting his friend on the back, in appreciation at the experience. The engine laboured to reach the peak where Alfred was mesmerized by the breath taking beauty of the scenery, the ground was white with frost and the trees were covered with a light dusting of snow. Alfred turned to Yuri and smiled at the pure joy of the scenery, the juxtaposition of the bright blue sky and the white-topped mountains was like something from his own imagination. The slow journey down from the peak was no less exhilarating and Yuri appeared to share Alfred's pleasure at the experience. The stop at the inn was the only stop they made and Alfred's thoughts began to centre on the question of the return. As if to sense what he was thinking, Yuri explained that they must return to the exact same spot where the journey began, or a return could not be made. Once they had arrived close to the correct location Yuri shut the engine off and from a nearby wooden cabin a man appeared, he was tanned and wore a long Hillbilly beard and the uniform of a railway employee. He ambled over to meet Yuri and they shook hands, after exchanging a few words, he boarded the train and as Yuri and Alfred walked along the platform, the engine could be heard building up power before moving off down the line. The two friends sat alone on the platform and in the waning sunlight, closed their eyes.

Soon enough, Alfred felt the soft cushion of the couch and on opening his eyes he saw the miniature engine in front of him and Yuri sitting next to him. Yuri smiled reassuringly and beckoned Alfred to follow him upstairs. As they sat to talk over what had just happened, Alfred became aware of the long time they had been away and looked down at his watch, thinking that it must now be the middle of the night but to his utter amazement only a matter of minutes had passed since he arrived. Seeing his confused look, Yuri explained that when travelling in the alternate reality of the railway, time was meaningless. You could spend a week on the railway and return just moments after arriving. They sat and chatted for some time and Alfred was given more vital information concerning the maintenance and care of this priceless piece of machinery.

He had lost track of the time and a worried mother voiced her concern when he finally arrived home at after ten. He was soon in bed and fast asleep, where his dreams were an assortment of being wide awake in a wonderful alternate reality and of dreaming of embarking on a magical adventure.

He decided that now was not the time to tell his young grandson the whole story as he would be compelled to tell anyone and everyone, not that he would be believed. The truth was, Yuri had created such an impact when warning Alfred about the need for secrecy that he had not told his own wife the full story. He realized that Matthew, like any boy of his age, was inquisitive, plus the whole family knew of Alfred's obsession with his railway. He also knew he would have a problem keeping the secret of his railway a secret from his grandson for much longer. For the time being, Matthew could see that no matter how he implored, he would not learn more until his grandpa was ready to tell him. Some days, Matthew's stop offs at The Spinney turned into a sleep over. The phone would ring and it was either his mother or father saying they were working late or going out for dinner. Matthew was always pleased when this happened, although he loved his mum and dad dearly, so that he could hear more of grandfather's stories.

His mother had lived all her life in Whiteash Green, attending Halstead high school for girls and taking the first local job she found when leaving school at sixteen. She had started on menial tasks in the head office of a large electronics company and over the years had graduated to a managerial position. In her mid- twenties she decided it was high time she saw something more of the world than Halstead. Having lived with her parents all her working life, Wendy had saved a tidy sum and bought herself a yellow Volkswagen Beetle and decided to drive across Scandinavia.

After driving from west to east Denmark, she caught the ferry to Malmo but careless deckhands had not secured her car correctly and in transit it had moved, colliding with two other vehicles. The ferry company accepted liability and would cover the cost of the repair of the cars, which would take a couple of days and the hotel accommodation. The arrangements were taken care of very professionally by the handsome and debonair Lans Henrick, the on-board ferry manager. Wendy was instantly smitten and during her brief stay, which happily extended, she was shown the sights of the city and treated to the delights of Swedish cuisine. He had told her that after fifteen years of service, he was about to lose his job. Over several years both a tunnel and bridge from Nordhavn to Malmo had reduced ferry traffic across the Sound, to below a profitable level and at the end of the current season the ferry line would close.

With plenty of prior warning Lans had sought a position with one of the world's largest ferry lines and with his track record and CV, all he needed to do was decide where to be based. He told her with a questioning look that the company had offices the UK. She had teased him by saying that he should just go and work wherever he wanted but added, she would not be unhappy if he chose England.

CHAPTER 2

THE EARLY YEARS

They had named their daughter Wendy, for no other reason than they liked the name. She was a perfectly contented child and rarely cried. Cynthia gave up her teaching job in London to be nearer home to spend more time with her daughter and of course, having Daphne living with them was a great help in those early years.

Whilst flicking though a copy of Country Life magazine, her attention had been drawn to an article about a billionaire industrialist, named David Longcroft, who had purchased Pickford Manor, a nearby 18th century stately home. Mr. Longcroft had announced his serious intention to return this eighteen bed roomed, dilapidated Mansion and extensive grounds, to its previous splendour. It was his plan to reopen Pickford Manor as a conference centre with residential facilities plus as a venue for weddings and other social occasions.

What particularly caught Cynthia's eye was the item detailing the recruitment of range of people, from builders, carpenters, plumbers, plasterers to security consultants and landscape gardeners plus somebody to initiate an environmental impact study, who could liaise with the local planning authorities. The job would include reforestation of the small wood on the estate, demolishing some run down out-buildings as well as rebuilding them, plus landscaping the gardens and the possible introduction of livestock. On impulse, Cynthia had called the number at the end of the article and by the end of the week she had met with David Longcroft and depending on receipt of positive references, her appointment as the Environmental Manager of the project was confirmed.

As Cynthia devoted her time to work and child rearing, Alfred's work on his railway was nearing completion. Yuri had passed over the engine and Cynthia had accepted Alfred's passion for all things connected to trains and passed off his fascination with a miniature train as an extension to that passion. Daphne was showing signs of tiredness, which Alfred put down to her active lifestyle but sadly that was not the case and following a particularly bad spell of breathing difficulties, she was persuaded to visit the doctor. She was subsequently diagnosed with bacterial pneumonia, which they were reluctant to pronounce as fatal but warned it was advanced and serious. Initially she was prescribed some strong antibiotics and told to drink a lot of fluids. After four weeks of this, his mother developed a bad cough and Alfred drove her to the hospital where he was told she would be admitted for observation.

27

Daphne was released in time for Wendy's forth birthday but sadly passed away before her fifth. Alfred was distraught at his mother's passing and following months of him grieving at the loss, Cynthia persuaded him to take some of his accumulated holiday. She suggested that the three of them should go to the seaside for a week and this they did, renting an apartment on the sea front at Walton-on-the-Naze. It was the tonic Alfred needed and life returned to normal.

As the years passed, Wendy achieved high grades as she moved from the junior to senior school and left with a bright future ahead.

The renovation and refurbishment of Pickford manor was complete and the dry opening was a great success, with many column inches in the regional press, praising what had been achieved. All in all, life was good for the Munros, Alfred continued to love his job and was forever adding to his front room railway. He had built a mountain range and planted a forest, installed a lake, plus a dairy farm and a small town, complete with stores and a tavern, as well as liberally spreading around people and animals. And around the whole landscape a railway line was laid.

Wendy had curtailed her holiday and returned to the UK to wait Lans's reposting. His new employer had an office at the international port at Harwich and Wendy found a job one floor above him as personal assistant to the Passenger Services Director. Her parents were delighted on meeting Lans and her father was instantly pulling the man aside to learn more about his years in the ferry business and for his part, Lans was equally as interested to learn about her father's years with the railway. They were both happy in their new jobs and in the following year he proposed. Cynthia spoke to David Longcroft and arranged the wedding at Pickford Manor, which was the perfect venue and preparations were made to invite family and friends, with the overseas contingent being able to stay in the main house. They choose a May wedding and the weather, whilst bright was chilly was too cold and pre-dinner drinks in the garden were abandoned. The hundred plus guests fitted comfortably into the smaller of the two large dining rooms and those attending said it felt more like a royal wedding.

When the time came for the couple to find a home, Lans was more than happy to live in the countryside near his work and for Wendy to be near her parents. Seven miles east of Whiteash Green was the village of Shirebridge and on a prior drive through to visit her parents, they had stopped at the village pub for a drink. Parking was an issue and they ended up finding a narrow gravel road near to the pub, which led down to the banks of the river Colne. There they noticed an old timber-framed house, which had been boarded up.

Now they were looking for a home they remembered what a lovely village Shirebridge was, close to the river and geographically in the area where they were happy to live. They returned to the boarded up house but saw no agent's signs or any indication that the property may have been for sale. Calling at a neighbour's house, they learned that the elderly woman, Anne Postlethwaite, who had lived there for decades, had passed away. She had a son who lived in Canada and about whom Anne had boasted, was a member of the Royal Canadian Mounted Police, living in Toronto. Wendy reasoned that there would not be too many members of the mounted police named Postlethwaite from England and living in Toronto. Back in the office, she placed a call to Toronto and before long had tracked down Sergeant Allen Postlethwaite. He told Wendy he had been wrestling with the problem of dealing with his deceased mother's estate from some three and half thousand miles away and was more than happy to proceed with a sale to her and her husband. He passed on the name and contact details of a company of solicitors who were dealing the matter and said they should make an offer through that office. They subsequently agreed a price and contracts were drawn up and exchanged. The next few months were a busy time for the Hendriks, both settling in to new jobs and once they had completed the purchase of their new home, beginning the work to achieve the desired look and feel. There was much work to be done with many minor jobs such as cracked window panes, a broken back door, a several broken floor boards and more seriously, the need to find a roofing contractor to look at the broken tiles on the roof and check the gutters. A new kitchen and bathroom were also of necessity and they agreed to extend their tenancy in rented accommodation until their new home was habitable. As if that was not enough to deal with, what Wendy thought was the stress of their frenetic lifestyle, turned out to be a pregnancy. The couple agreed that they were not averse to learning the gender of their baby and were told it was a boy. Lans was overjoyed at the thought of becoming a father and doubly so because it was a boy and it was all he could do to stop his parents coming to the UK to support or as Wendy suggested, to smother her with attention. After running through a number of options for boy's names, they settled on Matthew, happy in the knowledge that if it were abbreviated, then Matt was acceptable. This news engendered their renovation work with a greater sense of urgency but Lans was unfazed and felt sure all would be completed in plenty of time.

Wendy considered working up to her thirty eighth or thirty ninth week but by week thirty-five she was feeing both nauseous and hormonal. Her line manager was very sympathetic, having had her first child within the previous year

31

and urged Wendy to begin her maternity leave without waiting any longer. They had both put a great deal of effort to getting their new home ready and apart from some minor hitches in the arrival of a bed to sleep on, the project was completed in good time. As her pregnancy progressed there was little that Wendy could do and she co-opted her father to lend a hand with the finishing touches, such as decorations and gardening tasks. He was more than happy to lend a hand and they were pleasantly surprised by his rendition of a steam train, painted in watercolours on a wall in Matthew's bedroom. They had left the walls painted rather than papered, thinking that their son would doubtless try his hand with drawing on the walls, not thinking it would be his grandfather who would be first.

Alfred was the doting grandfather from the start, whilst never one to be bored, he was constantly busy with his railway and his garden but still, his first grandchild and a grandson, would take over a large part of his life. Once Matthew attended his junior school at five, he could not wait to visit his grandpa to help him in the garden or to look at his wonderful picture albums and hear his stories about life on the railways.

Cynthia's time at the Manor was drawing to a close and she told David that after so many years she would like to retire. He asked her to stay on to oversee the redecorations he had planned for the bedroom suites and she agreed. He had acquired several old tapestries that he wanted hung in the rooms but they required some repair work. Cynthia was on a tour of inspection and entered the Baronial Suite on the second floor and was taken aback by the sight of a young girl, perhaps five or six years old, with tightly cropped hair and dressed in a traditional African dashiki, brightly coloured in red, yellow and green and with multiple gold and beaded bracelets which jangled on her writs as she extended her hand and introduced herself, in perfect English, as Benesha. Almost immediately, from under a huge tapestry that covered a large area of the empty floor, emerged what would appear to be the young girl's mother. She was dressed in similar garb, a loose fitting multi coloured top but with a nod to western influence, a pair of denim jeans. Whilst her bright eyes and pearly white teeth would attract attention, so would two unfortunate scars that ran down either cheek. It took a few moments for Cynthia to gather her composure and to inquire who the young woman was and what she was doing. Kanika Mabweni introduced herself and Cynthia immediately detected a French accent but knew it certainly was not from France. It transpired that Kanika had been sent by a specialist restoration company to work on Mr. Longcroft's art works and tapestries. Kanika told Cynthia she was from Kinshasa where she had fled with a six week old baby, some seven years ago, when youth gangs began terrorising the city but she had not escaped without being attacked, hence the scars. A United Nations aid agency had arranged for her safe passage to the Netherlands and put her in touch with the Congolese community, in Amsterdam. After a two-year stay, where she learned the basics in restoration work on rugs and tapestries, she decided to move to the UK to seek better opportunities and initiated the long and winding road to gain entry to the country. Through a junior position working with experts at an auction house, repairing damaged tapestries and picture frames, she became adept at the work and the old craftsmen and women around her were more than willing to pass on their skills. She passed through several auction houses and antique businesses, arriving at Hargreaves and Goodman, a most reputable purveyor of quality, restored artworks. One of their long-time clients, Mr. David Longcroft, had approached them to discuss a major venture he was involved with that would require their very special skill set. Kanika had rented a small cottage just on the edge of the estate but struggled to survive, sending a large part of her earnings back home to support her ailing mother. When her spell at the Manor ended, Kanika was reluctant to return to London. She had fallen in love with living in the English countryside and had resigned from Hargreaves and Goodman. With Cynthia's help, she had approached David with a proposition to open a small gallery in

Halstead which in addition to selling artworks also provided a restoration service. Cynthia offered to invest in the venture and that together with David's favourable impression of her work at Pickford Manor, gave him confidence to also invest and that sealed the deal. A retail unit was located and with minimal work on both the interior and exterior, Thou Art could open for business. The upper two floors contained a small apartment, which was ideal for living accommodation for Kanika and her daughter. Kanika decided that if finances permitted, she would learn to drive and purchase a small car as her business and a growing daughter, needed the mobility.

Cynthia thought of Kanika and her daughter often and told Matthew of them. She suggested that Benesha was probably attending the same school and would not know anybody, perhaps he could befriend her.

In hindsight Matthew often found himself pondering what force of nature had brought him and Benesha together, both to be mesmerized by the total and wonderful other otherworldliness of the front room railway.

Alfred retired on his sixty fifth birthday by which time Matthew was twelve years old. He had seen most of his grandfather's albums, which initially covered engines, tracks, signals and rolling stock but latterly and far more interestingly, covered the places he had visited on passenger trains. These pictures included the flora and fauna of the English countryside, as well as many rural stations, which in bygone years had been tended and cared for by station masters, as if it were their own homes and gardens. Competitions were held to find the best kept stations and platforms and those with the best floral displays or the most comfortable waiting rooms.

After much nagging about Yuri, his grandfather relented and told how he had first met the Russian and how they had become firm friends.

Within the first year, Wendy and Lans had turned a rather run down period house into a beautiful family home. Whilst Lans had attended to the exterior, Wendy turned her hand to decorating the interior walls with artworks and putting up shelves on which she stood figurines and ceramics. They had a large shed installed in the back garden and it did not take long for it to become crammed with, a barbecue, deck chairs, two bicycles, a lawn mower and the latest addition, an inflatable dingy. Living so close to the river, Lans thought it would be fun to spend time travelling up and down the water way. He had purchased a small outboard motor but for Matthew, a small pair of oars would be more suitable. Matthew was not yet old enough to take charge of an outboard motor and so his father tied a long rope to a tree on the bank and attached the other end to the dingy. In that way Matthew could row the dingy, as far as fifty yards, in either direction, before the rope would prevent him going further.

Matthew did discover that Benesha and he attended the same school and he introduced himself. They quickly became good friends and he told her he would be happy for her to call him Matt and she replied, in that case, he could call her Ben. Whilst in different classes, they would meet up at break times and sometimes sit under the large oak tree on the edge of the playing field and share their snacks. Ben had told Matt that she became bored after school when she would be dropped off at the gallery and sat for two or three and sometimes four hours until it closed. Matt suggested that as Ben was bored sitting at the rear of the shop, just maybe, if his grandfather agreed, she could go with him after school to his grandfather's house. Matt explained that his grandfather Alfred had worked for British Rail all his life and had so many albums detailing his travels, which he told Matt about and showed him wonderful photographs of the places he visited. Ben was immediately interested in the idea but said she would have to get her mother's permission but there was the problem of how she could get from his grandfather's house back home. Ever resourceful, Matt offered the services of his mum or dad by saying that when they picked him up, they could also take her home. The plan was set and nothing remained but to obtain parental agreement, as well as Alfred's agreement to feed another child. With minor reservations, the adults agreed to the plan and the first date was set for the two of them to have tea and stories at Grandpa Alfred's. As luck would have it, the school bus stopped in Whiteash green and was a short walk from The Spinney. On their first joint visit, tea was being prepared when as they arrived. Ben thanked Alfred so many times on that first occasion that he had to tell her that he would accept just one thank you, to cover everything. The two of them chatted away between mouthfuls of egg and baked beans on toast, Ben had a healthy appetite and was never known to refuse a second helping when it was offered and always helped with the clearing up. Once done they eagerly awaited for the moment when Alfred went to the dresser and lifted out the next volume of his life story on the railway. They sat around the large wooden kitchen table and Alfred lifted the cover of the album.

On Ben's first visit the opening page of the chosen album, was an eight by six inch photograph of the iconic Flying Scotsman, a Doncaster built, Pacific steam locomotive. As Ben's eyes locked on the image, she appeared to become mesmerized and both Alfred and Matt were fascinated by the look on her face and told her so. She said she had never seen such a magnificent looking machine and her enthusiasm never paled as Alfred began another tale. This first visit of the two of them turned into a regular occurrence and as the weeks and months passed, the two friends never lost their enthusiasm to hear more stories.

One sunny day, snacking in the shade of the oak tree, on the school playing field, Matt casually mentioned the front room railway his grandfather had spent three decades building and perfecting. Ben was at first surprised that a grown man had spent more than half his adult life building a toy railway but then incredulous when Matt admitted that he had never seen it. He told her that on asking, his grandfather told him that firstly, it was definitely not a toy railway but a miniature train and secondly, it was not something that a young child should see. Matt admitted the foolishness of this, thinking at the time that is exactly what a young boy would want to see. They agreed that when the time was right they would jointly ask Alfred to explain why they could not see the railway.

And that time came on the day that Alfred took from the dresser drawer an album but one, which charted the building of his own railway. Alfred went into finite detail as to how he had managed, over the span of three decades, to plan and build an entire town and miniaturised, mile after mile of countryside, including a lake, mountains and a working farm. The album detailed where he sourced ready-made items, such as buildings, farm vehicles, boats for the lake and when he could not find something, he just made it. There were endless pages that he slowly turned and each one outlined in finite details such things as the climate he envisaged and the seasonal snowfall on the mountains. Matters that served to confuse Matt and Ben and they asked why such matters were of any concern in the front room of a house and a model at that. In reply Alfred offered that in time they would learn how important such matters are but before they could bombard him with questions, the doorbell chimed and his mother was there to take them home.

She dropped Ben off at the gallery and on the journey to Shirebridge asked Matt what grandpa had been talking to them about. Matt found this quite curious because he had never been questioned before as to what they had talked about, always asking if he had a nice time and what he had to eat but not the detail of the stories that grandpa told. After he recounted to his mother what he and Ben had seen and been told that afternoon, he asked why she wanted to know. Once home, his mother appeared keen to continue the conversation and Matt soon learned why. She told her son that when she was a little older than he was now, she remembers vividly one day, returning from school, her father had been working in the front room and had left the door ajar, believing the house to be empty. He had obviously forgotten that school was only open for half the day, as the afternoon was allocated for some teacher training. She had a key and had let herself in and as she did so, she immediately saw that the front room door was open slightly, a very unusual occurrence, as her father was fastidious in ensuring it was closed and locked at all times, including when he was inside the room. She had silently approached the open door and peered inside and what she saw she would never forget. Before her, covering every inch of the room was an amazing landscape. It was as if she stood on a hilltop and was looking down a grassy hill to a railway below and beyond the track was a lake on which a number of small craft bobbed about on the water. Past the lake, a range of snow-capped mountains rose higher and higher and disappeared in the darkness above.

She was transfixed at the reality of what she saw, there was just so much to take in. As she scanned around the scene, she was suddenly shaken back to her senses when her eyes settled on her father who lay slouched on a small couch, pressed against the wall, with a panel of switches, levers and flickering lights in front of him. Wendy's first reaction was one of shock, he was so very still and she did not have the immediate presence of mind to notice if his chest was rising and falling as he breathed, she was momentarily frozen to the spot. Throughout her entire young life, her father had installed in her the command that on no account must she ever enter the front room, without being accompanied by him. She had obeyed but had always been curious about this iron-clad rule.

She was instantly calmed at the sight and sound of his breathing and the realization that he had merely fallen asleep. She gently shook him and called to him. Slowly, he roused and his first reaction was of alarm, almost as if he had seen a ghost. He looked frantically around before settling his eyes on his daughter. He sternly asked what she was doing in the room, against his most strict instructions but quickly calmed down when she explained the open door and her concern at seeing him lying on the couch with his head on the side and eyes closed. They left the room and as he prepared something for them to eat. Whilst they ate he filled in some of the gaps to his daughter's knowledge of the railway. However, in all the intervening years, she had never been entirely convinced by what he had told her and gave this by way of an explanation as to why she was questioning Matt. She added that if the railway were ever mentioned, her father would just talk about his model railway and nothing more and so she put her thoughts down to childish imagination. They spoke no further about it and Matt went to bed more than a little perplexed at the conversations that he had with his mother and grandpa over the railway. The following day at school, Ben told Matt that she and her mother were taking a vacation. She said she had no memory, in her life, of ever having had a holiday but her mother had explained that she had a friend, an artist, who would be happy to mind the gallery and it would be a good opportunity for them to take some time off. It was approaching half term and so Ben would not miss any schooling. Her mother had found a holiday home to rent in Lytham-St-Anne, a short distance from Blackpool plus they were five minutes from the beach.

Ben was concerned at missing any elements of the railway story or further adventures and made her friend promise to make careful note of what he heard whilst she was away. Alfred continued where he had left off and Matt was now familiar with how the railway had come together and why it took so long to get it perfect. He reasoned with his grandfather that now he knew so much, what could be the problem with him being shown the railway. Whether it was the logic of his grandson's argument or perhaps something else that was nagging at the old man but to Matt's utter amazement, Alfred told him that when next he visited, he may well be in for a surprise, no promises but a strong maybe. In truth, Alfred was remembering his conversation of many years ago when Yuri explained the need for him to find a new home for his engine and its secrets. Alfred was getting older and his bond with his

43

grandson had convinced him that all would be in safe hands when the time came. He did not know why but Matt never told his parents what had transpired between him and his grandfather. Perhaps it was his grandfather's words of caution that resonated in his head. He decided to wait and see what the front room railway was all about before he considered whether to keep his lips sealed. Oddly enough, a couple of afternoons later when he and Alfred sat down for tea, his grandpa asked him if he had mentioned to his mother any of their previous conversations. He saw the perplexed look on the boy's face and put a comforting hand on his arm and Matt told him of his mother's questions and her own experience with finding her father asleep in the front room. Alfred smiled at the recollection and told his grandson that the railway but more especially the engine, has a strange effect on people that was not easy to explain but the one thing that was a strong and abiding rule to stand by was, that the less said the better. When people were told about something they do not understand they tend to speculate and that can lead to a dangerous outcome. Alfred had decided that the time had come to confide in his grandson and disclose more about the engine and its provenance and whilst all Matt wanted to do was go and see the great front room railway, the seriousness of what his grandfather was saying, made him curb his enthusiasm just a little.

44

Alfred began the story of the engine with his first visit to Yuri's home. Matt was now familiar with the old Russian as he had popped up often in the early life of his grandfather and his work on the railway. The story was pre-empted with a request that the boy did not ask any questions because the answers were sure to follow. Matt was concerned that the telling of the story had eaten into the time until he was picked up but his grandfather told him not to worry and that they had plenty of time. They cleared away the dishes and with a noticeable break to routine, grandpa did not go to the dresser to fetch an album. His grandpa smiled down at him, took his hand and led him to the front room.

He withdrew a key from his rear trouser pocket and unlocked the door. Before entering, he turned to his grandson and bent over so that their faces were close. He told him that what he was about to see was a miniature railway the likes of which he had never seen before and will never see again but all is not as it appears. Matt was told that he will have an irresistible urge to ask questions which could not be answered, as confusing as this might be, he grandfather told him much would become clear very shortly and above all, not to be afraid.

With little more to be said, Alfred opened the door and lead Matt in by the hand, turning and locking the door behind him. It was completely dark inside the room but the shaft of light from the doorway had momentarily illuminated a small couch wedged against the wall, behind a bank of dials and switches and wedged against the wall, close to the door. Matt was instructed to sit down and again, not to be frightened which he said he was not and Alfred joined him on the couch. He told his grandson that what he was about to tell him would not only appear very strange but completely unbelievable but the boy should just listen to the old man and not question him. With that he told him that the engine he would shortly see has some extraordinary mysteries attached to it, one of which was its ability to sense if people seeking to board it were mentally and emotionally in accord with the engine and if their inner beings were in harmony. Only then would it reveal its full panoply of mysteries. Otherwise, it would forever remain a miniature railway engine.

Finally, again placing his hand on the boy's arm, he told him to close his eyes and relax, he would soon hear a faint and pleasant musical sound. Matt closed his eyes and with little effort cleared his mind and relaxed and presently he could discern the faintest of sounds, it was a mixture of ethereal notes, pulses and musical notes but not from any instruments he could name. He subconsciously thought his grandfather had put a record on but this thought was instantly dismissed, as the sound very gradually became louder and at once, appeared to be all around him. As he sat and listened Mathew realised that not only was his sense of hearing acting strangely but that his sense of smell had completely scrambled his thought. In the millisecond before he was forced to open his eyes, he knew he was no longer inside a house but in the open air. This transition had taken but a fleeting moment and Matt's opened eyes confirmed what his senses had told him. He now sat on a wooden bench at one end of an empty railway station platform and as he rapidly attempted to gather all of his senses, he jumped at the sound of a shrill whistle, one unmistakably attached to a steam engine. The second shock was wondering where his grandpa had disappeared to. The previous sounds and been replaced by the puffing of a steam locomotive and the unmistakable rhythmic sound of the wheels interacting with the track. Matt raised his gaze along the track and could see a magnificent engine, entering the station and slowing to a halt, puffing and hissing as the driver released the safety valve and vented the built up steam. Matt sat aghast as the driver, his grandfather, climbed down from the cab with a beaming smile on his face. His grandfather came and sat beside him, putting his arm around the boy and welcomed him to his front room railway and he laughed heartedly and looked happier than Matt could remember.

He asked him if would like a train ride and Matt who

up to that point had not spoken, in fact had not been able to speak, blurted out a yes. He swiftly clambered up to the driver's cab and once aboard started bombarding his grandfather with questions. The train slowly gathered speed but hardly ever reached more than a brisk walking pace, Alfred explained that he planned it to be more of a leisure train, allowing people to have the convenience of free transport plus the ability of hopping on or off, whenever or wherever they desired. Each carriage had the normal couple of steps up from the platform but on this particular train, the carriages had an extra step which almost reached the ground which extended for use for non-platform boarding. Matt interrupted his grandpa and said he really wanted to learn all about the place they were in but more importantly wanted, no needed, to know how it was possible. As they sedately journeyed on, his grandfather told him to not be so impatient, as important as the question was, he would not have to wait too long for the answer. However, he cautioned, when he hears the answers he may well have more questions but those questions may not come with answers. They passed through an expanse of cultivated fields and he asked what was being grown and was told it was a wide-ranging list of vegetables, including lettuce, cucumber, squash, marrows, sweet corn as well crops such as wheat, hops and barley. Alfred added that he had planned that they should grow all that they would need and they were truly subsistence farmers. At each revelation all that Matt could do was shake his head in disbelief and yet, who in the world wouldn't give a king's ransom for a healthy dose of magic.

He told Matt he had a house, close to the town and he would cook him a meal when they finished their ride. He added that everything he ate would be produced locally and in time he would meet all the people who contributed to making his grandfather's dream a reality.

They made their way in a long arc along the edge the lake and presently Matt could see a sandy beach appearing, a golden border to the blue waters of the lake. As they drew nearer and slowed to a crawl, the shouts and laughter of children and adults playing could be heard and as if to answer an unspoken question, Alfred said that the beach was a regular stopping point for the train and he duly applied the brakes. Alfred said it was a thirty-minute stop and they disembarked, together with a few passengers, crossing a narrow coastal path to the beach. There were a number of sun shades, all uniformly placed in a line and tilted against the blazing sun. Matt ignored the shades and like anybody who had not seen a beach for a long time, made for the water's edge. Alfred ambled behind him and they both removed their shoes and socks and stood there, ankle deep and allowed the warm water to gently lap over their feet. Matt was curious, how could a lake, by the side of a mountain have warm water and his grandfather laughed and asked in reply, why would he make the water cold. He told his grandson that he was sure to have a pair of swimming trunks to fit him, back at the house and next time he could take a swim. They could see, far out in the middle of the lake, several small boats bobbing to and fro and fishermen casting their nets and hauling their catch of rainbow trout, carp, bream and even catfish. As Matt squinted against the bright light, his grandpa told him he would teach him how to fish and the boy just grinned at all the new and exciting experiences he was adding to a mental list. With this trip turning into more of a holiday, Matt wondered how long they could stay and Alfred explained the dynamics of time in this fantasy world. He told him that there were a couple of simple but important rules connected to trips on the front room railway, firstly, they must return to the exact point at which they entered and he emphasised the word exact, because failure to do so would just mean they would not return to the real world. Most significantly, on returning, the time would be a matter of a second or two later than when they arrived. In other words, his grandfather added, as if he wanted to, they could stay a day, a week or a month and the time when they returned would not have changed and they would not have aged. After cleaning the sand off their feet they boarded the train, Alfred gave three blasts on the whistle and presently the train continued its journey. It was exceedingly hot in the cab with the heat of the sun adding to the heat of the firebox but Alfred told Matt they would presently be turning into the shade of the mountain and that part of the journey would be cooler.

Before that, they approached a suspension bridge over what Matt was told was the Yuri River and the boy smiled at the familiarity of the name and Alfred admitted he had not been very creative when naming places. They passed a large shunting yard and railway works, where welding sparks shot into the air and the sound of hammering echoed. The rail then took a tight right hand bend and Bay Mountain appeared rising in front of them. Alfred glowed with pride, saying that it was one of his proudest achievements and Matt could see why, two cable cars past each other, the one ascending carrying skiers and the one descending empty to collect more.

The nursery slopes were a haphazard display of youngsters at varying degrees of skiing ability, upright, falling over or just having snowball fights. Higher up, the more accomplished skiers were drawing artistic tracks in the snow as they zigzagged their way to the base. Matt had become quite an accomplished skier, having holidayed with his father's family at Safsen, north west of Stockholm virtually every year, since his fifth birthday.

Another brief stop followed as a holidaying school party and family groups plus single skiers, disembarked or returning passengers banged the snow from their boots and stepped aboard. Matt was in total bewilderment at the incredible and undeniable reality of all he was witnessing including the ease with which his grandfather accepted it as perfectly normal. He repeatedly asked his grandpa if he was dreaming, knowing full well he was not but still incredulous that all that he saw could be possible. Alfred could only sympathize with his grandson, telling him he had spent decades attempting to rationalize this situation and was no further to finding an answer. The entire circuit of the lake, including the various stops, took approximately six hours and the sun was waning as they made the final turn towards Alfred Town. On the outskirts, Matt could smell, before he could see, a farm, which he was told was a dairy farm, home to both Herefords and Ayrshire's. He was familiar from his grandfather's tales of his evacuation, that he had very fond memories of his days on a farm and milking cows, a skill he enthusiastically told Matt he would gladly teach him. Alfred Town station was in the middle of town, at the water's edge and by the side of a dock where some small sailing boats were moored and a rack of kayaks was secured. They ended their journey in the town's station and

Alfred explained he would be about an hour attending to the engine, shutting down the boiler and waiting whist it cools and checking the pressure as well as draining the water and generally ensuring all was well for a repeat journey later in the day. He told Matt to explore the town if he wished and make his way back to the station in an hour. He suggested he starts with the church which they passed a short distance back and work his way along the back streets, returning along the houses and shops that front the lake. He fished around in his pocket for some money, which he gave him, adding that he would find several shops with refreshments or snacks. The town was populated like many rural English towns, there were no bustling crowds but a number of people coming and going into the provision stores and coming out laden with bags of groceries and other sundry provisions, standing around chatting or where he came across a café or a pub, most of the outside tables and chairs were occupied, it being that time of day when folks generally desire something to eat and drink. He bought a chilled soft drink from a small confectionary store and noted that whilst the people he interacted with were both polite and pleasant, nobody appeared interested in a visitor who nobody knew.

He took some time to look in the window of a clock repairers that had a large collection of clocks displayed, from

53

large grandfather clocks to small brass alarm clocks and all sizes in between. After thirty minutes he cut through between the buildings to reach the lakeside and turned to return to the station. The walk back struck Matt as akin to a scene from a Cornish coastal town but instead of the sea there was a lake. There was a thin coating of sand across the road and the nearby shops displayed a range of beach toys, inflatables, swimwear and lotions and potions to protect against sunburn.

There were a number of restaurants which consisted of the fast food variety, such as a pizzeria and fish and chips but nicely appointed with white table cloths on the outside tables flapping in the breeze and uniformed waiting staff, standing out front with menus, inviting people to dine. There was a steak restaurant and a fish restaurant, both of which had the appearance of fine dining.

Smiling with the pleasure of his short jaunt around town, Matt arrived back on time and his grandfather appeared to have had a wash and cleaned himself from his sweated labour of driving a steam locomotive. He said they would need to buy some provisions for an evening meal and they returned to stores Matt had passed earlier. Alfred was greeted as a dignitary, which was not surprising as the town was named after him and he duly introduced Matt as his visiting grandson. Laden with all he needed to cook dinner, Alfred led the way between a dental surgery and what looked like a cross between a clothes shop and a craft shop and up a steep path. The path continued up a hill that cut through a meadow, on top of which stood a neat thatched cottage, with a pretty planted garden out front and a sign on the garden gate that said Woodland Cottage. Alfred put a hand on his grandson's shoulder to stop him and recounted that the name came from his first home in Camberwell, also called Woodland Cottages but in that case it was a terraced house.

To say that Matt was surprised would have been an understatement, as he was served a delicious meal of steak and lightly steamed vegetables, plus fried potatoes, all cooked almost as good as his mother. The boy was tired after the day's exploits and after helping his granddad with the dishes, he was shown his room for the night. It was one of the front rooms and as darkness fell, Matt could see from their elevated position, the lights from the town below and the faint twinkle of illumination from across the lake to the mountain resort. He was asleep the moment his head touched the pillow and the next thing he remembered was his grandfather waking him gently at the crack of dawn. Today was the day he would show his grandson how to milk a cow. Following breakfast, they had a brisk walk to the farm, just outside of town, where a pot of hot tea awaited. Introductions were made and Farmer

Claybourne instructed his son Daniel, a few years older than Matt, to show him around the farm and they would join them shortly at the milking shed. Alfred gave a good display at the art of milking a cow and Matt made a vain attempt to copy him. The cow appeared as displeased with Matt's effort as the boy was but everyone laughed and it was good experience.

Daniel had a word with his father after which he told Matt he had to go into town to pick up some supplies; he was allowed to take the tractor and asked if Matt would like to tag along. He did not need asking twice and the two boys were seen walking towards a barn, deep in conversation as if they were old friends. It was lunch time by the time the boys returned and Betty, the farmer's wife said a chicken casserole she had cooked the day before was today's lunch, if the two visitors were happy to stay. Matt remarked that he had eaten so well in the past two days, especially when making the comparison with school dinners which he rarely ate. As lunch was ending a panicked farm hand came rushing in and in between gasps for breath, told them that Jemima was about to give birth. Matt looked around wondering who that was and was told Jemima was their youngest heifer. The farmer and his wife were experienced in the matter of delivering calves and as they all arrived at the barn the farmer could see Jemima was ready to give birth. Hot water was provided for hand and arm washing and Jemima was held firm. In no time the front legs of the calf were visible and a rope was deftly attached to assist with removing the calf from its mother.

Once the calf was breathing well, it was carried to a nearby bed of clean straw and her momma was led to be with her new-born. Matt remarked what an exciting day it had so far been and Alfred suggested they relax on the beach. They were given a lift back to the cottage where Alfred rummaged for some swim wear and towels. They made their way back to the station where the train was preparing for the second trip of the day. Alfred greeted Sanjay and introduced him to Matt, as the regular driver. They took seats in the last of the three carriages and presently the train left for the lakeside ride to the beach. As they took the slow ride, Matt found the opportunity to pose a few more questions, one concerned the weather and asked if it was sunny and hot every day. Alfred laughed and replied asking, what country did his grandson know of where it was hot and sunny every day of the year but Matt argued that this was a fantasy land. His grandfather conceded the point but said for the sake of the crops and livestock, as well as the residents, he conceived of a Mediterranean climate, with warm to hot summers and cooler, wetter winters. When they arrived at the beach, they found a vacant shade and two loungers, dropped off their belongings, disrobed and raced to the water. Matt was so happy so see his grandfather, behaving and enjoying himself like a younger version of himself. Being a lake there was no tidal drag and Matt swam more than he had for a very long time and felt invigorated by all the exercise. They collapsed onto the loungers and chatted happily until the sun began to sink. As the light faded still further, Alfred suggested they dressed and returned to their arrival spot to depart for home.

CHAPTER 3

A RETURN TO NOMALITY AND
A RUDE AWAKENING

It took Matt a while to accommodate the sensation of having been away for a couple of days and yet returning just after having tea with his grandfather two days prior. As they exited the front room, Cynthia was just arriving home from work, she smiled at the two of them and remarked that they looked as though they had been having fun. Matt could not hide telling her the truth, in one way it was the truth. He told her that his grandfather had finally shown him the front room railway and that he was completely mesmerized at what her saw. He was no less amazed at his grandfather, who had built it and he could spend endless hours playing in the front room if he were allow to. They laughed at his bubbling enthusiasm and as they walked down the passage to the kitchen, Alfred turned to Matt and winked. Cynthia went upstairs to take a bath and Matt and his grandfather sat in the kitchen and discussed all that had occurred but Matt detected something troubling his grandfather.

His mum and dad duly arrived to pick him up and on hearing the ring on the door bell, Matt composed himself. To erase the experience from his demeanour of what had happened was no easy matter but the intervening hour or so had helped. On the short ride home, they chatted as normal and with the prospect of some good weather on the horizon, his father suggested that they inflate the dingy and venture out on the river on the weekend.

Whilst life continued in its normal way, Matt's thoughts kept returning to the railway and the growing urge to return. With several days of the school holiday still remaining, Matt did not visit his grandfather but he came over and joined them on a day out on the river. Lans had fitted the outboard motor and ensured it was working before they carried the inflatable to the water's edge. His mother had filled a wicker basket with a variety of homemade food, which they pecked at the minute they were afloat, although it was not yet ten o'clock. They meandered leisurely along the river until Lans spotted a convenient place to stop for lunch and whilst he tied up the dingy, Matt and Alfred carried the picnic and deck chairs a short way up a grassy bank and laid out the picnic rug. The sun made a welcome appearance and Matt and his grandfather decided on a short riverbank walk before lunch.

There was plenty to eat for everyone and Wendy was complemented on the delicious spread she had provided. They dwelled for a good hour just chatting and continuing to nibble at the food and Alfred dropped off for a short nap.

Lans had calculated the time it had taken them to reach their present location and factoring in the slower pace returning, against the current, they had best turn around to ensure they reached home in plenty of daylight.

Both his mother and father were going to work the following day and Matt, still on holiday, argued that he was old enough to look after himself. There was no disagreement that he was old enough and mature enough to take care of himself and he happily occupied himself for the day. During one of his visits to his grandfather, Matt had asked him if Ben could accompany them on their next ride on the railway. At first he was adamant that it was a bad idea, reminding the boy of the need for secrecy. However, as the days passed and with Matt's gentle urging, the old man, who after all had grown very fond of Ben, appeared to be weakening in his resolve. Alfred had been ruminating over the circumstances by which he took possession of the engine and how he too now found himself considering the need to find a new home for the engine. Whilst Alfred knew his grandson would be a competent keeper of the railway, he was still rather young.

On his first day back at school, he immediately sought out Ben and at break time they hurriedly attempted to recount

61

their individual exploits of the past days. They laughed as they both spoke over each other in the attempt to tell their stories. At lunchtime, afternoon break and at the end of the day, they talked incessantly. Ben enthused about her trip and said there was just so much to see and do but the first thing was to go to the top of the Blackpool tower and in the middle of telling him of the amazing trampoline park she stopped and changed subject. She told Matt with all the fun she was having, she missed him and their time with his grandfather, learning about the front room railway. It was Matt's turn to tell her just a little of what had happened. He said he had seen the railway but gave no more details other than to say how truly amazing it was, with the lake and mountains and a whole town. Ben almost forgot about her own trip as she urged her friend to tell her more. He told her to be patient and that they would visit his grandfather's presently and then she could catch up on what she had missed.

As luck would have it, Matt had discovered that a country bus route would allow them to forgo the school bus and travel from school to Shirebridge. He asked his parents if Ben could have a sleep over one night and they happily agreed. The day they chose was dull but dry and they took the bikes from the shed and with a little wobbling they set off. Ben had brought a snack for them and they stopped after a half hour ride, to sit on the bank to rest, eat and throw sticks into the river.

Alfred was visibly pleased to see Ben on their first visit to The Spinney but to Matt's disappointment, his grandfather did not mention a word about another train ride nor about his friend joining them. Instead after tea, he pulled out the album detailing his construction of the front room railway and to Ben's delight, filled her in on what she had missed, which included the details on how and where he had sourced the material needed and the painstaking years it took to complete the mammoth task. Matt took the opportunity, when he was alone for a brief moment with his grandfather, to ask why they did not discuss another trip. All that his grandfather said was that in good time they will make a plan. Matt was obviously disappointed with his response but at least it was not a complete reversal and he had not said anything to Ben to build up her hopes.

As the weeks passed Matt noticed a slight change in his grandfather. It was difficult to pin point exactly what had changed, just that he treated his grandson and Ben more as young adults and less as children. Sure enough, as the year progressed, they kept up their visits to Alfred and on one momentous occasion he asked if Ben would like to see his front room railway. Matt could hardly contain himself as she replied

63

excitedly she would not love anything more. Neither of them wanted to waste time eating their tea but Alfred insisted, so they duly ate and cleared the plates before finally, Alfred told them to sit whilst he spoke seriously, mainly to Ben. He was at pains to explain that what she was about to see was a miniature railway the likes of which, in her wildest imagination, she could not picture. She must dispel all thoughts of what is and what is not real and just allow her imagination take over.

She knew it had taken decades to complete but was still curious as to why Alfred had been at such pains to emphasize how extraordinary the railway was. Somewhat perplexed by the old man's words, Matt took her hand and told her not to be in any way concerned and that he knew that what was in store was the opportunity of a lifetime. Without disclosing any details he gave the merest hint of his previous visit and assured her that it would be the trip of a lifetime, emphasizing the word 'trip'. With his words ringing in her ears, the three of them walked along the hall passageway to the front room and Alfred unlocked the door.

With all that had been said, Ben was not prepared for the darkness but Matt held her hand tightly as they moved inside to the small couch and sat on the small couch. Alfred closed and locked the door and joined them, telling them as he sat, to close their eyes and relax. Matt could feel that Ben was shaking a little and whispered to her that she should calm herself and listen for some wonderful soothing sounds. Presently the process began and the harmonic notes floated all around them and he felt his friend noticeably relax and released her hand.

As her senses told her that the environment had changed, she slowly opened her tightly-shut eyes. She slowly turned her head from left to right, taking in the magic and the phantasmagorical scene as it appeared. She turned to Matt but was unable to speak and just stared. They sat on the platform bench in bright morning sunshine and without the slightest acknowledgment at the sudden appearance of the three, an assortment of people milled about close by. A young boy and girl excitedly announced that they could see the white smoke of the approaching train and slowly the half dozen passengers, picked up their belongings and moved towards the platform edge, looking in unison towards the now visible approaching train. As it slowed to a halt, Sanjay popped his head from the cab and waved at Alfred, they exchanged a few words and Matt took Ben's hand and led her slowly along the platform to a carriage with available lakeside seats. As they sat, she gradually recovered her composure, finally regaining her power of speech, she began to ask her friend the most obvious of questions. As best he could, he told her all that he had learned about the train, the engine, its history and how his grandfather had inherited this wonderment and created this fantasy land. Alfred remained in the cab and Matt acted as tour guide, explaining the time conundrum. He said he would ask his grandfather if they could stay for at least a couple of days and maybe he would teach her how to ski. This was all too much for Ben and all she kept saying was that she didn't believe what was happening. He counselled her, repeating his grandfather's advice, on the need for her to suspend her belief in what was and what was not real and just live for the moment, enjoying what her senses told her about her surroundings. Gradually his words had an impact and she noticeably calmed and he could see she was starting to enjoy the experience. By early afternoon they arrived in Alfred Town and whilst his grandfather attended to his train, Matt took his friend on a tour of the town. They stopped on the lakefront for a drink and as the day cooled they made their way to the cottage where Alfred had set a table on the veranda. Over mouthfuls of food Ben said in good humour that having only dined on Alfred's beans on toast and poached eggs, she was seriously impressed by his spaghetti bolognaise and Matt was happy to agree. Alfred took the compliments in the good spirits they were made and topped up their glasses of wine. The three talked animatedly and Matt was visibly delighted witnessing the pleasure Ben had derived from the day's experience. As they sat and discussed plans for the following day, Alfred stood and gazed down the slope, his attention was drawn towards a distant figure heading their way. As the man drew nearer, Alfred gripped hold of the back of his chair so tightly that his knuckles whitened.

At first he murmured that he thought he was seeing Yuri, who his fellow travellers knew of but whilst the similarity was startling, he knew it was not him. As the old man of some indeterminable age reached the cottage, Alfred remembered the picture he had seen above Yuri's mantelpiece all those years ago. He was staring at Yuri's father and whilst accepting in this fantasy land that anything was possible, this broke the bounds of all that he had come to know and understand. The old man opened the gate and extended a sinewy hand in greeting. He told the astonished three that his name was Marat and that he was indeed, Yuri's father and his appearance was a predetermined event, he asked if he could sit and requested a glass of water.

He sat and sipped his water and almost in a whisper began to explain that he did not bring ill tidings nor to cause alarm, it was he said, a precautionary visit. The engine had been made by a highly advanced race of people, many light years distant from planet Earth and using a metal not found on this planet, called zergonite. Scientists working for the Czar at

67

the time discovered some rare properties of this metal, which coated the engine, such that it was totally impenetrable to sound, light and was indestructible. As the years passed and technology advanced on Earth, even using more modern methods available at the time and as further techniques were developed, the same results were found. Scientists had been experimenting on samples of zergonite, which had been discovered in a large meteorite that had crashed to earth in the northern Urals. It was believed that it was more than a coincidence that the arrival of the meteorite and the appearance of a magical engine were not inexplicably connected. In a similar vein, he continued, a Cossack in the pay of the Czar was familiar with the properties of zergonite, which had been used in the construction of the engine. For this reason and others, rumours abounded at the time as to who this Cossack was, or even if he was a Cossack. In addition, Marat had come to learn that the Cossack and the engine had a more than natural connection, almost as if the engine had a sentience about it and was cojoined with the Cossack. In time Marat and the Cossack became friends and confidants and when the Cossack told his friend he had to leave, he passed over all he knew of the engine and Marat became imbued with the special relationship necessary to operate the engine. Such a relationship manifested itself in the engine's ability to summon first the Cossack and then Marat, if the circumstances demanded.

As the three listened, entranced by the old man's words, he was at pains to tell them that he had no portents of impending harm, only that it were time to take precautions. He had been summoned from the netherworld of his eternal rest to impart to the present keeper of the engine, the knowledge to take steps to protect it forever more. At the time of its creation pure zergonite had been used and it was believed that if this were used to coat the engine it would be masked from prying eyes from this world or any other. All that Marat could tell them was that samples of the meteor containing zergonite had been collected on Earth and they must source this valuable metal. He also gave Alfred details on how to test for the metal and how to reduce its constituency to enable the engine to be coated

After the old man satisfied himself that they understood the importance of their mission, he bade them farewell and hoped there would be no need for them to meet again. They watched in silence as he slowly ambled his way down the path and then disappeared before reaching the buildings below. They sat in silence, contemplating all that they had learned and decided that they had best return to the real world and put into action the vital task they had been given.

Once gathered around the Spinney's kitchen table, Ben grabbed Matt's arm and asked him if what had happened was real or just a dream. She said he and his grandfather were acting as if it was very normal but her head was fit to burst with trying to fathom out what had just occurred. It was Alfred who answered by telling her that there is so much that happens in our little universe that is beyond our comprehension, to try and contemplate what may exist in the multiverse is not something we mere mortals are equipped to do. All we can do is accept what happens to us as a new experienced reality and not try and understand the how and why of it. Ben let out a deep breath and said she would digest what he had said. Returning to the matter in hand, Matt said in all likelihood it would be the Natural History Museum where such samples would be found. He added that in the final two years at school, they were invited to propose a thesis that they would prepare for submission. Matt suggested that he and Ben should produce a joint thesis on rare earth metals. They could make a strong case for the need to visit the Natural History Museum in this regard and in the days that followed, they prepared a document outlining the growing importance to the technological world of rare earth metals. Their proposal was persuasive enough and was accepted by their tutors, thus the first part of their plan was accomplished. Kanika, Wendy and Lans were all happy with the story they were told and even supportive of their joint endeavour. Alfred said he would accompany them to London and after padding out their thesis, which they agreed they would have to complete, they planned to head south the following week. Cynthia suggested she would join them as it would be nice to spend some quality time with her grandson. Whilst the disappointment showed, Alfred managed to dissuade her, telling her they would be spending most of the day in the basement of the Natural History Museum undertaking studious research. It only remained to hope and pray that they found what they were looking for.

They arrived at opening time at the museum, bearing a letter from their school, explaining their thesis and requesting assistance. The first official they met was unsure about the request but her superior, one Bartholomew Higgins, was more than happy to oblige. He was also apparently only too happy to impart to them the importance of his curatorship.

He was a scholarly looking individual, used to holding sway over visitors to his domain. He wore oval framed spectacles with thick lenses, perched on the end of his rather large nose. His poor eyesight was evidenced by several food stains that were noticeable on his navy suit jacket and the accompanying waistcoat. He said they occasionally assisted with third party requests from both the UK and overseas, as their collection was world renown. Eventually they were led to a flight of stairs leading to a basement where desks and chairs had been placed at the centre of a large storage room. Bartholomew explained that this area was closed to the public so they could work undisturbed but they must not touch any of the stored items encased in a large number of boxes and crates. The curator would not take his leave and continued to display his encyclopaedic knowledge of the museum. They unpacked their bags and laid out an array of note and reference books on a table. It took them some time, sitting and writing copious notes of no relevance, to prompt Mr. Higgins to take his leave and Alfred suggested he would loiter at the foot of the stairs to the basement and alert them if anybody looked likely to intrude on their questionable endeavours. It was Bartholomew who did just that twice but a rehearsed cough from Alfred sent the two scurrying to a table with open notepads and within seconds they were seated and writing.

It took some considerable time for the two to discover that this store room housed the museum's rare rock and meteorite samples. They sifted through the voluminous containers of rocks and meteor samples, which were all scrupulously labelled, according to date acquired and location found. Several hours' later three crates were located bearing Russian text stamped on the exterior, in which samples from the Ural Mountains were contained. After heavy lifting and sorting through the contents, they landed on several smaller boxes indicating they contained meteor samples. At this point Alfred came over to where they had made their discovery and unbuttoned his coat. He had attached to his trouser belt several cloth bags with pull strings and after a quick look around to ensure they were alone, he produced a small bottle and deposited a few drops of fluid on the rock samples, as instructed by Marat, to confirm the samples contained zergonite. With a positive test completed, he deftly dropped a number of samples into the bags.

They returned to the ground floor and found Mr. Higgins where he had cornered some young, uniformed students and was holding court. They waved a swift goodbye and headed for the exit. Once on the pavement, they all breathed a sigh of relief and Alfred suggested they find somewhere to eat before heading home.

Alfred had received additional instructions from Marat as to extracting the zergonite which involved grinding the hard meteorite to fine granules and mixing it with an advanced silicone adhesive, further adding a number of chemicals which Alfred would need to produce. Alfred had converted a large garden shed into a workshop and hung along one wall was an impressive array of tools and attachments for cutting and drilling, screwing and fixing, basically everything required for the mammoth task he had set himself when building his railway.

However, he did not have the correct grinder attachments that would reduce the meteorite samples to the granules required. He knew of a company of monumental masons in town and made a call to see if they could offer some advice. After some research, he found a geologist in the vicinity who, on being told that Alfred had some meteorite samples, was able to lend him the appropriate tools. It took him five long days of sweated labour to finally fill a small bucket of zergonite granules. He next toured the area visiting chemists and hardware stores looking for the correct chemicals. After mixing in the solution of adhesive and adding the chemicals, they were reading to complete the task. Applying the coating to the miniaturized engine was a simple task and when completed, Alfred said he needed to disclose one more secret, perhaps the most important one so far. They sat around the kitchen table and Alfred explained that Yuri had told him when he was handed the crate containing the engine, there were six tracks included which must not be joined with any others but should be stored in a secure location. A small remote would, when the time came, activate the rails to join together. He said that he had only been told but never experienced, what would happen should the engine ride those six tracks. Yuri had told him that the engine would be transported through a portal to places far beyond our space or time, to realms unknown to mankind and through dimensions unknown.

Matt and Ben listen to these words of science fiction but the seriousness on Alfred's face remained. He told them he was unable to talk to them of the multiverse or multiple dimensions nor the myriad of unknown galaxies in our own solar system. This knowledge was far beyond his ability to contemplate. However, what Yuri had told him was that we lived in a multiverse, which has twelve full dimensions that span a multitude of frequencies and our physical universe is the first full dimension, made up of the bottom of the twelve frequencies. Whilst on the train the occupants would create energy around themselves, which would allow them to move from one frequential state to another. The energy we create is the very geometry of our construct, as we move between the dimensions, that construct will change but will be an anathema to what we truly are and will invoke a force to draw us back to the engine, where we will reconstruct our geometry and which ensures our return. The full power of the engine would allow true trans dimensional travel between the full dimensions in the rest of the multiverse. At this point Alfred fell silent and allowed the enormity of what he had just told them to sink in.

He restated his inability to comprehend much of what he had imparted but recalled being enthralled when being told of yet another component to the awesome power of the engine. However, he felt sure that in the fullness of time, should they desire to explore further then all would become clear. As if preempting the questions hanging on their lips, Alfred said he had repeated what Marat had told Yuri and what Yuri had then told him but could offer neither explanations, nor details of what lay beyond, should they take the next step.

CHAPTER 4

THE FRONT ROOM AND BEYOND

It appeared that none of them had built up the courage to take the monumental step they knew that awaited them. Matt discussed the matter with Ben and they arrived at The Spinney with renewed determination. Matt told his granddad that it would be wrong to be in possession of such a powerful item and not take the opportunity of revealing any and all of its mysteries and powers. And so it was, on a bright spring day and with some degree of trepidation that they filed down the hallway and into the front room.

Following the now familiar process, the train appeared and Alfred explained to Sanjay his intention to take the engine to the sheds for some routine maintenance and that he should take the substitute engine to continue on his way. Alfred took control and dropped Sanjay off by a siding to pick up engine number two, he was shortly on his way and Alfred took his engine the short distance into the shed. He stopped at the end of the rail, which terminated some hundred feet from the facing shed wall. The three stood in the cab in silence, Alfred explained that he needed to connect the six tracks to the track they were on and climbed from the cab. As he reached the ground, he turned and suggested to Matt, almost as an afterthought, that he may want to close the rarely used cab doors and windows. They quickly attended to Alfred's suggestion and then looked down and watched Alfred uncover the six rails, from under a tarpaulin in front of the engine, removing a small remote from his pocket. He pointed the remote at the rails and several moments passed when nothing appeared to happen but then a grinding noise could be heard as the tracks connected and began to move towards the engine.

They continued at a snail's pace until, with that familiar metallic clank, the connection of the tracks was complete. Alfred looked up at his grandson but never moved and with a resigned tone in his voice he told Matt he would not be joining them on this next leg. Matt began to protest but Alfred, stood his ground with his mind made up, he explained that he had many adventures in his life but was now tired and did not feel able to confront the enormity of what he felt lay ahead. He considered that Matt and Ben were more than able to face, whatever came next, well enough without an old man to look after. Matt continued to object and told his grandfather that it just would not be the same without him. With tears in her eyes, Ben climbed down from the cab and hugged the old man, Matt did the same. He told them not to worry that he would be here when they returned and ushered them on their way. He counselled them to be careful and not to lose connection with the engine and looked forward to hearing their tales. The rail beyond extended the remaining one hundred feet, before it met the shed wall and Matt engaged the engine and slowly moved onto the extended rails. Once the engine was fully on the extended rails, all sound ceased, it continued its slow progress forward, in complete silence, as if it floated on a cushion of air. Halfway along he became noticeably nervous as in an instant, the four hundred ton engine shot forward with the thrust of a jet aeroplane. Neither Matt nor Ben had the time to contemplate the brick wall hurtling towards them. In a nanosecond the wall had evaporated and they sped forwards towards an impenetrable blackness that surrounded them. They moved without sound and at a speed without wind and devoid of heat or cold. They gazed around in awe at a multitude of coloured jets of light, flashing past on all sides. They marvelled at stars without number, some shooting across their view or shining so bright it hurt their eyes to look at them and a blanket of twinkling lights far beyond. And then the light show ended, the engine stopped moving and only blackness remained. They stood in the cab and looked at each other; unable to vocalize what they thought had just occurred and only the sound of their heavy breathing pierced the silence. Matt spoke first and just said he wished his grandfather could have seen what they just saw. As a natural reaction, Matt shut the motor down and walked to the cab window, trying to discern what lay beyond. He opened the window and extended an arm, withdrawing it rapidly as it appeared to touch a soft and pliable like substance. He inspected his arm and with no discernible effect, he did the same again but with both arms straight, he moved them about and as he did so, shards of rainbow light streamed through before the black curtain closed. Matt took Ben's hand and opening the door he cautiously descended the steps where he tentatively extended a foot until he felt a soft but solid surface. He turned and signalled that it was safe but said that he was unsure what kind of surface he was standing on. Ben followed close behind and as they proceeded, in a just seven steps the blackness again parted before them and they appeared in bright light but were rooted to the spot, transfixed at the sight before them and the sky above.

They stared upwards at two enormous whirlpools of clouds of red, yellow and blue, layer upon layer, at the centre of each appeared a moon. The light they saw and the heat they were feeling came from not one but two Suns, the one to the west of where they stood and one to the east. Across this breath-taking canvas of light and colour there were shooting stars, hurtling across the sky in every direction and in numbers never witnessed in their world. What completely assailed their senses was the feeling that if they reached up, they could touch the clouds or one of the moons. Matt had not let go of Ben's hand and now gripped it even tighter, as if this were his only hold on reality.

The need to proceed came to both of them and they looked around to check on their surroundings, all Matt could see was an endless expanse of a pastel landscape, which appeared to merge with the sky above. They could breathe normally and the atmosphere was remarkably earth like. He looked behind and could detect no evidence as to where they had come from or indeed where the engine was. He returned his gaze forward and could see in the middle distance a forest. It was a forest populated by lofty trees, maybe fifty feet tall or more, each was perfectly straight and all exactly the same height. At regular intervals, starting approximately halfway up each trunk, there sprung bunches of large bright red pods. Presently the trees began to quiver and then shake, the tops started to sway to and fro, from between them emerged several huge theropods, which looked to all intents and appearances like the ancient Allosaurus that Matt recognized from his natural history study books. He knew such beasts lived a hundred and fifty million years ago on Earth but the pictures he had seen looked remarkably like the beasts they were staring at. They stood high on their hind legs but what astonished them both, was that they had not front claws but what could only be described as hands. At their distance, they could not discern the detail but could see these amazing creatures extending their upper arms and dexterously wrapping finger like extensions around the pods, which they plucked and dropped in their mouths. As they stood and marvelled at the creatures, first one then all turned and looked straight towards them. They took a deep intake of air and held their breath, the creatures stood their ground and then, without moving, each returned to their feeding.

The two relaxed and decided to move and explore the place where they had randomly arrived. They looked around scoping near and far, Ben pointed, saying she thought she saw something on the horizon to their right. This was a good enough sign to set them off but immediately she took the first step and put her right foot down, it was repelled with a force that lifted her off the ground and she landed as if on a foam mattress. She lay there laughing and Matt attempted a first step but far more cautiously and whilst his foot involuntarily lifted his body a foot or two off the ground, he maintained his balance. Ben stood and they proceeded, quickly becoming accustomed to what was almost zero gravity. The harder they landed their feet the higher they were lifted and by leaning forward that height was converted to a forward motion. In such an environment they crossed the distance at speed and it took little time to reach what Ben had seen. They stopped to try and comprehend what they were now looking at.

There appeared many spherical and transparent globes, suspended motionless in the sky, closest to the ground were exceptionally large ones perhaps fifty in number which reduced in size as they looked higher and higher. They moved closer and estimated there were many hundreds of these globes, of multiple sizes. As they surveyed them they realized they were not completely motionless but shimmered and the light reflected revealed that the globes were rotating very slowly. They remained rooted to the spot not sure whether or not to make a closer inspection but that decision was made for them. There emerged from one of the lower globes, a floating entity which as it moved towards them took form. To their utter amazement the form that appeared in front of them was to all intents and purposes humanoid, an androgynous being of considerable stature. Its hair was silver and silken, skin the colour and texture of white marble and dressed in a flowing toga that covered its feet and lay in folds on the ground. It stood momentarily staring from emerald green eyes, which suggested significant intelligence.

Its unwavering gaze penetrated their minds and without their realizing, learnt all it could from both of them. After a matter of moments, a smile appeared on the beings face and a hand was raised, as if in greeting. It did not speak but they telepathically received a welcome and that they should feel neither fear nor alarm. They were informed that they had arrived at Philax 10, in the constellation of Lunorar and populated by a highly advanced and peaceful race known as the Philadrons, who had achieved osmonological perfection, the ability to change their physical appearance at will and it did, in this instance to human form, to place the visitors at ease. They were androgynous and whilst they had no requirement for names, the visitors not being proficient at telepathic means of identity, could refer to their host as Yamnus. Matt attempted to speak to introduce himself and Ben but quickly realized that his natural and instant mental compiling of the words he wished to speak, had been picked up by Yamnus and no words were spoken. They had been observed, they learned, the moment they entered the dimension, as were all movements in the realm monitored. The Philadrons, Yamnus informed them, took a semi solid form which many millenniums of development had proved, enabled a greatly extended life expectancy to about two hundred and sixty Earth years, as well being impervious to harm and giving faster movements on the surface or above it. They were beckoned to follow and moved towards the globes, finding themselves presently on the underside of the lowest and largest of them. Yamnus placed a gentle hand upon each of their heads and they were gently lifted to find themselves inside what could only be described as a paradisiacal scene. They were told that the Philadrons had mastered geokinesis and subterra capabilities which enabled them to move solid matter and create physical scenes, such as they were witnessing. The natural extension of such powers also ensured the Philadrons had been at peace for many hundreds of thousands of Earth years.

The size of the globe they had seen from outside bore no relationship to what they were seeing inside. They stood on the shore of an azure blue lake and filling the view of the far shore was a red planet, with multiple rings, half above their line of sight and half disappearing below the horizon. Yamnus explained that the dimension they were in had existed from a time long before human kind arrived in their own dimension. He was aware of the world from which they had travelled and was able to tell them that the dimension they found themselves in was in the realm of a million of their years further advanced. And long before Yamnus' learning, they had devoted themselves to the development of one's self and a semi-metaphysical state. The power of their minds was all they desired for a perfect existence and so in the passage of their early development they had decided that a physical presence did not prove conducive to their preferred ideals and in ensuring an exceptionally long existence. Over the passage of many millenniums they developed the ability to alter the molecular structure of all that existed around them and in turn, themselves as well. Whilst in their current state of being they did not require sustenance in the form that his guests understood, however, they appreciated that their guests may well be desirous of food. The two having quickly adapted to this non-vocal means of communicating enthusiastically agreed, at the mention of food realizing how hungry they were and with that their host disappeared.

They sat on the sandy shore and spoke of their inability to reduce their current experience into words that would make any rational sense. Matt told his friend that the only person he could speak to of this extraordinary adventure was his grandfather and he would be nothing short of amazed. Although only having just arrived, they thought it prudent to discuss with Yamnus how they could make their return trip, having lost sight of the engine at the point of arrival. They became aware before they saw, a different being had appeared, on this occasion the individual with the same bright green eyes but with golden hair and in stature was smaller than either of them but slightly built and dressed in western style clothing by way of a checked shirt, denim jeans and highly decorated, pointed toed cowboy boots. They were introduced to Nonzaid, who had taken on a distinctly feminine appearance. She hoped they were impressed with her appearance, which had taken some considerable effort, following detailed researching of vast databanks of information from planet Earth, on clothing and attire. Nonzaid carried or rather guided a floating tray which hovered in front of her and which was now lowered to where they sat. They saw a selection of items, some of which the two could reasonably determine, were possibly fruit but perhaps not fruit they were familiar with. As it was placed before them, it was explained they had produced food that they believed the guests would enjoy, perhaps the shape and consistency differed from what they were accustomed to but it was hoped it would be to their satisfaction.

The two of them had forgotten when they had last eaten. As Nonzaid stood and beneficently smiled down at them, they ate with murmurs of delight and swapped guesses as to the identity of what they were eating and drinking. Round balls of a yellow substance tasted of freshly baked bread and the clear liquid they drank was indistinguishable from freshly brewed coffee. Oddly shaped items, of black and brown turned out to taste of bananas and passion fruit. They laughed and gorged themselves and Nonzaid was visibly delighted with the culinary success. As the two friends sat there in a totally surreal setting, they discussed how they had, in relative terms, assimilated much of what that had happened to them in the past twenty-four hours, with surprizing ease. Matt admitted that whilst he was a little impatient to return to his grandfather to impart all that they had experienced, he also admitted that he was just as eager to discover what more there was to discover of their current location.

As if his thoughts were read and who knows, they may well have been, Yamnus returned to inform them that their engine was proving somewhat of a mystery to these highly enlightened beings. They sat and listened in amazement as they were told of the enormity of the multiverse and that Yamnus had been in existence for approaching two hundred Earth years. Half his life to date, had been spent studying many of its dimensions, universes and planets. He had visited and explored in excess of one hundred thousand planets whist by means of remote research had investigated a further one million. It was explained that they had terms for the vastness of the multiverse and the possible number of universes, all of which would be meaningless to Matt and Ben. What was not meaningless was the matter-of-fact statement that they had discovered a multitude of planets on which life, in its broadest sense, existed, some highly advanced but on others no life as advanced as theirs but which had the potential to develop over many millennia. They had been alerted to the arrival of the engine into their dimension and were prompted to investigate its properties and what beings it was transporting. Whilst they recognized Matt and Ben as humans and from where they came, a fact Matt was determined to explore further, they could not ascertain exactly who had constructed the vessel that transported them but they could hazard a well-informed guess. The builder was likely to be from another far more advanced civilization than existed on planet Earth and they believed they had determined from whence the builder had come and also why it had visited Earth.

Again Matt's thoughts were read and they learned that previous incarnations of Philadrons had visited Earth when civilization first appeared, some five thousand years ago. They had returned during its early development to observe and learn but they determined that their temporal and dimensional travels should remain unobserved. They had attempted at communications on other planetary visits but considered it unwise to interfere in the development of other dimensions or worlds.

They had discovered a planet in a universe some one thousand light years from Earth and known as Druxivis, which had reached an advanced stage of development. The Drux too had ventured to other universes and galaxies but their search was for an alternate home. The three suns that were the providers of all life and sustenance on their planet had been in an expanding elliptical orbit, taking them further and further away from Druxivis and they had known that a time would come when their planet would die. The Drux had sent out a multitude of highly complex and advanced probes, to distant universes to find a place to escape to but had not been successful. However, long after Druxivis and the Drux had ceased to exist, the probes had continued their journey and one, they believe, had found its way to planet Earth. And the Philadrons were sure that this probe had been found and ultimately used to produce the engine that brought the visitors to Philax 10. Whoever had discovered the probe, as likely or not, also a visitor from another world, recognized the power of their discovery and the interplanetary and trans dimensional travel capabilities it possessed. At that point both Ben and Matt thought of the Cossack in Alfred's tales. The level of planet Earth's technological development at that period was quite primitive and whoever had located the probe, knew that it was a discovery of immense value and should not be shared. Matt and Ben could piece together what happened following its discovery and why it had remained secret ever since.

Yamnus explained that their engine was cleverly cloaked and hidden from view but they would be able to locate it and they would be taken back whenever they wished and assisted in the reversal of their trans dimensional trip. However, Philax 10 was a vast planet some many times larger than planet Earth and Yamnus suggested they may wish to see the wonders on offer. Matt looked at Ben and was pleased to see she was as eager as he was to lengthen their stay and he communicated this desire. Yamnus then presented the two with a shattering but awesome proposal. On Philax 10 it was the power of the mind that governed life and the Philadron's very existence. Before departing, to explore the planet, it would be of great benefit and even essential, to equip them with the requisite skills to operate their transport globe plus other essential requirements, it would also give them an immense benefit when they returned to their world. Yamnus added that their research had led them to conclude that the brains possessed by the people from Earth, could be considerably enhanced. With the available capacity the Philadrons possessed the technology to transfer a number of their skills and powers to the two visitors.

Unfortunately, their brains were not developed enough to receive the full extent of what their host's mental powers were able to exert. However, Yamnus cautioned, they must decide for themselves if they wish to be availed of such enhancements. They would be alone in their world with such skills and it could only be speculated on the ramifications which could ensue, being placed in such a unique position. Yamnus advised them to take some time to consider what they had been told and when and if, they were ready to proceed, he would return with a further explanation and with that he was gone. Matt and Ben sat without speaking for several moments not knowing what to say. What powers and skills was Yamnus referring to? What would they do with such powers? To be unique on a planet of almost eight billion people was an immense responsibility and would dramatically affect their relationships with family, friends and all they knew.

To be so unique and to possess what Yamnus alluded to placed a heavy responsibility on their shoulders. To counter this, they reasoned, incalculable benefits could ensue and maybe such an offer should not be declined. The two discussed the matter for some time and were moving towards a positive decision. Presently Yamnus returned and they could see from his expression, that, once again, their thoughts had been read.

Yamnus beckoned them to join him and as they stood, placed a hand on each of their heads and they rose through the globe and found themselves in a smaller globe above. In this space, large marshmallow like chairs floated above the floor and from around the chairs long tendrils snaked upwards. Yamnus began to transfer details of what the two could expect and if they were in awe on hearing the proposal, the details that they were now receiving were beyond description. There was yet another additional aspect of the procedure they were about to undertake. Yamnus appeared to choose his words carefully, in proposing what could be described as a cerebral cortex expansion; there would be a side effect. Naturally, this term immediately produced a red flag in both of them, which Yamnus immediately assured them was unnecessary. The nature of the skill set they would receive would require that the four lobes of their brain plus the cerebellum must be advanced exponentially in order to accommodate powers that their current abilities could not accommodate. In this process, the side effect of which he spoke, will be to greatly enhance the function of your hippocampus, the learning and memory part of your brain. I can only counsel you to be circumspect how you display and reveal all these new abilities you are about to be given. You will be, he again repeated, unique amongst your people and they will not be able to understand and maybe find it difficult to accept that you are now of a different species to what you were. With these sobering words, Yamnus explained he would now send them a comprehensive vision of all he had told them, together with the details of the powers they have chosen to accept. They took their respective marshmallow seats and the multiple tendrils automatically attached themselves to

93

their heads. Effortlessly, they drifted into a receptive state and information poured into their brains. Firstly, they would possess the power of telekinesis, the ability to move objects, words and formulae were accompanied by images, which further explained the full extent of what this meant. Each new feature assailed their minds and senses but somehow all was assimilated, as if it were a most natural process. There followed a concept that was far beyond their comprehension, that of apportation which would enable them to appear and disappear. Detailed scientific information told them how molecular analysis and rearrangement enabled this act to be achieved. Next the power of levitation of which they knew but considered it mere fiction. The following wonder was just as unimaginable as the previous, that being the ability of psychic surgery. By mere touch, one could see at a molecular level, into every part of a human body and thereby detect matters that would be cause for concern and have the ability to treat them. Finally, the advances to their current abilities would enable them to consume, learn and interpret vast amounts of data at unimaginable speed. They heard the voice of Yamnus, who like a surgeon about to undertake a major operation, informed them that the procedure was estimated to take approximately three of their hours and throughout every moment their brain functions will be closely monitored to ensure a seamless acceptance. He told them that long before their visit, many decades have been spent studying the composition of human beings, he further informed them and they possess finite detail of the molecular composition of their brains and so no adverse reactions will be permitted. Without realizing, they began to slip away into a complete state of semi consciousness.

In this state, they were able to feel and even visualize the very action of their sensory neurons pulsating, as power and energy was received and travelled to their brains. At the appropriate moment, the tendrils detached and floated aloft as they regained consciousness. The acceptance of such voluminous data left them slightly dazed and they remained seated as they contemplated what had just transpired. Slowly they regained their composure, realizing they were fully apprised of all the changes that had taken place and felt an amazing awareness and feeling of enlightenment.

Together with Yamnus, who with great insight was helping them to craft their acceptance of these gifts. He further counselled that they use their moral and ethical judgment, on the extent to which each or all of these skills and powers should be utilized. There could be no denying that so enabled, they could have a material impact, in a positive way, on the future of their planet. They communicated their happiness with all that had transpired and what they had been told and were prepared for whatever came next. Yamnus trained his radiant green eyes, first on Ben and then on Matt, satisfying himself as to their preparedness and told them that they had taken a brave decision to proceed with the enhancements. With new found insight, Ben told him they when they return, they would need to remain exceedingly close and vigilant to ensure they stay harnessed, as best they could, to the reality of their ordinary lives.

They later recalled the sensation was as if they were watching a film at ten times the normal speed, a blur of sights and sounds, all of which disseminated into a blinding awareness of every word spoken and action taken. When the sensation had subsided somewhat and relative normalcy had returned, they were greeted by yet another Philadron, this time introduced as Ukvul who explained that with their new enhancements, the functionality of their transport globe and their onward journey would be far more easily accomplished. Ukvul had adopted the visage of a 1950's American movie star, she sported platinum pin curls and a figure hugging white cocktail dress, was fully made up with ruby red lipstick and long mascaraed eye lashes. Finished off with impossibly high heels, the whole image, whilst perfect on a film set, was totally incongruous considering their present location. The two of them could not help themselves but just stared which had the effect of making Ukvul look very uncomfortable. Ben rescued the situation by conveying how they were dumbstruck by her stunning beauty, this worked and a wide white toothed smile, appeared on her face. With that delicate situation resolved, Ukvul explained it was her role to monitor the multitude of globes that traversed the planet and would guide them to their personal transport globe. They were handed what looked like headphones but with pads, which they were instructed to attach to their temples. These would be used to communicate with the globe. Once installed in the globe their mental transmissions would be paired with the globes operating system and would react accordingly. Ukvul explained to always be brief, using concise instructions. There is a built-in safety module, which is fully aware of all and every possible danger that Philax 10 possessed. They were guided upwards to a platform along which were many small globes lined up, as far as the eye could see. Amazingly, the number three hundred and eighty two came into his head, Ukvul told him that was indeed the number of globes currently docked.

A smile appeared on Ukvul's face as she cautioned that some trial and error may be required, although unlikely, until proficiency was accomplished in their instruction technique. In time they could dispense with the headpieces and just by means of thought transference, operate the globe seamlessly. Each globe appeared capable of accommodating perhaps four or six human sized forms. Further along the platform there was a constant arrival and departure of globes, with Philadrons boarding or alighting. Matt was curious how these globes were propelled and Ukvul looked at him and momentarily considered the question in her mind. She advised him that there were many things on Philax 10, which were too advanced to offer an easily comprehensible explanation to species from far less developed worlds. Ukvul politely offered to attempt a simplified explanation by directing his attention towards the base of the globe. By means of offering Matt a pictorial as well as a text explanation, she portrayed a system, which harnessed opposing forces to create power. Within a sealed unit no larger than a small suitcase, was a system using antimatter-matter annihilation propulsion.

The antimatter was harvested in deep space but could propel the globes at unimaginable speeds, if required. Matt turned to Ben and could see she had received the same information and was similarly as nonplussed as he was. Ukvul apologised that she was unable to offer a more simplistic explanation.

They were directed to a globe nearby and instructed how to gain access, by means of placing a hand on the surface and projecting the demand for an opening to appear. Both of them made attempts but failed. It was evident that their heads were occupied with a number of conflicting thoughts when instructions such as the one they were attempting, could only be achieved with a clear mind. Several attempts later, it was Ben who was successful as an opening appeared in front of her and she stepped aboard. There were four sculptured seats behind two rows of blank screens. They entered and took their seats, Matt instinctively stared at one of the screens and it lit up to reveal a panoramic view of the planet spreading out from where they were docked. Ben took his lead and looked at another screen, it too lit up but this time the display was of a huge waterfall of unimaginable height but at the bottom of the fall was a black void, which swallowed the cascading water.

Ukvul explained that each of the screens had a different function and they would soon learn what the function was, by pairing with the screen. One in particular, second from the left on the top row, Ukvul explained, was for geographical information, by simple interrogation it would tell them of all the places to visit and what to see on arrival, how long the trip was and much more. On the lower row were screens, which provided various on-board services such as their particular food requirements, or health and safety needs. Ukvul undertook a short demonstration by swiftly lighting up each screen in turn and explaining the different functions that each displayed.

She explained that they had developed these globes for

guests visiting from worlds that were possessed of different skill sets and who may not be able to operate the globe by the simple power of thought. They reviewed the multiple screens and discovered everything from strange looking items of clothing to what looked like propulsion packs for individual use and detailed explanations of particular items in their line of sight. Ukvul next drew their attention to one particular screen on which appeared a strange symbol, this they were told would enable them to return to an available docking station along the platform. Another option would offer them immediate protection, at which point the two of them looked at Ukvul questioningly, wanting to know, protection from what. She suggested there was no real need to worry in that all climate related matters could be dealt with by the impenetrable nature of the globes structure but there had been known to be incursions from beyond Philax 10. Expanding and collapsing planets which may exist vast distances away would occasionally cause planetary debris to pierce their outer limits. The globe had sensors which would warn occupants if such an occurrence were imminently expected and they must activate the screen to which their attention had been directed. The globe would then move at hyper speed to a protected location, deep in the planets core, until any danger had passed. They were assured this had only occurred twice in the last thousand years and on learning this, the pair visibly relaxed. Ukvul continued that there were also large predators on the planet who could, if they felt threatened, pose a small element of danger, the safety protocols would likewise be deployed. And with no more apparent communication from their instructor, the globe was sealed and they were ready to depart.

CHAPTER 5

ONWARDS AND UPWARDS

The two friends sat there, looking at the screens in front of them and the endless vista all around through the clear globe. The longer they spent on the planet, the more adept they became at telepathically transmitting their thoughts. Ben was the first to move, she inclined forward and focussed on a screen, which depicted the immense waterfall and without being aware of exactly what she did, nor how she did it, the globe gently lifted into the air and without a sound sped forward. They were both slightly alarmed and Matt, now without speaking, congratulated her on her first telepathic instruction. By way of an experiment, Matt instructed the globe to stop; instantly the globe came to a standstill, in mid-air and remained stationery waiting for another command. It was agreed that it would be sensible for only one of them to instruct the globe and they would confer who that would be as each occasion arose. Ben agreed and told Matt she wanted to continue to the waterfall and transmitted the instruction, which instantly caused the globe to again propel forward.

Initially they saw a rising mist in the far distance but as they approached, they realised it was a fine spray caused by millions of litres of water pouring over a sheer cliff face and dropping into a black hole beneath. They guided the globe to hover over the top of the fall and then slowly lowered, at a safe distance, following the path of the falling water downwards. They stopped, maybe a hundred meters above a black hole and stared. It was impossible to fathom out what the makeup was of this feature, whether it was natural of not. The humongous volume of water just silently fell into blackness, looking like the massive mouth of a thirsty monster. Surrounding the black hole, stretching in every direction was dense, lush vegetation and looking further outwards, vast swathes of land given over to crops which on Earth they would have thought to be cereal crops. They moved away from the black hole and lowered the globe to a few feet above the gently swaying crops, the similarity to corn from far above was no longer apt, in their estimation the plants were around two meters high. Ben activated a blank screen and directed that it viewed the plants below and with a minor tweak to her instruction, they were delighted to discover what they were looking at. There appeared the image of a single stem with the description informing them it was a Norlanda plant, edible for entities with a digestive tract. They assumed that this may apply to the animals that inhabited Philax 10 and visitors such as themselves.

Matt suggested they inquire if there were a place where they could see what animals there were on this planet. The screen, which had depicted the waterfall was now showing numerous pictures of strange and bizarre looking animals. Directing attention on one animal, they could then learn anything and everything about it. Having now mastered the ability of instructing the globe, they sped off at great speed, rising to scale a mountain range and then slowing as they reached the top. The summit flattened to reveal a massive crater, several miles in diameter, which was covered in parts by lush forests, made up of the trees they had seen on their arrival and others of a more prehistoric nature. There were massive ferns but with brilliant, coloured flowers at the tips of each blade and innumerable luminescent yellow Lilies that had attracted hordes of what looked like, flying lizards that popped in and out of the flower cups. At their current height they were unable to make out much detail below and dropped to a level that allowed them to see the myriad of small reptiles that were feeding from the flowers rather than pollinating them. They were suddenly aware of a growing vibration, they enquired of the globe which produced the image of something called a Kalidon, they rapidly learned this colossal beast stood twenty plus meters tall and its preferred method of attack was to propel a paralyzing and deadly acidic bile, with great velocity and from a distance of a hundred meters from its prey. No sooner had the pair digested these mind-boggling statistics, than the globe, enacting its safety protocol, shot skywards but not before they felt the impact of a gelatinous fluid landing on the globe and the interior darkened. With their heightened awareness, Matt told Ben they were safe and no damage had been sustained to the globe. They glanced towards the ground and to their utter amazement saw this behemoth staring vehemently up at them, with giant globules of its deathly bile dripping from its cavernous mouth.

They were delighted and relieved to see Ukvul appear in a seat behind them, only this time more soberly appearing in checked shirt and corduroy slacks. She noted their rather impromptu introduction to one of the larger carnivores, a member of Kalidon family, but told them not to fear as they were never in danger. They told Ukvul they were grateful the sensors had removed them from the proximity of danger. However, Ukvul was concerned that the beast was able to approach as close as it did and shall report the incident, requesting that the safety systems be reviewed. She had picked up a message from the globe and thought some assistance was needed. Ukvul took charge of the globe and sped across the range to a lake, at which point the globe plunged into the water.

The dip not only served to wash clean the globe but

they were also treated to a spectacular sub aqua panorama. Matt excitedly looked around through the clear water and was intrigued to learn what some of the sea freshwater creatures they were looking at were. However, when names and details appeared on a screen, he was none the wiser. Ukvul informed him that some creatures of Philax 10 found their origins on other planets and others were the creation of their geneticists, whose advances allowed them to create new species, although they had encountered some issues with the reproductive cycles. She pointed out one sea creature, which did strike a familiar chord, Ukvul told them they were looking at eel-mastigodryas. On enquiring, this creature had indeed been created by the geneticists from samples brought form planet Earth. As they exited the lake with all signs of their recent unpleasant encounter erased, Ukvul suggested a more pleasant place to visit. There was a location where Philadrons, who had embarked on detailed research of other planets residents, would go and replicate the beings they had discovered, not only their appearance but customs, habits and speech. Ben was most intrigued at this idea and they both welcomed the opportunity of Ukvul escorting them onwards.

The topography below them changed rapidly and as they left the mountain range, a vast desert opened out below them which stretched to the far horizon. There were dunes as high as mountains and they could see a distant sand tornado zigzagging across the dessert. Here and there they could pick out rocky outcrops and it was towards one of the larger ones they now headed. The globe slowed and as its altitude decreased, they could make out a cavernous entrance, which they presently entered. Expecting total darkness, they were surprised to see a pleasant lightness, which Ukvul told them was artificially generated. This place had been chosen because some of Philadron's elders scoffed at the pastime of those gathered here, considering it hardly in pursuance of their ideas of intellectual and scientific advancement. Whilst the location was not a secret, it was sufficiently discretely located as to remain less offensive, to the critics of the practice. Thus informed, the globe settled on a sandy bed by the edge of a lake on which large half coconut shell like crafts haphazardly criss-crossed the surface. Some made their way to an island at the centre and for the first time, Matt and Ben could hear not only voices but music. Their curiosity was greatly aroused and taking his cue, Ukvul explained that it was not only the customs, habits and speech that had been replicated, but other diverse cultural aspects of their lives, which included music and food. As they stood, totally intrigued by the sight, one of the strange craft drifted towards them. Sitting aboard was the strangest being they had seen to date, marginally humanoid in appearance but with reptilian features, such as a scaly face and hands, almond shaped eyes, no nose but two small apertures and no apparent ears and wearing a naval uniform. After spending some time assessing the human visitors he welcomed them in a guttural, passable and comprehensible English. The two of them could not help themselves and finally, bust out laughing which had the effect of causing the boatman to turn to Ukvul with a look of hurtful despair. Matt was the first to realize their rudeness and spoke aloud with eloquent apologies, explaining their laughter was more a sign of joy, having not heard their own language spoken for quite some time. At this a smile broke out on the boatman's face and he stood, bowed and introduced himself as Nimmiks. He explained that he had never met an earthling before and that his linguistic achievements had been garnered from his planet's archives. He said he would be most grateful if they could spare some time to converse with him, so that he may learn more of their language and manners.

Ben told him they would be delighted to talk with him and with that he jumped ashore and helped them aboard his coconut shell boat. Once seated, they noticed that Nimmiks tapped a small keyboard affixed to the side of the hull and the vessel turned and headed towards the island. As they sedately got under way, it was Matt who asked Nimmiks why he had chosen to adopt reptilian features. In a matter-of-fact manner, he told them that he was unimpressed by the appearance of humans and during his research he happened upon the planet Porilia, in the Raloona constellation and there in the Waters of Claresino, there dwelt the most attractive race of sentient reptiles. He was captivated by their looks, which was why he decided to adopt certain of their features. To this, there was little either of them listening to his explanation, could say.

As they reached the island, the music became more discernible and what had appeared from the shore to be a familiar sound, was on closer listening most certainly otherwise. There was a primal beat that both Matt and Ben recognized but the overlay of unknown instruments and less than rhythmic sounds, left them bemused. It was in short a complete unmusical cacophony of sound. They followed the boatman along a narrow sandy path, lined by what appeared to be palm trees and eventually came to a clearing. The two visitors stopped in their tracks and stood transfixed by numerous individuals that were gyrating in the centre. For the most part, the majority had adopted variations of human appearance, in a variety of colours and hues but there any similarity in appearance ended. Others were decidedly animal in their appearance but of which kind was impossible to say. The attire, much less the gender of each was impossible to discern, it was a strange mixture from traditional and even formal dress, to battle garb and what could only be described as medieval. There were two in particular, that caught both their eyes and one appeared to be wearing chain mail and armour chest plates and another in a tuxedo, complete with top hat. It would be impossible to describe their movements as dancing, as well as to suggest that it was the music that had prompted such movements. However, having said that, all those gathered appeared to be having a good time. They were both captivated and amused by the sight and vocalized such to both Ukvul and Nimmiks. They were beckoned to some traditional looking seats and were pleasantly surprised when an individual, dressed as a waitress, arrived and asked if they desired refreshments. Ben asked what was available and the waiter appeared stumped for an answer, turning to Ukvul for assistance, presently, with a pleasant smile and in a totally unfathomable accent, told them that whatever they desired was available. At this Matt laughed and told Ben that they should have known that the inhabitants of Philax 10 could conjure up whatever the imagination thought of. The two of them ordered a Hawaiian punch and waited in anticipation to see what arrived. They did not have to wait long before the waitress returned with two tall glasses of a yellow liquid, complete with a slice of what looked like pineapple and a cherry on a tick plus a cocktail umbrella. Amazed the couple sipped their respective drinks and announced, with honest delight and pleasure, what an expertly made cocktail it was. As for their associates, they would need to ask what they had ordered. Nimmiks held a large mug which veritably boiled over with foam and following a noisy gulp, was left with a white moustache. Ukvul, who the two friends believed, no longer possessed a digestive system, was served a cocktail glass filled with a clear fluid. The nature of the mysterious drinks was explained, Nimmiks described his as being the extract of a local plant mixed with a strange sounding liquid which neither Matt nor Ben was prepared to sample when offered. Ukvul was consuming with apparent relish, an extract from the stomach of the Namongo fish, which she said they may have seen in their brief underwater foray earlier in the day. It was a medium sized bulbous eyed fish, white in colour and covered in blue dots. It was a description that neither of them recollected but neither of them was inclined to sample that drink either, when offered.

On impulse, Matt stood and took Ben's hand coupled with a request for a dance. Laughing, they joined the throng and made a brave attempt to pick up a rhythm to dance to. Finding that impossible they just improvised and became totally lost in the absurdity of where they were and what they were doing. They happily remained on the island for some time, enjoying the dancing spectacle of others and taking turns in speaking slow well-enunciated words for Nimmiks benefit.

111

In addition to the drinks on offer, they were offered food and the friends now appreciating the limitless availability of instantly produced fare, ordered cheeseburgers and fries but were asked to explain in more detail exactly what it was they were ordering. Whilst not a hundred per cent perfect, with some peculiar colour differences, the texture and taste were remarkably close to the real thing. They had warmed to Nimmiks for his repeated thanks for their patient tuition and congenial manner. The time came for them to depart and he took them back to the shore and their globe. Yamnus was waiting for them when they arrived back and they were excited to convey how much they had enjoyed their trip and all of the sights they had seen. Both of them conveyed they were tired and would welcome a chance to sleep prior to making a return journey to their home. Yamnus offered them a comfortable resting place and they were taken to yet another globe, nearer the ground, which was gratifyingly equipped with beds. He explained that should they wish, just transmit the command for darkness and the globe would become opaque. Yamnus explained that they did not use water in their daily lives but demonstrated the use of a cubicle that emitted a pulsating sound and a purple light, which he said would serve to cleanse their bodies. They took turns and marvelled at a technology that effectively cleaned and refreshed them as water did but with the use of sound and light only.

They briefly discussed the amazing experience of their time on Philax 10 and how and if, they would disclose any of it to anyone, including Alfred, only thinking of the safety of those they loved. Too tired to stay awake, Matt effected the darkness command and sleep came quickly to the friends and they slept soundly. They were awoken only when a mental awakening announced coffee and something to eat, was on its way. Nonzaid appeared before them and they had not realized how hungry they were until they started to eat not bothering to disseminate what it was they were eating and drinking, accepting that it all tasted perfectly nice. Matt communicated with Yamnus that the time had come for them to take their leave and in return he displayed a positively human trait by expressing the pleasure he had derived in meeting with them and the hope they would return. They reciprocated the sentiments and they boarded a globe to be reunited with the engine. Before departing they conveyed to Yamnus their gratitude for all he had done for them and he conveyed the hope that he would come to see how they used the gifts he had given. Without explaining, Yamnus replied that in the long future that lay ahead he felt sure he would learn of the mark they would leave upon the planet they called home.

They boarded a small globe and directed it to the

arrival spot. The globe settled in what appeared to be a barren area but they spotted the distant forest they had seen on their arrival. Yamnus told them this was the location of their transport vessel and in their absence, he had visited the spot and acquainted himself with the operating functions of the engine. It would appear that all that was necessary was for them to exert their now amplified mental powers to direct the engine and a homing device will transport them to their point of departure. Matt said to Yamnus that they had arrived at Philax 10 completely randomly but could the engine be programmed in any way to predetermine its destiny on any future trip. He considered the matter and that he believed it was Matt who could dictate where the engine would travel, in the same way as they controlled their globes. However, in order to avoid total randomness, he would need have some familiarity with his desired location.

With combined concentration they slowly walked forward and were presently engulfed in total darkness before seeing their engine before them. They climbed aboard and agreed that whilst it had been the most incredible journey, they both were looking forward to be returning home. Although, possessed as they now were, with incredible skills, it would take all their human attributes to manage and utilize them. Matt fired up the boilers and instinctively reaching out took Ben's hand, he engaged the engine and they closed their eyes in concentration. They sensed rather than felt movement and opened their eyes to take in a repeat of the light show they had seen on their outward journey.

Seamlessly and with the passage of a few minutes they found themselves seated on the small couch, in the front room. Regaining their composure, they exited the room and heard Alfred moving about in the kitchen. He stopped what he was doing and came to meet them, with a quizzical look on his face, he gave both of them a hug and kiss and said how happy he was to see them. He locked up the front room and told them to come into the kitchen, he needed to know what they had seen and done. They looked at each other, still unsure what to say and Matt told Ben, without the need to speak, to leave it to him, he would think of something.

CHAPTER 6

BACK TO NORMALITY OF SORTS

Once again there was the need to assimilate the fact that they had only been absent from the real world for a short time, exactly seven minutes. They sat around the familiar kitchen table and whilst Alfred busied himself at the larder, they told him they were not hungry and he stopped what he was doing and joined them. Matt composed himself and began by telling his grandfather that what they had seen and experienced was beyond imagination. What he had given them, by allowing them access to the engine and so much more, would change their lives forever. He then began with the jaw dropping light show of their brief trans dimensional trip and then their first experience of arriving at Philax 10 and the meeting with Yamnus. Matt was graphic in his story telling, only considering to reveal their dramatically enhance mental powers, may be a little premature. Ben had silently suggested this was wise, for the time being. Alfred was left speechless by their tales, only speaking once to suggest what he was hearing was beyond science fiction. Nevertheless, he listened patiently to all they had to say and apart from his initial amazement, accepted all that he heard with an exterior calmness. When Matt commented on his ready acceptance of what they had experienced, his response was that in all the time he had spent with Yuri and travelling on his railway, he knew in his heart that there must be so much more to the mysteries of the engine than just providing him with a pleasant train ride in his own make belief world. However, he could never have dreamt that such an amazing revelation would have awaited them and was so very happy for them and was truly interested to know more. By emphasizing his interest to know more, told Matt and Ben all they needed to know as how much Alfred accepted what they had told him as being the whole story.

It became increasingly difficult for them to remain focused on their normal daily routine, as their respective minds demanded attention in many other directions. Attending school presented a particular challenge and at the first opportunity they found a quiet spot on the far side of the sports field to talk. They conversed silently and agreed that they would harness their greatly enhanced acumen and ensure that their future schoolwork would open up new opportunities.

It was a swift transformation from average to good students and then to levels of excellence that confounded both teachers and fellow students alike. Such a transformation lead to a summons from the head mistress, for what transpired to be a most congenial chat. They had rehearsed a response to the obvious question regarding their rapid intellectual development, which was that the concentrated and intense amount of extracurricular studying together had born fruit. Whilst it may have been a less than compelling explanation, nobody who heard it could offer a counter reason. The school was receiving positive publicity, as the two began achieving extraordinary results and were only too happy to bathe in the reflected glory. Within the passage of the following year Ben became head girl and Matt head boy and their respective parents were left dumbfounded by the array of achievements from their children.

When they had first returned from their trip, Matt asked if Ben had experimented with any of her powers, she told him that on the day they had returned, she made the excuse of being tired and went to her room at the earliest opportunity. It had not been difficult to summon but more difficult to control, her powers. She was able to move inanimate objects and told Matt that after just a couple of attempts, she had successfully lifted a hairbrush from her dresser and transported across the room and into her hand. Her attempts at levitation had not been so successful and whilst she felt a definite lightening in her body, the extent of the effort enabled her to rise a mere foot but the exertion was too much and she gave up. She decided, at that point, she would be happier if they could trial their powers together and stopped trying.

For his part, Matt's attempts at telekinesis were also as good, as far as it went but he admitted to a better result with levitation. He had laid on his bed and closed his eyes, cleared his mind and practiced deep concentration. He told his friend that he stifled a cry of alarm when he realized that he was about to bump into the ceiling light in his room. He had raised himself off the bed and had not been aware of having done so. He suggested that on the very next occasion they were to visit Alfred at The Spinney, they would get off the school bus a mile or so before, where there was an entrance to a small country park. Assuming they could find a discreet spot, they would work on their skills and powers, particularly the one neither of them had attempted, that of apportation, appearing and disappearing at will.

It was a sports afternoon where they each played key roles but claimed, with forthcoming exams, they wanted to concentrate on other subjects and no objections were raised. Too early for the school bus, they took a taxi to the country park. They could see in the distance some young children running about and mums sitting on benches, Matt pointed to a thicket with a number of small trees in the middle. They made their way over and it proved perfect as the trees opened to a small space, just enough for the two of them to stand in and be shielded by the dense undergrowth of the thicket. Matt had his school bag with him and removed a textbook which he then placed on the ground, just a couple of paces away. He suggested they took turns to raise the book and transfer it to each other's hands. It took just a couple of attempts to perfect this small display and Matt suggested it would be interesting to see at what distance their power would extend. With some trepidation, Mat offered to try apportation first and closed his eyes to assist in concentrating. Beth watched him intently but was alarmed at hearing a voice close by. She turned in the direction of the voice to hear a woman calling her dog that was scratching around in the thicket just a couple of feet away from where they stood. The dog returned to its owner and Beth turned to an empty space where Matt had been standing. Without shouting, she said his name and before she had time to panic, he reappeared a foot in front of her, wearing a huge grin on his face. He admitted that his only fear had derived from the not knowing where they would go when they disappeared but the answer he said, was nowhere. In fact, he heard the dog, saw her turn and felt an almost out of body experience. He did not realize he had achieved disappearance until she turned and he saw the startled look on her face and only realized at that point she could not see him. He was not frightened about the return and just closed his eyes thought in clear and precise terms

120

about the desire and it was fulfilled.

He urged her to try and seeing his confidence, she was immediately reassured. To witness a human being disappear in front of his eyes was an amazing experience for him and he told her when she returned that if and when they did such a thing with others present, it was inconceivable to imagine the reaction. At this she smiled and said that raising a chair and sending it across the room was just as likely as to have them burnt as witches, at which they both laughed. The remaining power of psychic surgery was the last to be attempted and neither of them knew how to go about testing this power. He suggested they just attempt a deep body investigation and without further ado, he placed his hand on Ben's wrist, again closing his eyes. He swiftly removed his hand and his eyes shot open, his alarm, he told her, was the most stunning mental images of seeing her various vital organs. As he imagined her heart, he saw her pumping heart valves and the image was so stark and detailed, it came as a shock. Ben decided to wait until a later occasion to test such a skill. They also discussed the need to test the full extent of their powers before there was ever any need or requirement to use them. They also spoke of how far would they be able to remotely raise objects. If they were to disappear, could they reappear at another location? They agreed they had much to discover whilst remaining cloaked in secrecy.

121

They left the thicket and walked across the open field in the opposite direction to where the children and parents were. On the edge of the park Matt said he wanted to try further apportation skills and told Ben he would risk a transfer to the top of the tall oak tree they were now standing next to. Ben urged him to take care but with no hesitation Matt vanished and she looked skywards. At the very top of the eighty foot tree she could make out Matt waving at her and the next instant he was standing by her side. He told her the key to deploying each skill was to totally clear their minds and apply deep concentration on the desired outcome. With that in mind, Ben closed her eyes and disappeared, Matt knew where to look and with greatly enhanced vision could see a smiling Ben sitting atop the tree.

Feeling a little tired from their exertions they made their way towards the park exit gate. Matt touched Bens arm and pointed to a plinth on which was placed a World War 2 floating mine. They walked over to it and saw a brass plaque which explained that the mine was found, still live, on the beach at Clacton-on-Sea on the 15 July 1944. It had been dropped in the River Rhine three months earlier, by the British Air force, in the hope it would float through Germany and explode on contact with any German vessel. Apparently it missed everything and no contact was made, the mine reach the end of the river and floated into the North Sea and across to

Clacton. At the bottom of the plaque was stated the mines dimensions, including a weight of 440 lbs. It was this that caught Matt's attention. He looked around three hundred and sixty degrees using his enhanced vision, to ensure they were out of range to the few distant people in the park. He then stared at the mine and concentrated hard and within a matter of seconds the mine effortlessly lifted to a height of a hundred feet, before he quickly and gently returned it back onto the plinth. He told an impressed Ben how easy it was and she must find another weighty object and try.

By now the first school bus should be arriving and they waited at the stop to continue their journey to The Spinney and Matt told Ben he wanted to disclose to Alfred the full extent of what happened on Philax 10. When they arrived his grandfather was, as usual, busying himself at the stove, preparing something for them to eat and it allowed them a little time to come to the agreement that Matt would choose the right moment to tell all. It was almost as if Alfred had played along, having dwelt longer in preparing their food and intermittingly going to the larder which was at the other end of the kitchen to where they sat. He returned with plates of grilled tomatoes and sardines on toast and a pot of steaming tea.

He smiled and suggested that they may well have more to tell him about what happened to both of them during their recent travels. Between the two of them, they told all and not for the first time Alfred was taken aback by the enormity of their revelations. He had begun to counsel them on the need for great caution and not to allow a frenzy to occur over their overt use of these gifts, as he called them. He said that just by looking at them he could see they had changed, carrying themselves with a heightened degree of self-confidence and awareness and if he could see it others will also. They must train themselves to disguise all these outward signs. They were dismayed, as much by Alfred's astute observations and their own failure to recognize these tell-tale signs and thanked him for the warning.

They were interrupted when the front door bell chimed and it was Wendy arriving. With that his mother breezed in, kissed her father and they exchanged a few words. The friends gathered up their belongings and Wendy ushered them to the front door. They drove to Halstead and dropped Ben off but before continuing their journey home, his mother confronted him with a curious question. She said that she and his father had been astounded by the change in Matt and Ben and what they were both achieving at school. They frankly were unable to understand how such a transformation had been possible. He could do no more than keep to the script he and Ben had agreed upon and that it was just a new found desire to make something of his life. His disappearing to his room and his somewhat withdrawn demeanour were just a consequence of that. He explained it all away, adding the heightened pressure of additional schoolwork and assured her nothing at all was amiss. She smiled and told him that she could not be happier that her son was turning into such a clever young man and with that she put the car into gear and off they went.

Both Matt and Ben had discussed a growing hunger to learn and a desire to master everything they attempted. In that regard, Ben was passing some fellow students in the school refectory who were playing chess. She stopped and began to consume each and every move the opponents made, she pulled up a chair and sat, watching each game with the same intensity. She discovered that she could recall not only every game she had watched but every single move. With the desire to play and no less, master the game she joined the school chess club and shocked herself, as well as some of the older members by her rapid grasp of not just the game but the more intricate strategies required to win. Within a week she had consumed the strategies and winning moves of Magnus Carlsen, Kasparov, Fisher and other world Grand Masters. The Science teacher, Mr Hedges, who ran the chess club and fancied himself as quite an accomplished player, was taken aback by Beth's stunning aptitude at the game and the speed with which she learned so many of the billions of moves.

The club met three times a week, with different students attending on different days, however, Ben was at every meeting. Mr Hedges stood over her as she played and shook his head in disbelief. After dismissing three opponents in rapid succession, he asked Ben to join him in his office. She remembered Alfred's sage advice and adopted a demure manner whilst he enquired where she had learned to play, explaining that some of her moves were text book moves from grand masters but others were quite unique. She lied by telling him she had been reading chess books and playing against herself for some time. Whilst he appeared disinclined to accept this explanation, he could not deny his own eyes and said he would like to spend some time mentoring her. He was heard to say some time later that if he had not seen her progress himself, he would not have believed it possible.

Within six months of first being introduced to the game she ceased attending the chess club and was entering local competitions. With consummate ease she won game after game, culminating in winning the County Chess Tournament. Her mother was besides herself with pride and with the gallery turning a more than reasonable profit, took her daughter out and lavished her with a new wardrobe. Within a week of her success appearing as a banner headline in the Halstead Gazette, the phone rang at the gallery. At first, Kanika assumed it was a wrong number until the heavily accented voice mentioned Ben by name. Nicholas Bartofski, a UK Grandmaster, explained that he was a member of The World Chess Federation, known as FIDE (Fédération Internationale des Échecs) and whilst currently based at Warwick University, he was looking for chess prodigies. He had heard of her daughter's amazing and rapid mastering of the game from her science teacher, who he knew. He went on to say he had never come across an individual who within six months of being introduced to the game, had reached the standard of her daughter and in the process had beaten players who were National competition winners. With Kanika's consent, he requested a meeting with Ben, just to meet and talk and understand how she had achieved what she had. And so it was, Mr. Bartofski appeared at the gallery within two days and sat playing chess with Ben for the next week. At the conclusion of the week, Mr. Bartofski appeared visibly shaken but effused with admiration and compliments. They had played in excess of forty games and he had lost all but three. He paid no heed to his trouncing, imploring Kanika to allow him to speak, on her behalf, to the powers that be at the World Chess Federation, in Switzerland. From what he had witnessed, he did not think it an exaggeration to suggest that Ben would likely be in Lausanne,

127

in the not too distant future, on the first step to a bright and exciting future.

As for Matt, whilst his achievements were undoubtedly less high profile, they were of greater import to the advancement of mankind. Since their ride in a globe on Philax 10, he had been intrigued by the propulsion the Philadrons had developed, that of antimatter-matter annihilation propulsion. Such propulsion on earth would achieve a manned trip to Mars in a month, compared with a current trip for an unmanned spacecraft of almost a year. He had undertaken extensive research on the topic, consuming vast tomes of highly complex scientific data and in the process discovered it was not the subject of total fiction. Scientists had been experimenting with the power of antimatter for several years but in order to build a matter-antimatter engine they faced one currently insurmountable problem, the lack of antimatter in the universe. Whilst the technology to create antimatter through the use of high-energy particle colliders, like CERN exist, the amount of energy created in one year would only be enough to light a 100-watt electric light bulb for three seconds.

He applied his enhanced ability to read and digest vast amounts of information in another direction, that of discovering if the lack of antimatter in the universe was only due to the limited knowledge of the universe or something else. He travelled to the British Library in London and spent untold hours over many days, in the science reading room, reading page after page and book after book on complex scientific subjects, centred around distant galaxies and space travel. Librarians and regular visitors to the library could not help but notice the mountain of books and papers that Matt was consuming, at the same time as making copious notes, consisting of complex equations and charts. The speed with which he was able to consume the vast quantities of data, certainly attracted attention but no onlookers wanted to disturb Matt's intense studies.

Following an intense nine months he produced a scientific paper, postulating on the plausible possibility, supported by convincing data, that their existed galaxies that contain naturally produced antimatter. Specifically, he named the Laxis Nebula, as revealing fragments of a super nova which he maintained, was expanding at near the speed of light, which suggested an abundance of anti-matter. In addition, he had also calculated that being in a galaxy much closer to earth than the Crab Nebula, it could be in reached within the decade. He distilled the volume of work he had completed, into a thirty page document in which he had studiously omitted to include vital elements of his overall findings. The scientific faculty at his school were left speechless by the works this, hitherto

129

unremarkable student, had produced. They further admitted it was beyond their abilities to comprehend much of the theories and arguments he was putting forward. What they did admit was that what was within their scope of comprehension, was so staggering, they were compelled to forward his work to the science faculties at both Oxford and Cambridge Universities.

Several weeks passed before there occurred a veritable explosion of interest and the school was bombarded by a frenzy of calls from noted professors and academics wanting to know more of Matt and how he managed to produce such a unique paper, highlighting discoveries the greatest scientific minds in the world had failed to make.

More and more was appearing in the local and even the national press, about the remarkable brainiacs from a rural town in Essex and they were becoming more concerned about the growing interest they had created. Eventually reporters from the national press were knocking on their doors. Kanika plus Matt's parents did their best to fend off this intrusion but all concerned agreed that Ben and Matt should independently make carefully crafted statements to damp down the fervour they had created. Alfred, whilst sympathetic to their plight could only offer that they respond to their inquisitors by suggesting the evidence is all they need to satisfy the mystery. In other words, he suggested that Ben could hold out that she had found an interest in chess and it had awoken a latent talent for retaining and practicing and creating tactics and moves. Indeed, this proved to be the case, under the watching eyes of several Grandmasters and officials of FIDE, Ben left a trail of defeated Masters in her wake and all with an astounding display of original moves as well as established openings, middle games and end games. And now that she had attracted the attention of the world's media she rose to the occasion with an impressive degree of maturity and confidence.

In a similar fashion but far lower key, a pinstriped, silver-haired gentlemen arrived at Matts home early one Friday evening. It was Lans who opened the door and after a polite exchange, the visitor produced an embossed business card, from his Cartier wallet, announcing that he was Richard D. MacAllister - BSc Hons (Applied Sc), Senior Project Development Manager at the UK Space Agency. Momentarily lost for words, Lans invited Mr. MacAllister in and led him through to the lounge where Matt, was engrossed in a book with a pile of at least a dozen others on the floor around him. Matt regarded the visitor with polite indifference and suggested that he was doubtless visiting to discuss Matt's recent scientific paper and that was without knowing who the visitor was. Mind you, Mr MacAllister's attire suggested he was not calling on the Hendrick's household to sell life Assurance. The visitor smiled and Matt noted the visitor's studious note of the books Matt was reading. He confirmed that the assertion was perfectly correct and repeated his title and the agency he worked for. His employers were seriously impressed with Matt's work and were interested to explore further his findings and any potential collaborative initiatives to build on what he had already achieved. Matt was happy to accept the offer but first would like to know what they had in mind as regards collaboration. Wendy had opened a small mahogany drinks cabinet and offered their guest a drink, which was gratefully accepted and she busily poured him a whisky and disappeared into the kitchen to fetch some ice. MacAllister sat thoughtfully for a moment or two and then, with upturned palms, said that in all honesty, the Agency had been so wrong footed by what Matt had published that they were at a loss to know how to proceed until they had the opportunity of meeting and talking with him. In view of this, he suggested, that he visit their head office in Swindon for an informal meeting and just see where it leads, if anywhere. Matt contemplated what MacAllister had said whilst happy to accept this proposal was quick to qualify that acceptance. He explained that the document MacAllister had doubtlessly seen was not complete, in that certain elements that validate his findings had been omitted in order to protect his ownership of the research. The work had taken a great deal

132

of time in both research and validation, accordingly he would in the first place look to be reimbursed for his endeavours and in any event, expect the Agency to sign a non-disclosure agreement such was the sensitive nature of his work. As MacAllister regarded this unexpected come back from Matt, he turned to his mother and father for their approval, however they had reached a point of accepting that their son was more than capable of arriving at the correct decision, on every aspect of his life and no longer required parental guidance. They engaged in small talk whilst Mr MacAllister finished his drink and stood to leave, telling Matt he understood his concerns regarding the nature of his work and would be in touch to agree on terms and a date to meet. He momentarily hesitated before explaining that should he agree to proceed then it would be necessary for Matt to sign the Official Secrets Act, as he would most likely learn of information of a highly sensitive nature but assumed Matt would not find this a burden in any sense.

The following week Richard MacAllister called and he and Matt agreed on a date for them to meet. He conveyed to Matt the basic terms of a collaborative agreement and Matt was more than happy with the monetary sums mentioned. At this point whilst Matt was old enough to drive, he had neither taken a driving test nor thought about buying a car, MacAllister said he would send a car to collect Matt on the appointed day. With the nature of his work and that of the Agency, both parties were not only happy but worked at keeping Matt's name out of the public domain. The first meeting, as Matt told his parents, was very congenial and they had reached detailed agreement on how Matt would be rewarded for passing over title to his work to the agency and how he would be remunerated going forward. The serious amounts involved would allow Matt to become independent, as was the case with Ben and as their school leaving date neared, they discussed their next moves. Ben's diary was filling with an increasing number of overseas trips, requiring repeated long hauls to Heathrow Airport and Matt's had the need to be close to the UK's major libraries and the repositories of scientific journals which were all based in London, as well as the UK Space Agency in Swindon. Their dramatically changing life styles led them to conclude that they had to move to London. They agreed that they would trade in their old mobile phones for smart phones, as they would be spending more time apart it was vital they kept in contact. At the same time what had first been proposed at an informal meeting with the UK Space Agency, was now turning into more of a serious discussion of National importance. At the Agency's expense, Richard had organized an apartment for Matt in Swindon town centre, as it was hoped that with the wealth of information to be discussed, a period of weeks would be required to fully explore the subject matter.

They spoke to their parents about their plans and in the light of their remarkable achievements, they were happy to acquiesce to their suggestion of a relocation. Whilst leaving home did not fill them with joy, especially Kanika being a single parent, there was no plausible argument to raise in convincing them to stay at home. When the school leaving date arrived, Alfred and Cynthia suggested that they all get together for a celebratory dinner in town and so a date was agreed with Wendy, Lans, Alfred and Cynthia plus Kanika and Ben. A private dining room was booked at the Gay Hussar steak house in Halstead and it appeared no expense was spared. There was much talk of the incredible success of their respective child and anecdotes a plenty were on offer which caused much merriment. As the evening moved towards the end, it was Cynthia who proposed a toast to the future success of both of them and to help them on their way, she offered to purchase an apartment for them to share in London. On that stunning announcement, the talking ceased and all eyes turned to her for some further words on what had prompted such a generous offer. Cynthia explained that many years ago she had inherited a sum of money from a deceased relative and in their twilight years, she and Alfred needed for nothing. As if on cue, both the youngsters stood and walked around the table to hug their benefactor and Ben looked at Matt and he answered a wordless no, to the question, asking if he knew his grandmother was going to do this.

CHAPTER 7

THE SERIOUS BUSINESS BEGINS

Matt, his grandparents and Ben travelled to London, armed with a number of properties to view. Cynthia had organised five viewings, the budget determining the areas. After an unsuccessful trapes around Farringdon, Barbican and Clerkenwell, the last remaining property was in south London. It was whilst they travelled across the river, to SE1 that Cynthia explained that the next place had caught her eye because it was an old council owned block that a private developer had bought and completely renovated. It was being sold on a shared ownership basis, which made the purchase of a better quality property more affordable. They stepped off the bus along Blackfriars Road and took a five-minute walk to Chancel Street. Only a stone's throw from the river and a fifteen-minute walk to Borough Market, the property had a lot going for it, before even stepping through the front door. They were met by a representative of the developer's sales company, a young Yvonne Fletcher, obviously new to the job, she had an honest approach which was refreshing and they were all happy to let her read from the glossy brochure she held. Her lack of sales technique was no hindrance as the property sold itself. It was located on the first floor, the block being along a narrow one-way street and far enough away from the overhead railway line, to offer a relatively quiet spot in a busy City location. Matt and Ben told Cynthia they really liked the place but as she was the one buying it, the final decision was hers. As the two friends walked around they discussed the suitability of the place. It had three bedrooms, none particularly roomy, one of which would make a very useful study and a fair sized kitchen with a breakfast bar. The bathroom was small and the bath too small for the still growing Matt but he was inclined to shower, in any event an in-bath one was provided. The lounge was a comfortable size and came with a small balcony overlooking the rear courtyard, big enough for two small chairs and a coffee table. The flat was at the end of a row of four, accessed along a corridor, open on one side and here they found one great bonus, facing them at the end of the corridor was a door and this, Yvonne explained, accessed a storage unit about six feet by four and was part of the property. The fact that they were the first buyers was very appealing, as all the fixtures and fittings were new and unused. Cynthia and the agent were huddled in negotiations whilst Alfred was checking the utilities, nodding with approval at the cost saving heating system and the triple glazing on the windows. Matt tapped Ben's arm as he saw his grandmother shaking hands with the agent and they both turned with smiles on their faces. It appeared that a deal, in principal, had been agreed and that barring any unforeseen problems, once searches and all the legal issues had been attended to, they would own a three bed, first floor apartment in SE1.

As was the norm in matters of property transfers, the exchange and completion process took almost two months and that was considered quick as there was no chain of buyers and sellers. Both their names were entered on the title deeds and Cynthia counselled them to come to an agreement, preferably in writing, as to what to do, should they decide to live together no longer. It was at this time that their visits to Alfred's place tailed off, as much because their impending move to London would make them impractical.

As the years ticked by Alfred remained in relatively good health but showed increasing tiredness. He had been taking afternoon naps, which turned into longer and longer day time sleeps. Matt's concern was such that he went to visit his grandfather one morning and said he wanted to undertake some investigations to ascertain if there was anything he could do but Alfred was quite hostile to the suggestion. He told his grandson that whilst he was immensely proud at all that he had achieved and knew he would exercise the use of his acquired skills with the utmost concern for a positive outcome and the good of all concerned, he did not want the natural passage of time interfered with, if his time on earth was drawing to a close, so be it. These words caused Matt great pain and it showed in his reaction, such that his grandfather, not known for being a tactile person, put his arms around his grandson and they both shed some tears. The old man was not in any pain and the results from a recent medical showed nothing more than the ravages of time taking their toll.

As he approached his seventy-fifth birthday the family decided to celebrate in a memorable fashion. Lans invited his parents over for the occasion and Cynthia had no problem in organizing a number of rooms at Pickford Manor. A local catering company that was a regular service provider at the Manor and who Cynthia had originally hired, were more than happy to provide a gourmet meal for the evening. Wine was provided courtesy of the De Beauvoir vineyard's and Cynthia's parents were generous to a fault, unloading a dozen cases of fine wines from their car when they arrived. Wendy's contribution was to track down a string quartet that she recalled assisting when their instruments were mislaid on one of the company's ferries. She had successfully located them aboard the wrong vessel and they were beside themselves with gratitude, well she thought, now was the time they could show their thanks. The evening was an unmitigated success for everybody, the fine wines continued to be consumed into the small hours and the music continued for longer than the musicians would normally perform.

Once they were notified that contracts had been exchanged on their flat, Matt and Ben were happy to put their busy lives on a temporary hold whilst they shopped for a multitude of necessities, furniture, cooking utensils, cleaning equipment, cutlery, glassware, bed linen, towels and a host of consumables and that excluded food. They also took the opportunity to take a limited number of driving lessons, as their aptitude for all things became second nature and they passed their tests within a short space of time.

They were busily unpacking numerous bags, having returned from another shopping expedition when the doorbell chimed. Matt opened the door and was shocked to see his grandfather standing there, he put his grandson at ease by smiling and giving him a hug. On ushering him inside, Arthur hesitated and said he had brought something with him to give to Matt. Matt followed him back outside and knew instantly what he had brought when he saw a wooden crate bound by straps and padlocked, sitting on a trolly. Stunned, Matt asked what had prompted this sudden gift. They pushed the trolly inside and after a welcome hug from Ben, they sat and Alfred explained with the simple fact that it was time. He may well live for another twenty years or one, the wisest knows not how long and he could not risk leaving the engine to be discovered by strangers, even if they would be prevented from accessing its inner most secrets. He suggested that the store they had would make a good repository but Matt would have to first put some additional security measures in place. The three of them spent some quality time together and ate at a local kebab house before Alfred said he wanted to miss the rush hour traffic and should be leaving. Before he left, Matt promised he would make time to visit The Spinney soon, it had been too long since he had seen his grandmother.

With the flat finally kitted out, Ben jetted off to New York for a US Chess marathon and Matt, after many and repeated requests from the UK Space Agency, finally agreed to spend some time at their Swindon headquarters. He packed a suitcase, rented a car and armed with the address that Richard had sent him, headed to Swindon. Matt found the rather nice apartment, at the taxpayers expense, on the edge of town and opposite a small green. Being just one bedroom it was on the small side but with all creature comforts. There was a small stand up kitchen with a stove, a fridge stocked with milk, eggs, bacon and jam and a microwave. He was pleasantly surprised to find quite a large shower cubical in the small bathroom with toiletries supplied. There was a fifteen-inch colour television in the lounge/bedroom and one armchair to sit on plus a divan sofa. Matt did not imagine spending too much time in the apartment and was quite content with the accommodation. Five minutes after arriving, there was a knock on his door. A motorbike courier handed him an envelope marked Private and Confidential with his name underneath. On opening the letter he pulled out a blank copy of the Official Secrets Act and wondered how they knew he had just arrived and hoped the Agency was not keeping tabs on him.

Arriving at the Agency the following morning, Matt was rather flattered to be welcomed at reception by name, handed a printed security lanyard and accompanied to a meeting room. Already seated were five serious looking gentlemen and three equally seriously looking ladies. Matt instantly noted that without exception each of those in the room wore surprised looks on their faces, he assumed at the image of one so young as Matt. He was in no way disarmed and knew he would have no problem in convincing them that his youth was no indication of his abilities. Richard came over to shake his hand and took the manila envelope Matt offered him, he then introduced Matt to the others in the room. With his current abilities, Matt rapidly committed the names and appearance of the other eight occupants of the room, committing to memory their names and faces plus any distinguishing features. Following polite introductions, Richard turned to Matt and explained that he had disseminated what he had learned of Matts findings and everybody present had studied his paper. He asked Matt if he would like to add anything to what his paper had already revealed. Richard extended his hand towards a lectern with a microphone. It was Matt's, first public performance but it held no fears for him and he decided to give them something other than anti matter propulsion to think about. He explained that in addition to the planets Kepler -62F, Kepler – 186F and Kepler- 442B of which they would be familiar, all of which ranged from 20 to 200 lights years away, there were other planets beyond that range, which contain traces of water and in addition, he postulated, could contain some signs of sentient life. These hycean planets, as they had recently been termed or waterworlds are large and easy to find and there may well be upwards of 4,000 likely candidates out of the 100 billion that exist across the Milky Way. In fact the closest hycean planet, he told the now hushed audience, was less than a light year away, some five trillion miles and he would soon share its location and why he believes it may contain aquatic life.

He would also fill in the blanks that appeared in the document they had all been given. At this, the silent listeners became animated with several posing probing questions. He respectfully asked that he be allowed to finish and would be more than happy to answer any questions at the end. He continued, telling them they would likely be aware of the Victor M. Blanco telescope at the Cerro Tololo Inter -American Observatory in Chili that had exposed 300 million galaxies. He would also in the coming weeks, reveal the location of several of those galaxies which contain planets able to sustain life, in one form or another and by the use of anti-matter propulsion, they could be reached well before the end of the century. Finally, he returned to his initial paper and expanded on what he had described as the farming of anti-matter.

He now invited questions, which came thick and fast but which he deflected with ease. Whilst he was unable to present empirical evidence to support many of his assertions, such was the detail of his submissions, supported by current thinking that nobody present felt confident enough to challenge him, least of all to brand it pure speculation at best and downright science fiction at worst. By this point he gauged that he had comfortably won over any initial doubts that had been held about his credibility. Whilst several of those present remained sceptical and who could blame them, an unknown individual with no recognized scientific qualifications nor published papers after his name had made some pretty wild claims. However, the more they questioned him and the more he answered their questions, revealing a deep and profound knowledge of the subject matter, the more the sceptics became converts. At the conclusion of the first day, Matt was stuck by the fact that everyone present had asked and even grilled him on his presentation, that is everyone but one. Seated at the back of three rows and writing notes in a reporter's pad, throughout the meeting, was a certain Edward Creighton, who Matt was to learn, represented the Ministry of Defence (MOD), who were joint funders of this division of the Agency. He studiously avoided making eye contact with Matt at any time and after three hours, a break was called for and a refreshment trolly appeared. At that point Mr Creighton made a hasty exit and Matt caught Richard's attention and moved to the side of the room to question him on the curious character. It appears that the man whilst a scientist by training, was not well versed in the subjects under review. He was tasked to report to his paymasters that their money was being well spent and that Matt should pay him no heed. However, his heightened senses suggested he do otherwise. The meeting resumed and at the conclusion of the day's business Richard was the one to suggest they it had be a most rewarding exchange and that further dialogue would be of value, all those present heartily agreed. As the meeting broke up, Matt was approached by many of those present, who were eager to talk with him, he had obviously aroused their interest with what he had to offer.

However, he also noted that one or two of the more senior attendees appeared to feel affronted by this young pretender and their subsequent questions appeared more a means to entrap him than to find answers. Matt saw through this primitive charade and politely dismissed their clumsy attempts. There were a further five days reserved for continuing discussions and as the days progressed, Matt was treated with increasing respect and what first appeared a distinctly dubious, even hostile audience, as much to their surprise as Matts, became keen supporters of his theorems and conclusions. The remaining days were spent covering how they could best develop a proposal to government to fund exploratory trips to obtain evidence to support all that Matt had presented.

It fell to Richard to deliver the joint findings of the group at the end of the five days. He said whilst the Agency deemed it was unable to accept the totality of Matt's findings as conclusive, it similarly stated it would be remiss of them not to move forward in some form of collaborative agreement, in that not to, may well result in missing a golden opportunity.

As Matt made to leave the meeting room, Richard pulled him to one side, appearing rather nervous as he asked Matt if he knew why Mr Creighton was suddenly and without notice, removed from the Agency and called back to MOD head office. Matt asked why Richard thought he should know

147

and in response was told that it was Matt who had mentioned Creighton's odd behaviour very early on in the current session. Matt was happy to explain to Richard, the salient points of what transpired but obviously had to rewrite certain parts of the story that would make it appear more credible.

It was early on the second day of the session that he became more suspicious at the man's behaviour and decided to pay a discreet interest in his activities. He was also additionally attentive to ensure he was not also being watched. Each day's business concluded at three p.m. and as the delegates left the room to return to their respective offices, Matt monitored the movements of the civil servant. Smartly dressed in a three-piece suit, crisp white shirt and what looked like a regimental tie, he donned a trilby hat and with a pronounced limp, left the building. From the reception area, Matt noted the jaguar that his target climbed into and quickly returned to his own vehicle. He noted the jaguar turn towards town and proceeded to follow. With sufficient traffic on the road, Matt was not worried that he may be spotted plus Creighton was unlikely to know what vehicle Matt was driving, ten minutes later the jag pulled into the Marriot Hotel in town and proceeded to the underground car park. Matt parked in the short-term upper car park, close to the main entrance and before getting out, disappeared. Matt was close enough to the reception desk to see the room number on the key handed to Mr. Creighton. Matt remained unseen in the room as the civil servant put the key in the door. He was now proficient in appearing and disappearing in the same location, which gave him the ability to be invisible but to remain *in situ* to see and hear everything. Creighton entered and immediately locked the door, walked over to the windows and drew the curtains, actions of a security conscious individual Matt thought. He removed his jacket and threw it over a chair, walking over to the room safe, which was inside the wardrobe, Matt made a mental note of the combination as it was punched in and the door swung open. The hotel phone rang and Creighton picked up the receiver and simply said yes twice, he then quickly closed the safe and wardrobe door, put his jacket back on and left the room. Matt was undecided what to do next and settled on opening the safe. He rematerialized and punched in the four-digit code, the safe contained a stack of new bank notes and a small tablet. He withdrew the tablet, which he quickly discovered to be password protected, ensuring he left no fingerprints, he returned it to the safe and returned to his car unobserved. He drove to his apartment, had a quick shower and changed and left for the short walk to a local pizzeria. Having not eaten since breakfast, he realized how hungry he was and enjoyed a pizza and a glass of wine. Matt decided it would not be prudent to carry on disclosing more of his findings to the Agency, until he had satisfied himself as to Mr Creighton's true intentions, which at this moment in time he was unsure of.

A couple of hours later he returned to the Marriot to check if Creighton had returned, by simply checking the underground car park. The jaguar was there and he apported to the room to see the civil servant busy typing at his tablet. He could see that he had accessed an encrypted messaging app called Lighthouse and in between typing, he was referring to the reporter's notebook on the desk that he had used in their meetings. A quick glimpse at the message and Matt was shocked to see he was transcribing some salient points of the past two days of the Agency's proceedings. The message was sent and soon after the machine chimed and a message was received. It was brief and simply said thank you and was signed DT. Creighton stood and went to the mini bar and took out a miniature of whisky, dropped in a couple of cubes of ice and switched on the TV. Matt wondered if it were worth staying but as he had left his tablet open, he decided to wait a little longer. Fifteen minutes elapsed and Creighton returned to the desk. He scrolled down his desktop and found an icon, which read, Hendragon Bank (Guernsey) Ltd, he opened the site and was prompted for a password, the details of which Matt duly noted. His suspicion was seriously heightened at the first figure he saw, it was a current account balance of £825,000. When the transaction page was opened, the first line had the current day's date and showed a deposit of £25,000 made minutes earlier. Matt had seen enough, Creighton poured himself another whisky and went into the bathroom to run a bath. At that point Matt departed.

Matt and Ben had practiced all of their skills extensively but not to the extent of the limits that each power could reach. He so wanted to discuss what he had discovered with her but had no idea if it was possible to transport himself as far as New York. Once in his car he called her, she was at once delighted to hear from him and just as quickly alarmed. He explained there was no cause for concern but just a matter he wanted to discuss but face to face. He innocently asked her exact address and said only he would see if he could get to see her very soon. She quickly understood what he was proposing and merely voiced a concern that maybe it was a little rash but he assured her he was quite comfortable with a swift journey and signed off. He drove to the apartment, drew the curtains, turned on a table lamp, made himself comfortable in the armchair and closed his eyes. He drifted off with the imprinted thought of room 3015 on the 30th floor of the Warwickshire New York Hotel at 65 west 54th Street at the forefront of his mind. His stomach churned, he had no idea what was about to happen. The furthest distance they had experimented with was twenty miles with no problem but this was nearly three and a half thousand miles. His first sensation was of being exceedingly cold, to a point of shivering but that lasted only a few seconds, next came blackness, of an intensity which sucked all the air from his lungs and could have caused a panic attack but for the fact that almost instantly it cleared. His next sensation was of Ben throwing her arms around him. Matt felt weak and sat before he fell, his first words were to ask for water. A jug and glass was placed on the table next to where he sat and he looked around, aghast at Bens accommodation and he then bust our laughing. He told her that what was so funny was that his apartment in Swindon, in its entirety, would fit into the corner of her bedroom. She pulled a stool over to be close and told he when he was rested she would show him around but that the software company sponsoring the tournament she was competing in, was paying for the room. Meanwhile, she was eager to know how the trip was but also why he felt it was urgent to make it. He dealt with both matters quickly and they sat in silence for a moment, he with his eyes closed and she now standing and pacing. They spent a little time catching up and then concentrated on the case of Mr Creighton. After some thought she suggested that he find a source at MI6 and hand over what he knew but cautioning that it was impossible to disclose how he came by the information, it would have to be done anonymously which would raise all sorts of questions in itself but deflect away from him.

Matt considered the basic premise of the idea sound and as the head of MI6 was a matter of public record, the information could be sent from an Internet café, perhaps outside of the UK to further mask the origin. Ben agreed the plan but suggested that hard evidence would be essential. This would require, at a minimum, Matt accessing Creighton's tablet again and copying at least a bank statement. He suggested this should not be a serious problem, other than choosing a time when he was away from the hotel. With that problem dealt with, Matt stood, tested his legs and asked for a guided tour. The huge hotel room consisted of lounge come bedroom some fifty feet square with a king sized bed, a couch and two armchairs, a small dining table and a forty-inch TV. A large lamp stood in one corner with a gold shade, which matched the gold drapes, gold bedspread and the gold cushions. Ben fetched them a drink from the fully stocked mini bar and told Matt she needed to broach a matter with him. She began by reminding him that they had spoken in the past of discharging their powers in ways that would benefit society and the world at large. In this regard, she had become increasing aware during her time in the USA at the high incidence of crime and gun violence. She picked up a copy of the New York Times and showed him the front page, the headline read 'Scarlet Serpents Strike Again!!', the body copy which he scanned, revealed that a brazen gang of bank robbers had so far pulled off four major bank heists in as many weeks and the police were devoid of any meaningful leads as to the perpetrators. In the first, a security guard was shot dead and in another a bank customer was shot and is in a critical condition. Matt listened to Ben and assured her he agreed it was as good a time as any to for them to dispense a little justice. He asked that he be allowed to return to the UK to ensure the protagonist at the Space Agency is removed, so as not to jeopardize what he was trying to achieve. As soon as that business was taken care of he would return and they would unite and see about bringing this gang to justice.

Before he left, she suggested they find a quiet place to dine, she being quite a celebrity at present, was reluctant to attract the paparazzi who were always snooping around and picked the hotel's steak restaurant. They enjoyed the short time together and were both a little melancholy at the time they were spending apart and hoped that they could both return to the London flat that had hardly been lived in, in the near future. They returned to Ben's room and with a final hug, Matt disappeared.

It was early evening when he returned and contacted

Richard McAllister, asking that the meeting planned for tomorrow be adjourned until Monday as his Grandfather was unwell and he wanted to visit home. This was indeed true but not the essential reason for putting the proceedings on hold. Now knowing what he knew of the nefarious activities of Mr Creighton, he was not prepared to feed him any further valuable information. He drove to the Marriot and without checking if he was in his room appeared outside the door. He listened intently but heard no sound, he reappeared by the wardrobe, opened the safe and withdrew the tablet. He swiftly logged on to the offshore bank account, inserted a memory stick and copied several statements and then on the spur of the moment decided to check his email account. It was also password protected but like so many people, Creighton used the same password as he used for his bank account. There were no incriminating emails in the inbox but assuming anything of interest would have been deleted, he accessed the bin file but nothing there. On returning to the inbox, he checked the sent file and his attention was drawn to an email addressed to DT, immediately remembering these were the initials on a message Creighton had received, during a previous chat. The email simply said that his wife was delighted on receiving the fresh flowers and confirmed receipt but it was the recipients email address that caught Matt's attention, ending as it did in the letters 'ru' identifying its location as Russia. The time of this sending was five minutes after the arrival of £25,000 into his account and Matt likewise copied this email. He froze on hearing the lift doors open down the corridor and swiftly logged out, shut down the tablet and returned it to the safe. He effected his disappearance at the precise moment the room door opened. He saw Creighton's eyes open in shock, he obviously had caught a momentary sight of something, he shook his head, rubbed his eyes and looked again. He rushed in with a panicked look on his face and checked the only other room, the bathroom which was of course empty, he checked the balcony doors which were locked and poured a large drink. He was visibly shaken and this brought an invisible smile to Matt's face. He returned to his apartment and decided the next stop would be Paris. He located an Internet café in the Montmartre district and with a little research found that one Bertram Fitzroy-Smythe was the current Chief of MI6. Further digging and he discovered an appropriate email address for the agency. He couched the email in the strongest terms he could muster, as regards it urgency and serious nature. He laid out the official details of Creighton's current assignment, the sensitivity of the information he was privy to at the Space Agency and the incriminating nature of his offshore accounts and a Russian email address. He also attached the copies of the bank statements and email he had found. In writing the email, he purposefully included a couple of French words and English grammatical errors. He would telephone MI6 the following day to ensure the email had found its appropriate destination.

With little left to do, he called Ben and suggested he join her, if she were free, they could attend to the matter they had discussed. She was about to begin a match but having researched her opponent, she was confident of winning in twelve moves at best and fifteen at worst, either way, she would be in her apartment in approximately one hour.

Matt considered the follow up to his plan and as MI6 probably didn't keep regular office hours, he decided to call before he met Ben. Again he considered it wise to make the contact away from Swindon and to add confusion as to who he was, he found a phone box in Edinburgh. Reception was not mindful of putting through an anonymous caller to the head of MI6 and Matt was prepared for this hurdle and outlined the nature of the email he had sent and was immediately asked to please wait. The next voice was that of a Major Digby Malholland, who without asking Matt any questions, confirmed that he was Deputy Director, he had been handed the email in question by the Chief. Matt had no problem in disguising his voice and conveyed in the most urgent terms that Mr Creighton must be removed from his current assignment, as a matter of

National security. Understanding that Major Malholland could not act on the information provided by an anonymous informant, Matt asked that he make a call to Richard McAllister at the Agency. The Major did not fill Matt with any confidence that his approach would be acted upon and decided on impulse, to issue an ultimatum. He told the Major that unless Creighton was investigated with immediate effect, the matter would be dealt with by a third party. He disconnected the call and then contemplated what on earth he had meant by that threat.

CHAPTER 8

THE EVIDENCE OF THEIR EXISTANCE

He arrived at Ben's apartment before she had returned and helped himself to a drink from the mini bar. He was watching the local news when she came in and she was in time to see the news flash that the Logan Mutual Bank in Newark had been hit, with a now customary note left by the Scarlet Serpents which was simply a drawing of two red snakes laid next to each other to form two S's. Ben wanted to know what progress he had made with his problem and complimented him on his ingenuity when he detailed his subterfuge. They agreed to head out to Newark and the scene of the latest robbery to see what they could learn.

It was their first joint operation and they admitted to being a little excited at the prospect.

They eavesdropped on the local FBI officers who were spearheading the investigation and picked up that the gang always used stolen get away vehicles which they torched after swapping to another vehicle. Eyewitnesses had spotted a speeding car leaving the scene and it was easy enough to find a burnt out Corvette, matching the description, located on a quiet road adjacent to the South Mountain Reservation, a public park just a ten minute fast drive from the bank. The two of them remained out of sight, in this case sitting on a low branch of a nearby sycamore. They watched the NYPD officers standing around close to the vehicle and heard one of them announce that they would stay by the vehicle until forensics arrived. Matt had been intensely scanning the area and said to Ben to look at a point some hundred yards further along the narrow road where it turned sharply to the right. It could be clearly seen that a vehicle, had left the road leaving tyre marks on the sidewalk, before cutting across the grass of somebody's front lawn. Whilst the grass was churned up, acutely enhanced eyesight had seen that there appeared to be tyre tracks where there was no grass but damp soil. The tracks could well have been made by another vehicle and he reasoned that they were likely made by somebody in a hurry. They waited patiently for the appropriate moment for closer inspection, this came when the officers decided to get out of the chilly weather and wait in their vehicle which was parked nearby but facing away from the spot the two wished to investigate. Matt took a number of close up photographs of the tracks and they returned to Bene's apartment. The Hotel had office services and Ben downloaded the pictures from Matt's phone and printed them off. Their next step was to locate a well-stocked tyre depot to identify what vehicle would use such a tyre. It may well be a needle in a

160

haystack Matt said but on the other hand, you would think the crooks would make sure they had a high performance car for a speedy onward journey.

Premier Tyres in Yonkers claimed to stock more tyres that any other company on the east coast and that is where they found themselves, a little over an hour since leaving their sycamore perch. Ben told Brian the assistant who greeted them that somebody, likely a drunk driver, had mounted the sidewalk, driven across her lawn, hit her car and driven off. She added that the police didn't appear interested and so she decided to act as a private investigator and produced the print of the tyre track. Brian was amused at the yarn but complimented Ben on her quick wits and beckoned them to join him in the office, where upon he took down a thick book from a stacked shelf. He dropped it on a table and together with the photograph of the print, starting to leaf through the pages. He murmured, as he moved his head form print to page and back again but half way through the book, looked up and said it may be the print did not show enough detail to find a match. He nevertheless carried on looking but came to the end without success. Matt asked if there were any other reference books that covered specialty tyres, he said wordlessly to Ben that maybe they had a sports car for a quick getaway. Brian agreed that was a good idea and he fetched another reference book, this one

161

much thinner. As hopes began to dwindle Brian turned to them with a toothy grin and said he believed he had found the trey with the tread they had found. He told them he had thought although it was a bad picture, being as the width was far larger than most tyres but in fact it had been spot on. He pointed to a Bridgestone X500, a ten-inch, low profile tyre, which he added, was often used by road racers. Matt asked where such a tyre could be purchased and was told that very few dealers he knew carried them in stock, as they were expensive and the market for them was limited. He guessed their next question and went to a directory, laying on the table next to the telephone and ran his dirty index finger down page after page until he stopped, looked up and told them that the only store likely to be able to help was on the east coast, between New York and Miami, in Savannah and went by the name of Rodriguez Racers. They thanked Brian profusely and were almost out of the door when he was yelling after them with the address. They knew they could locate the place without a problem and finding a quiet alleyway they disappeared, heading for Savannah. They had aimed for the centre of town and ensuring they didn't spook anybody by their sudden appearance, chose an alleyway to reappear in. Both agreed that before proceeding they needed to rest and take on board some liquids. They found a juice bar and ordered large fresh orange drinks, the vendor looked at them curiously when they returned twice for refills. The bar had a public phone and a directory hung on a chain, which Matt flicked through and found the address for Rodriguez Racers. It was a distance away and they decided to take a taxi, they conversed silently on the way and decided that to avoid arousing any suspicion they would access the sales records of the store, out of hours. They had no idea if this was a wild goose chase and even if it and the gang purchased tyres form Rodriquez, if may have been a year ago or never. With their ability to take on board data at an unnaturally fast pace, assuming the records existed, they would soon find out if they were on the right trail. They stopped the taxi along the street, after spotting the store and decided to find somewhere to eat, to while away a couple of hours. It was late afternoon and they suspected the store would close shortly and so they made for the rib shack just across from the store. There were only four solo diners, heads down and noisily eating and slurping. They ordered and took seats at a bar facing the street, occasionally glancing across the road. It was getting dark when they saw the roller shutter of Rodriquez's come down, paying their bill they left. Ducking into a nearby doorway they disappeared and made for the tyre stores office. There were contact alarms on the doors and windows but as they didn't breach either there was no problem.

Having no idea of what sort of accounting records the business kept, they rummaged around for a while until they discovered a box full of used invoice books. Apparently Rodriguez operated a pretty basic manual system whereby the customer was given a hand written invoice, with a duplicate retained in the small A5 book. At least, Ben said, after flicking through an invoice book, the name and address of the customer appeared at the top of the majority of invoices. Matt had better luck when opening a desk drawer, he produced a large day book which analysed all the invoices by name, value of sale and fortunately, by producer. He ran his finger across the first page and skated past Michelin, Continental, Goodyear Yokohama and stopped when he found Bridgestone. The specific tyre was not listed and so they would have to find all Bridgestone sales in the book and then dig out the corresponding invoice to find which tyre was sold. It was a laborious task and it was nearing ten o'clock when they finally had a list of four customers who had bought Bridgestone X500's in the past two years. They all appeared to be within the state of Georgia and they could make a quick visit to each in a short space of time. Both Matt and Ben had arrived independently at the same conclusions, as regards their powers. Firstly, the more they used them the more adept they became, specifically, telekinetic use required far less concentration than levitation. When it came to apportation, the ability to appear and disappear could be finessed to assure them of not being discovered, by becoming hyper aware of anybody close by. Secondly, they knew that by combining their telekinetic efforts, they could move objects of a far greater weight and size together rather than alone.

Armed with the information they needed, they quickly surveyed the office to ensure everything looked untouched and left. They would not visit their first suspect until morning and so thought it best to get a night's sleep. To save time and energy, they decided to remain in Savannah and bed down unnoticed in the Bayview Hotel in the centre of town. With almost a thousand rooms this huge hotel enjoyed only sixty per cent occupancy, the duo reckoned that if they occupied one of several hundred empty rooms, the likelihood of being discovered was exceedingly remote.

Constant use of their powers came with a certain degree of exhaustion and lying out on top of the bed, the two were sound asleep within minutes. Waking naturally as the sun was rising, they took turns to take a quick wash both agreed breakfast was in order before the work day began. Walking along West River street they were spoilt for choice with café, after restaurant, after breakfast bar and an all you can eat waffle house. They settled on the Two Cracked Eggs Café and before they had got comfortable, steaming hot coffee was being poured into two mugs. They ordered a light breakfast and whilst they waited, Matt recalled the four names they had gleaned from the tyre store. He could not see from the scant information they had which of the four was the most likely suspect. Ben reasoned that they could check all of them out within a short pace of time and so it was of no real consequence who they visited first. They had a coffee refill before paying up and leaving. By the time they stood looking across the river, the sun had already begun its work and a digital thermometer on the side of the convention centre opposite, told them it was twenty five degrees at eight thirty in the morning.

Matt once again recalled the four names and randomly selected Dale Cummings of 1525 Eucalyptus Avenue and knew immediately on arrival this was not what they were looking for. On the driveway was a Ford Camero GT, which only had two rear wheels, the front being jacked up on bricks. They surveyed the occupants of the house and discovered one heavily tattooed male of approximately 200 pounds, snoring loudly in a front bedroom.

They swiftly moved on to suspect number two which held better prospects. In the garage of 1748 Canyon River Road, was a spotlessly clean white BMW M2 3.0 BiTurbo, in the kitchen drinking coffee, were two well-built males, one likely to be Chuck Jones, the name appearing on the invoice. Their interest in these guys was dashed when the phone rang and one of the guys jumped up and grabbed the phone, they listened in on one end of the conversation. In an excited manner he confirmed to his partner their entry had been accepted for the forthcoming NASCA racing trials.

The third name on the list was Lionel Faras and he could be found at High Springs Farm in Fleming. They arrived in the small farming town of just over a thousand people and decided to remain unobserved. There were so few people around that their appearance would be conspicuous and so they made directly for the farm. It was now mid-morning and not only did they immediately find a Toyota 4x4 Land Cruiser parked at the rear of the main house but it ran on four Bridgestone X500's. Additionally there appeared two other vehicles, secreted away in a barn, just a few yards away. They quickly observed that the occupants had CCTV strategically installed around the property, also noting the blinking of small red lights, denoting passive infrared alarm beams. They drifted over to the house and found a vantage point on the veranda, looking into a large sitting room. Matt said with growing confidence that he believed they had located the gang's lair.

Sitting on a couch, facing the windows, were two guys of average build, both dressed in denim dungarees, common apparel for farm labourers but they were clean and scrubbed, one wore rimless glasses and both had unblemished hands and wore polished shoes. Whilst one was clean-shaven the other sported a full beard. There were two armchairs, one with its back to the window, was occupied but all they could see was a large head that protruded over the top of the chair as did a thick barrel neck. They could make out his hands, which were resting on each arm of the chair, a large chronometer was on the left wrist and several gold rings adorned the fingers of both hands. Opposite sat a large framed forth male of slightly oriental features, wearing a tightly fitting black short sleeved tee shirt that revealed the contours of a well-defined, muscular body and jeans. Along each arm were intricate coloured tattoos of dragons, breathing yellow fire. It was the member who they could not see who was speaking. They assumed this to be Lionel Faras and he spoke with a deep southern drawl. He spoke aggressively and with passion about their next heist. There was a trestle table set up in the middle of the room, littered with empty beer bottles but amongst the debris were several maps, drawings and what looked like blue prints. Ben indicated a staircase leading to the first floor and suggested they find a perch above the gathering and listen to the conversation from a better vantage point. Information flowed thick and fast and they quickly deduced the next job was to happen in three days' time. All that remained was for the two to ascertain where and when to waylay the gang. Settling in the shade of a tree, in an adjacent meadow, it was Matt who grinned as he suggested a somewhat outrageous solution. However, he first said that if they were to embark on a crime busting or disaster averting, course of action, it would be exceedingly difficult to be effective in total secrecy. He then laid out his plan, reminding Ben that as they entered town there was a monument, a five or six meter high square plinth, that stood in the centre of a roundabout. She was looking at him quizzically not yet following his line of thought, until he suggested using their kinetic skills to capture the gang's 4x4 and lodge it on the top of the monument. All they then need do was to alert the local law enforcement agency to come and collect this most notorious gang of bank thieves. She loved the idea but asked how they were to get the four protagonists into the vehicle. Matt thought on this for a short while and then suggested they disable the other vehicles, which would force them to use the 4x4.

Returning to the farm where the four remained inside, they decided to wait in the hope that none of them departed until the evening and in the meantime Matt attended to decommissioning the starter motors of the cars in the barn, telling Ben to keep watch and to warn him if anybody was approaching. It was early evening when the three members of the gang stood to leave and Faras remained seated with his back to the window. They made arrangements to meet up again the following day and the three others left by the back door to walk over to the barn and climbed in their vehicles, as first one tried to start his car, then the other. They cursed and furtively looked at each other and around the area, the one with oriental features suggested they go back to the house and check the CCTV. As they walked back, it was the one of the others who said that it was impossible for an intruder to have sabotaged the vehicles because they would have tripped the alarms. A surprised Faras finally stood and revealed a large and imposing man, well over six feet tall and likely as not, weighing over two hundred and ten or twenty pounds. The four made for a door off the sitting room, which led into an office where above a large desk and fitted to the wall, was a bank of half a dozen small monitors. Faras sat and deftly moved his fat fingers over a keyboard, which effectively rewound the recordings for each camera, covering several hours. He voiced the same thoughts as his associates and in his deep drawl, also confirmed that the state of the art alarm system would have been activated if a mouse had run into the barn.

Matt's plan was working out well, as by the time they had reviewed all the footage and found nothing, Faras said he would take them back to their places. He pulled on a leather jacket and took a bunch of keys from a rack by the front door. He told them to leave by the back door and he would bring the car round. Ben suggested they wait to see which direction they took before acting and as luck would have it, the Toyota turned left as it exited the property, heading for town. Just prior to reaching the town centre, the car veered right, off down a dirt track, kicking up clouds of dust, which gave the two a perfect opportunity.

They appeared by the roadside some distance in front of the car but hidden in the undergrowth. Together they combined their efforts and at first raised the car just a couple of feet off the track which had the effect of the car losing traction but the wheels carried on spinning. As the dust settled Matt and Ben could see a combination of bewilderment and fear had appeared on the faces of all the occupants. They saw Faras grab his door handle, as if to step outside to investigate and at that moment they raised the car by fifteen feet, which immediately had the effect of causing four grown men to scream in unison. The monument was a couple of hundred yards away, to the left of the town shopping mall. They decided that their best course of action was to transport the vehicle over the hedgerow that bordered the track, through the rear car park of the closed mall and then swiftly place the vehicle on top of the monument.

They effected this manoeuvre in under a minute and satisfied themselves that it was safely in position. The next part of Matt's plan was to place a call to the Georgia State office of the FBI and inform them the Scarlet Serpents had been apprehended and were awaiting arrest in Fleming town centre, this he did from a nearby payphone. The receptionist at the office was naturally sceptical of the call and told them to contact the local sheriff. This they did but by the time Matt's call went through, pandemonium was breaking out in the town centre. Numerous passers-by were craning their necks and pointing, asking each other how such a thing could happen. Matt and Ben had adopted a physical form and stood amongst the growing crowd as first one siren wailed and then others. First it was the sheriff who was swiftly followed his deputies, then the FBI and finally by a fire truck. The onlookers were ushered to a safe distance as the sheriff took off his hat and scratched his head. For a small town, Matt and Ben were amused to see a crowd of several hundred people converge on the centre. The assembled services were now joined by the late arrival of a several news trucks and a couple of ambulances, at which point Matt and Ben agreed they had seen enough and their work was done. Feeling pleased with themselves they left for New York.

Ben said that she needed to resume her chess matches

in the morning and he decided to stay the night returning to the UK, first thing the following day. It was unfortunate that Ben had to travel by conventional means, being in the public eye when competing and said she was likely to be back at their London home in two or three days' time. For his part, Matt would be stuck in Swindon for a few days more, assuming the Secret Service had taken him seriously and acted.

They ordered some Chinese food to be delivered and sat and watched TV whilst they ate. They were both somewhat surprised by the speed with which their exploits had made the national news, with a live newsfeed from Fleming, zooming in on the still perched vehicle. A large crane had been called and was currently positioning a frame, commonly used for removed illegally parked cars, swung beneath its extended jib on the end of a thirty foot boom. The scene changed to show four men in handcuffs being roughly pushed into a police van but not before smug officers had posed with their captives, for the front pages of the national press. Returning to the removal of the stranded vehicle, with small precise movements, clamps were secured around the four wheels and the 4x4 was lifted as if a toy and loaded onto the back of a police branded low loader. A police spokesman was having a hard job holding back the barrage of question being fired at him, asking for an explanation as to how the car ended up where it had been and who was responsible for capturing the gang. Although failing to answer the who question, as every expert asked would continue to fail to answer, he was at least pleased to confirm that the occupants were the much sought after Scarlet Serpents, who were now in custody.

Without regret, Matt told his partner there was no going back now, as there would be a massive investigation to ascertain how such an impossible feat was accomplished. They felt comfortable that there was no possible way either of them could be connected with the event but they agreed that, moving forward, it was imperative that they maintain that anonymity.

CHAPTER 9

BIG CHANGES AND TURMOIL

Matt was quite relieved to return to Swindon following the excitement of the past few days and Richard was surprised to take a call from him announcing that he was back. A few messages had appeared on Matt's phone, he made a point of not taking it with him when 'working' with Ben. He explained that he had been rather pre-occupied and apologized for not returning calls. Richard explained that it was not a problem as the Agency had welcomed the opportunity to lay down some plans for the next phase of their programme. He had been authorized, by no less than the Parliamentary Under Secretary of State for Science, Research and Innovation, whose remit covered space exploration, to offer Matt a retainer to continue his work and he added a rather generous retainer at that. It would not require him being permanently based in Swindon but if they could meet up he can run through the proposal for going forward. Matt was more than happy with the sound of the arrangement, particularly at the quantum of the retainer which averaged out at *circa* £15,000 per month and they arranged a meeting at Richard's office the following day.

Before hanging up, Richard adopted a somewhat grave

tone and told Matt, if he had not already heard that Edward Creighton was on remand, for breaches of the Official Secrets Act and espionage. He added he and his colleagues were grateful to Matt for bringing to their attention the somewhat curious behaviour of the civil servant, which had prompted further investigation.

He duly met with Richard and without too much debate they arrived at a mutually satisfactory working arrangement, following which, Matt headed back to London. The cupboards were bare and he took a walk over to Borough Market for supplies to stock up the fridge. With Ben returning in a couple of days he thought he would buy some of the things she liked and he enjoyed acting out the role of a normal Londoner going about his business.

Out of interest, he reviewed some of the newsfeeds from the US and noted that quite a number were still leading with the mysteries of the events that occurred in Fleming, with many carrying the photograph of the 4x4 suspended below the crane jib as it was being removed from the plinth. Scrolling through the articles he was able to determine that the combined might of the US law agencies and other investigatory bodies, were singularly unable to throw any light as to who or what played a part in the gangs apprehension and the bizarre location of their vehicle.

It was not long before he turned his attention to the engine and the desire, as much as the need, to find a more suitable home for it. In the meantime, the external store would need to be made into a safe and secure repository. He considered it unwise to find a contractor to make the necessary modifications he had in mind, as secrecy was paramount. He shopped around for the necessary tools and set about the task. He had decided to brick up the external doorway of the store but to reaffix the door back in place, so that it looked as though it remained the means of accessing the store. The external wall of the room they had designated the study, was a party wall with the store and with hammer and chisel Matt knocked through to the store, making an opening wide enough for access. He fitted a retaining beam overhead and a doorframe and made a passable job of rendering and after two full days of work, he was pleased with his DIY efforts. All that remained was to hang a small flush door at the opening, with a spring push opening and not a conspicuous door handle, as a finishing touch he had bought a book case in the market, to cover the tell-tale signs of his work, plus for good measure he added a movement detection alarm system. With perfect timing, as he was cleaning up the final mess from his labours, he heard a key in the door and his partner came in lugging two suitcases.

They hugged her and silently admonished her for not

177

contacting him to meet her at the airport but she explained that it was no problem to jump in a taxi. He showed her his handy work and she was suitably impressed. Tired from her transatlantic trip, Matt suggested an evening in and he cooked dinner for them, suggesting they had much to talk about. They drank multiple cups of coffee, which kept them awake and talking long after midnight, not realizing there was so much to discuss. They had been remiss in not returning to see their family and the first item on their agenda was a trip to spend time with their respective parents and Matt's grandparents. As it appeared a more frequent occurrence, they both began to have simultaneous identical thoughts, often about minor inconsequential things. Despite Matt's recent work on the place, he mentioned to Ben that maybe they should think of moving somewhere more spacious and a little more secluded. He told her of his new contract with the Space Agency and their combined income was now quite significant. Her eyes had widened and she said in surprise that she had the same thought very recently and that whilst she liked their small apartment, perhaps their future endeavours, whatever they may entail, would require more space and with less risk of prying eyes. It was also agreed they should acquire some personal transport. They went to bed in the early hours with much on their minds but there would be more to occupy their minds come morning.

The smell of freshly percolating coffee brought Matt shuffling into the kitchen where Ben was poaching eggs and buttering toast. He sat and switched his phone on and a number of messages appeared from his mother and grandmother. Thankfully, they were mindful enough to begin by saying he should not panic, however his grandfather had been taken into hospital, having suffered a minor stroke and was being well cared for. Matt immediately called his mother, quickly telling Ben what had happened, he told her that only last night they had made plans to visit and they would return that very day.

Shortly after breakfast they walked to the station and boarded a train to Halstead. Ben called her mother, who had heard the news about Alfred and told her she would be home in a couple of hours. Ben said she would dearly love to see Alfred and so they arranged to see their respective parents and meet up at the hospital, when afternoon visiting hours began. Lans was at work but Wendy was at home when Matt arrived and by her hugs and kisses, he realized how long it had been since he had been home. He secretly vowed to not let that happen again and they sat whilst he filled her in on all that had transpired since they had last spoken. She was both surprised and astonished when he told her of his contract with the UK Space Agency and whilst the Official Secrets Act prevented him telling her of his work, he could tell her of the generous remuneration that came

179

with it. They drove to the hospital and Alfred was overjoyed to see his grandson and similarly on seeing Ben. They in turn were relieved to see him awake, alert and in no discernible discomfort. He was almost dismissive about his stroke, although admitted it gave him a scare but with a speedy admittance to hospital and a rapid procedure that cleared the blood clot, he was optimistic at leaving hospital in two or three days. Matt and Ben agreed they would remain local for the next few days and suggested that the families have a get together.

Whilst Matt sat at the kitchen table at his parent's place researching suitable vehicles on his mother's laptop, she fussed around preparing dinner. He also found time to brief some property agents, giving them a detailed specification of the type of property he was after and the desired locations. Lans arrived home early, knowing his son was visiting and suggested they adjourn to the local for a pint before dinner. Matt was more than a little embarrassed when the landlord began congratulating him on his achievements in interplanetary travel. He looked at his father in mocked reproachment and his father shrugged, as if to say, cannot a father be proud of his son. They took their pints into the garden at the rear and both enjoyed the opportunity to catch up, and Matt asked his father's advice regarding a car. His father was quite knowledgeable in this area and gave his son convincing reasons, if his budget could stretch, to go for a 4 x 4. He was taken aback by his son's heady progress at the Agency and the rewards he was reaping for his endeavours.

His parents had kept his room as it was when he left home and he enjoyed reminiscing, opening the chest under the desk containing all his toys and flicking through a scrapbook he had kept as a youngster. He had found a local dealer and his father accompanied him to test drive a demonstration model Range Rover, Lans was more than a little surprised when his son declined the credit terms the dealer offered and said he would be paying cash. The dealer required twenty-four hours to undertake a pre-delivery inspection and within two days, after confirming they had received the funds Matt had transferred, he collected the vehicle.

He picked up Cynthia in his sparkling jet-black 4x4 and drove to collect Alfred when they learned he was being discharged. His grandfather loved the car and couldn't help himself, switching every switch and turning every dial. They detoured via the gallery to pick up Ben, he jumped out of the car to give Kanika a swift hug and she stuck her head in the vehicle and gave Alfred a kiss whilst cooing approvingly at Matt's new toy. On the short journey to The Spinney, the four of them talked incessantly and continued once home. Matt told his grandfather, as much as he could, about his work and their

181

crime fighting exploits. Alfred beamed with pride and told he grandson as much. Matt added that now he and Ben had the resources, they had agreed to find a more suitable home, preferably in the countryside, in which to install a railway. This pleased him no end and he said he hoped to live long enough to see what his grandson would achieve.

A week went by during which the families did enjoy a reunion, this time hosted by Matt and Ben, following which the two drove back to London. Ben was saddened but had to agree she had noticed when Matt mentioned it that his grandmother had become rather forgetful and he made a mental note to talk to his mother about it. He told Ben he had briefed a number of agents to look out for a suitable property along the lines they had discussed and hoped that Ben would be in the UK for long enough to view anything that came up. She told him she had been considering a tentative offer to write a book about chess for beginners and that may well keep her off the circuit for a few months. Once back in SE1 they were happy to remain ensconced in the apartment, tapping away on their laptops. Matt was busy expanding on his theories of interplanetary travel and was composing additional papers for the Agency to consider. He found time to help Ben in lay out some basic rules for the writing of her instruction book for chess novices.

As was typical of property agents, he received

numerous properties, which exceeded their budget or which in no way fitted the brief Matt had given. He studiously ploughed through all of them until he finally found one worthy of sharing with Ben. Bawdsey Manor in Suffolk was a late 19th century manor house set in fifty rural acres; it occupies a prominent position at the mouth of the River Deben, close to the village of Bawdsey in Suffolk. The agents blurb waxed lyrical, describing how it stands in a magnificent position on a red crag, Pleistocene cliff, overlooking the River on one side and the North Sea on the other. However, it was not the impressive manor that interested Matt but the Summer House, which was located on the southern border of the estate and close to the river side, a good half mile from the main house. The owners were desirous of selling the run down property not being willing to invest the necessary funds to renovate it and also seeing the opportunity of topping up their coffers by selling it. In the first instance, the primary requisite of a good location was met in spades and secondly, the accommodation was more than adequate with five bedrooms, two sitting rooms, a study, two bathrooms, kitchen and scullery plus an all-important basement. Matt quickly notified the agent of his interest and arranged a site visit. Whilst it was too big for their current requirements they hoped to grow into it and that family would come to stay in the future.

They undertook the three-hour drive on the appointed day and were pleased to see that the property was accessed via a public road, around the western perimeter of the estate, with an access gate close to the house. They had chosen a pleasant day, weather-wise, to make their trip and they both fell in love with the location, at first sight. Facing the river, with an overgrown lawn sloping down to the river's edge, there were no other dwellings in line of sight in any direction. The front door was padlocked and they meandered around the exterior, whilst waiting for the agent to arrive.

Matt withdrew a notepad from his pocket and began to make notes as he slowly made his way around the building. There was much to do and he hoped between them they could make it work at least, financially. He picked at a rotten window frame and Ben pointed out a broken tile on the ground, which had fallen from the roof. There was little doubt that the vendors had set the sale price primarily based on the location and significantly less so, on the condition of the property. They were alerted to sound of a vehicle approaching and made their way to the entrance. A portly, smartly suited, young man pulled himself out of the small compact he had arrived in, apologised for being late and immediately launched in selling mode. Ben considered him pleasant enough and he was well versed in all aspects of the property from local rates and taxes to the urgent need to modernise the bathrooms and kitchen. Once he had removed the padlock, Matt and Ben took off alone to explore, strategically going from room to room and leaving the all-important basement until the last. Whilst the super structure appeared sound enough, a number of rotting floorboards and the primitive plumbing and wiring, suggested a considerable renovating budget was required. They discussed their plans at length, especially with regards to the basement. The agent may have been curious at the time they spent down there but did not mention it.

At the end of two hours they found the agent sitting on a window ledge and he revealed he was greatly relieved to hear they were interested. They had ascertained that the property had been on the market for well over a year and Matt stressed that with the huge budget required to restore the property he would make an offer considerably lower than the asking price. In addition, he required specialist contractors be permitted on site to estimate the costs involved prior to any legal formalities were entered into. All this was agreed and between the two of them they found a number of local artisans who had the requisite skills to attend to the exterior and interior. It was three months following their initial viewing by the time they had finalized a budget and were able to submit an offer. Matt was happy to give the agent a schedule of his refurbishment costs to pass on to the owners, in the hope that they would understand why the offer was so much lower than the price they were asking. Matt had spoken to Cynthia, saying it was only right for them to give her the sale proceeds, when the flat was sold. She was adamant that one did not return gifts and in any event, she had no use for the money and they would need it for their new home. The two of them knew that without those funds it would be near impossible to consider the Summer House purchase and Matt was prepared to seek a loan from the bank for any shortfall. As is the natural order of things, with property negotiations, there was offer and counter offer and long lapses in between but eventually an agreement was arrived at. Whilst it was a fair price they were still short of funds and both met with their respective bankers. They could both submit an impressive CV's and proof or earnings and both bank managers were aware of the notoriety of their clients, consequently bridging the gap on their finances was not a problem.

Wanting to preserve the original look of the property, although it was not listed as being of special architectural and historic interest, would take just over six months. They made a point of sourcing the correct materials and replace less than adequate trades people with better ones. Only once the main refurbishment work was complete, could Matt turn his attention to the railway. Alfred had insisted that Matt take as much from his front room as he wanted and whilst it filled only half the basement at the Summer House, at least the engine had a rail to run on and it gave Matt a good base to work from. With all the additional basement space he and Ben swapped ideas on how to fill it. They became excited with the idea of an extended forest, with timber holiday lodges and extending the mountain range at a lower altitude to include foothills and pastures with more leisure pursuits, such as camping. All these plans involved endless trips, near and far, to source and collect the various items they needed to bring their ideas to life.

There was little problem in selling the London flat, although Matt's modification of the storeroom access, raised a few eyebrows. A delayed completion on their purchase was required to allow time for the Summer House renovation and refurbishment to be completed.

The owners of Bawdsey Manor had accepted the need for the new owners to erect a perimeter fence and only required prior approval for aesthetic purposes. Matt was happy that electronic security would be more appropriate than physical security which in any event would arouse more interest. With the passage of time and a healthy dose of patience, the Summer House regained much of its former beauty. Matt had co-opted his grandmother to help by bringing her expertise to bear to the garden and interior design of the house and whilst her mental abilities diminished, she retained much of her practical skills and the finished product could grace the pages of house and country magazines. Ben wanted and sourced a large gazebo and a replica of Rodin's The Thinker plus a birdbath. They took the limited furniture from their flat, which was lost in the much larger space they were moving into. However, it would suffice in the meantime and on upturned crates they sat in the gazebo on their first day in residence, drinking their way through a bottle of Malbec and snacking on a Chinese takeaway, silently watching the Deben as it slowly emptied into the North Sea. There was little river traffic, just a few passing kayakers and the flapping sails on small craft, moored up at the sailing club on the opposite side of the river. It was almost to the day a year ago that they had agreed on the purchase of the house and they sat and mused on all that had happened in their lives in such a short space of time.

Getting further entrenched into the world of science and technology, Matt had another idea to purchase some serious radio receiving equipment, to monitor the national and international emergency services bandwidth. He reasoned with Ben that whilst occupied on their own work, it would be wrong not to pay attention to what was happening in the wider world and to help out in emergency situations if they were able. Ben agreed and he undertook extensive research but it was not long before he discovered that what he sought was difficult to obtain. He took the somewhat unorthodox approach of visiting GCHQ, the UK's spying headquarters to see if he could learn anything about the equipment they used. He came away with the name of Beacon Electronics and sourced their location. Having now been given personal business cards from the Agency, he had no problem seeking a meeting at the Surry head office of the company. A suitably impressed sales manager was only too happy to entertain Matthew Henrick from the UK Space Agency and to demonstrate their range of transmitting and receiving equipment. At the conclusion of his meeting he was satisfied that he had found the kit he wanted. He asked that a pro forma invoice be emailed to him and he would pay by return, confirming the delivery address. Matt confirmed that a full set of user manuals would accompany the delivery as he was a little unsure of his competency in operating such sophisticated equipment.

Ten days later a large truck pulled up at the gates to the Summer House and both Matt and Ben were a little surprised at the number of crates that were unloaded. It took Matt the best part of a week to assemble the kit and he still needed to install a receiver dish and antenna on the roof. It still remained for him to access the dark web to obtain details on how to access the range of emergency services broadcasts for the UK and across

Europe, such information not being in the public domain and coming at a price. Finally, he called Ben into the room he had now designated the Communications Room, for the switching on ceremony. He powered up the system and waited as a multitude of lights came on and static poured from the speakers. He twirled the location dials until he heard a broadcast from somewhere on the north east coast, calling for medical assistance at a motorway accident. One of the four screens he had mounted on the wall would tell him where the broadcast was coming from but their problem was the ability to rapidly extract emergency matters in need of their special talents, as against those quite easily dealt with by more traditional means.

They sat and experimented with picking up various broadcasts from various locations across the country and overseas. They became blatantly aware of the language problem and needed to consider how best to address it. Their astute abilities were able to detect that in the case of the more serious emergencies, the channels used and terminology differed, which in addition required different services to be looped in, whether it be the health services or the police, serious crimes units or coast guard services, issuing the messages.

It took a degree of trial and error before they were able

to hone their skills sufficiently, so as not to race to the scene of a cat stuck up a tree which only happened once. They assisted in a number of what they would term, minor emergencies, such as extinguishing a house fire and saving the trapped family, in advance of the fire services arriving. They also spectacularly pulled a school bus of thirty-two children that had become trapped when torrential rains had caused a mudslide in a small hamlet in Western Germany and were only able to get involved due to Ben rapidly brushing up on the German she had picked up from her language course at school. The various agencies that attended the miracle rescue had assumed that the force of the cascading water and mud had somehow caused the bus to be washed clear. It obviously gave rise to questions being asked and more than one or two claims of divine intervention but the duos identity was always scrupulously protected. In the meantime, Matt began work on enlarging the basement railway and creating his own landscape. Ben was also enthusiastic to be included and with two such highly competent individuals involved, the development assumed a breath-taking pace.

Several busy months passed, during which they managed a long weekend trip to Halstead, The Spinney and Shirebridge. Kanika had become quite the entrepreneur, opening mini galleries in three different five star hotels plus putting on shows for young and aspiring artists at venues in the locality. Alfred had recovered well and it was only his age beginning to take its toll but he was now confiding in Matt his concern for his grandmother. It took some cajoling to persuade her to visit a specialist at a cognitive neurology and dementia centre in London but being an intelligent woman, she realized all was not as it should be and finally agreed to a visit.

Meanwhile, Lans and Wendy were more than happy with life, Lans having been promoted to CEO of the UK division and Wendy deciding to retire. Ben managed to make good progress on her book and with the advance she had received they had been able to further furnish their home. Matt took up a temporary teaching position at Kent University, adding considerable gravitas to the course subject of astronomy, space science and astrophysics. In addition to their busy schedule they had made further progress in the basement and an appealing landscape was appearing. The frenetic point of the year was passing, or so they thought, when they rushed to the comms room on hearing a frantic mayday call. They listened intently placing the coordinates of the distressed call as coming from a vessel, close to the shore and two miles south of Scarborough. They were at the scene, scouring the coastline within a minute of listening to the call. Matt spotted a stricken twin-masted yacht, wedged against the rocks and almost totally submerged. They moved down to the shoreline, to a position a short distance from the vessel, which was stuck fast against the rocks and being pounded by the waves. Checking for signs of life, Ben pointed to a comatose male figure, half covered by a ripped sail and lashed to a broken mast, bobbing up and down as the angry sea worked to dislodge him. With nobody yet at the scene, they combined their efforts to raise the figure from the water and lay him on dry land. The male was in his early twenties and barely alive, his breathing was shallow, almost imperceptible. Following some rapid psychic surgery they discovered water filled lungs, five broken ribs, a broken arm and a damaged kidney. They agreed only immediate attention was likely to save his life and they set to work. Both placed their hands on his body and whilst Ben concentrated on emptying his lungs, Matt began repairing his rib, setting his arm was not a problem but his kidney was. Matt looked at Ben and said that the damage to his kidney, probably caused by blunt trauma, required specialist attention but was not life threatening. He was now stable and breathing far better, any further surgery was best left to the doctors. They transferred their body heat to him and he began to stir, finally gasping and coughing up sea water, finally opening his eyes. As Matt looked into the man's eyes, which appeared to dart around fervently, he silently said to Ben that the man was blind. In a rasping voice, he asked where he was and who they were. Ben put him at his ease and explained they had fished him out of the sea but regrettably could not find any other survivors. It was then they heard in the distance the sound of sirens and the whirling of a helicopter, they told him he was out of danger and that help was now at hand. The two prepared to leave the scene but told him as they stood that they must depart but would find him, to check on his recovery. Again he fought to speak, asking them again who they were and Matt, bent down and said in a calming voice, they were friends but then they were gone, as paramedics came running down from the roadside. He was lifted onto a stretcher and taken to a waiting helicopter to be airlifted to hospital. Matt and Ben, sat drinking a hot cup of tea at home, wondering at the many questions their recent escapade might attract. It was impossible for them to decide how to help those in dire need and simultaneously deal with the storm of questions, which would be left in their wake. They both knew the time would come when that square could not be circled and they would have to devise a convincing scenario.

As expected, the national news media carried headlines the following day which either spoke of the tragic loss of life when a stricken yacht sank off the east coast or the miracle saving of the blind son of those missing, presumably lost at sea. There was television footage of the treacherous rocks and incredulous reporters unable to even speculate how a blind man, half drown, was able overcome pounding waves and massive slippery rocks, to make dry land.

Lying in a hospital bed, he was now fully conscious but could not answer any questions, from the police or the media, on how a man in his perilous position had managed to haul himself out of a raging sea and scale perilous rocks to the safety of dry land. They scanned the various articles and watched the TV news reporting the rescue, they determined who the lone survivor was, one Loris Balcombe and that his trauma had been amplified by the fact that he was blind, having been so since birth. As the days past since the rescue, Matt and Ben watched with mild interest, the frantic searching for clues by a myriad of sleuths, whether they be tabloid journalists, the police or would-be amateur detectives. The bewilderment of all concerned was heightened by the increased mystification generated by the medical fraternity, attending to the lone survivor. Despite the drafting in of specialists of all kinds, they could not agree on any one idea as to how newly broken ribs and a broken arm had set without medical intervention. To add to the mystery, here was a body that had been immersed in the freezing North Sea, during which time, by his own testimony, he was unconscious and yet there was no water in his lungs. However, the duo was in turn mystified as to why Loris had made no mention of his rescuers.

His silence and their wish to check on his recovery, prompted them to visit Loris, without appearing and were happy to see he was fully conscious and fielding a constant stream of visitors, predominately press, they surmised. They decided to pay him a second visit but out of hours and arrived one evening with just a nurse at the entrance to the ward and out of line of sight of Loris's small private room. They found him sitting up in bed with a set of headphones on. Matt tapped on the door and they both slid in. Having regained his voice, a well-spoken Loris, a little startled, removed his headphones and asked who his late night visitors were and looked in their direction. Matt spoke first and said they were friends and then fell silent when Loris said how pleased he was to meet his saviours. Ben asked him how he had deduced that and Loris smiled, explaining that having been bind for almost twenty five years, he had developed his other senses, particularly his sense of hearing and recognized the voice that had spoken to him on the sea shore. Matt followed with the pressing question, asking him why he had not mentioned their coming to his aid. Loris firstly thanked them profusely but then added that he did not say anything, assuming they must have had a very good reason for not wanting to be found with him. Remaining silent, he added, was the very least he could do in return for their saving his life. Matt introduced the two of them and reminded Loris that he did tell him they would find him and asked what his plans were once he leaves hospital. Loris told them that the boat was the family home since his parents had sold their modest home and bought the yacht to sail the world. Loris had been in rented accommodation which he let go and flown to the coast of Newfoundland, to join them on the last leg of their trip. He now had no home, no siblings no living relatives and no job. Impressed with his apparent resilience and after silently checking with Ben, Matt picked up a note pad and scribbled down his cell number, he passed the note to Loris and told him to have the hospital call him on the number he had noted down, when he was ready to leave. He thanked them but before responding further they had vanished, Loris strained his hearing to detect if he were alone or not, perplexed at not hearing them leave but assuming they had. He smiled to himself, thinking that these two were racking up some serious mysteries to be solved.

They heard no more from him and assumed he had decided to get on with his life without their further intervention. It was only later they would learn that he was kept in hospital, following a full recovery, for observation for a further three weeks, when the truth was he was more than able to walk out after ten days. Vested interests were so flummoxed at his miracle recovery, they were determined to undertake more tests to find some answers but of course failed. When Matt's phone rang and the unknown number message flashed on the screen, he suspected it may be Loris. It was and he was calling from the hospital, Matt told him there was a coffee shop a hundred yards west of the hospital and he should take a slow walk, have a coffee and Matt would pick him up in about an hour.

When Matt entered the coffee shop he noted that almost instantly Loris had looked up in his direction and then greeted him with a cheery smile. As clever as Matt was, he was impressed by this man's skill. Loris apologised to Matt at the state of his attire but his wardrobe had gone down with the boat and the hospital charity shop had provided the clothes he was wearing. Matt told him they could pick up something on the way to his place, where he could recuperate, as he had mentioned that he had nowhere to stay. He told him that he and Ben were more than happy to put him up until he finds his feet. As they left the coffee shop, Matt noticed Loris produce a telescopic white cane from a pocket, whilst simultaneously putting an earpiece in his ear. He told Matt that the company that produced the cane had read about his case and gave him one as a gift, thereby earning some free publicity. The cane was an ultra-cane, which emitted tones of different frequency as he approached objects in his path, the frequency varying according to the object's size and whether it was moving or static. They arrived at the Summer House, laden with carrier bags and Ben came out to greet them. Loris's obvious appreciation at being offered temporary accommodation was accompanied with his burning curiosity as to who his benefactors were.

As if Ben had read his mind, which spooked him more than a little, she said that he doubtless had many questions about who they were but perhaps he would like a bath and to put on some fresh clothes first and then over a meal they could chat. She placed a hand on his arm and led him upstairs to one of the spare rooms, explaining the paucity of furniture was due to them only recently moving in. She placed the bags of new clothes on the bed and directed him to the bathroom placing a bath towel on a stool by the bath. She told him to yell if he needed anything, otherwise dinner would be in about an hour.

They had managed to furnish their home quite extensively, however, it was a large place and required still more in the category of soft furnishings and a few sundry pieces of furniture. They spent a lot of time in the expansive kitchen, which housed in its centre, an eight foot long solid oak table, where Matt sat nursing a glass of wine whilst reading a scientific journal. Ben was busying herself over the Aga, stirring a simmering casserole, when Loris entered the room. Matt and Ben exchanged the thought that he was a handsome man with a confident and self-assured bearing. Matt told him that there was a chair directly in front of him and offered him a drink, both telling him they approved of his chose of clothes. Loris explained he did not drink alcohol but would be grateful for a soft drink. Ever curious Matt asked how he found his way around the house without the aid of his cane, to which Loris replied that with light touch he could visualize and retain the layout of places quite quickly, plus the sounds made and the smells produced assisted. Navigating stairs was easy he said, as was the noise a kitchen makes.

Ben had cleared any eating preferences and served the chicken casserole, which Loris was quick to compliment her on. They made small talk over dinner but it was Loris who was eager to find out more just as soon as coffee was served. Matt deferred to Ben and she briefly chartered her meteoric rise in the world of chess. When she had finished a potted history of her short adult life, Loris let out a whistle and paid her repeated compliments on her achievements. Matt began with an apology by explaining that his main line of work was covered by the Official Secrets Act, to which Loris showed surprise and told them he thought he had been rescued by a comic book dynamic duo. Matt was at pains to explain it was not quite as glamorous nor as mysterious as it might at first appear and it was the UK Space Agency he worked for and not the Secret Intelligence Service. However, they did indulge in other projects and he spoke about his recent teaching assignment and Ben her book.

With little surprise, Loris wanted to know what had happened to him. His last memory was of his father diving into the sea to save his mother who had been swept overboard by a freak wave. He had yelled at Loris to strap himself to the boat and he would be back as soon as he found his mother and that was the last he heard of him. Meanwhile from what Loris could hear and feel, the sea was getting angrier and he sensed a storm was brewing. He said he lost track of time but guessed that around an hour had passed and he felt a violent shudder pass through the boat followed by an ear-piercing crack as the hull was breached when the boat hit the rocks. The beleaguered yacht was buffeted from rock to rock and closer to the craggy shore until it became wedged. Loris recalled losing consciousness but not knowing for how long and remembered being suddenly aware that the boat was leaning at a perilous angle and had begun to capsize. He remained tied to the main mast, being whipped by a ripped wind driven sail and feeling his life ebbing away, that was the last he could remember. Whilst he was a good swimmer, he had swallowed too much water and the waves crashing against the rocks prevented any safe passage, which in any event he was unable to see. He lost consciousness several times and so now, as he finished his recollections, he wanted to know how he ended up on the shore

201

and all that followed. Matt and Ben exchanged ideas on how to proceed and it was Ben who offered the unsatisfactory reply that they had both taken lifesaving courses and were able to find their way across the rocks to pull him from the sea. In addition they had a comprehensive first aid kit in their vehicle, which greatly aided them once they were all ashore. Loris obviously did not buy into this explanation but followed by responding, even if he was to accept that part was true, there was no doctor or surgeon who could explain how his injuries had been treated. At that point all that Matt could offer was that if Loris stayed a while he may well find the answers to his probing questions.

Loris appeared to be contemplating his options, although they were somewhat limited and with a congenial smile and opening his arms to indicate his surroundings, said it was an offer he could not possibly refuse and would be most grateful to accept their generous offer. With that said they adjourned to the main sitting room and whiled away several hours, talking over their respective lives, with Ben and Matt, naturally editing theirs accordingly.

Ben remained at home working on her book and Matt left early the next day to start his stint at lecturing. Loris was not one to be idle and with little coaxing from Ben set to on a number of small jobs she found him to do. She was transfixed, watching how dextrous a man without sight could be and at times embarrassed herself warning him of the nearness of the river or the large rose bush Cynthia had planted. On each occasion he thanked her for her concern but he knew where the water was and was aware of most obstacles around him.

The radio receiver continued to broadcast and Ben could not avoid answering some of Loris's continuous barrage of questions. She fabricated her and Matt's CPR skills and the fact that it was the radio that brought them to his rescue, although the geographic conundrum remained. Taking a break, Ben took Loris into the study and sat him in front of the radio set. She guided his hands to the various controls explaining how it all worked, adding that it was powerful enough to receive broadcasts from Europe. She watched as he lightly ran his fingers across the dials and buttons, asking her questions as he did so. A plan began to form in her head and when Matt arrived home she told him of it and his agreement was instant. They invited Loris to join them from the gazebo where he sat enjoying the country air. Ben said she had a proposal, as he had appeared keenly interested in their radio set up, suggesting that for a trial period, he might like to act as their radio and communications operator. They would give him a smart phone and he would monitor the airwaves. They would provide a detailed brief of what to listen for and if and when he picked up a call deemed of crucial interest and according to the brief, he could use the smart phone to contact them. They would load it with voice activation software and he could alert them immediately. During the trial period, his food and lodgings would be provided for, plus a payment for the three months of £10,000. For a somewhat talkative individual, Loris was momentarily speechless but he finally replied that his silence was not for the want of what to say but what to say first. Owing them so much, he would love to help and contribute in any way he could and thanked them profusely for the offer which as well as being generous, was certainly of interest. However, before either of them spoke, he went on to say that he felt there was so much they were not telling him. As if by way of example he said that if the radio receiver picked up an urgent call from Dusseldorf or Zurich, how on earth they could assist when Matt was maybe teaching in London and Ben playing chess in Birmingham. Of course, it was a very pertinent question that Matt thought deserved an immediate response. He told Loris that they had a network of agents across the UK and Europe, who preferred anonymity and who they could call on at any time. Whilst Loris accepted his explanation, neither of them felt he was convinced.

CHAPTER 10

ANOTHER CRIME BUSTINGB CAPER

When they had first embarked on building the railway, they stood in the large basement and agreed that their primary aim was to get the railway installed and the train running and whilst they would layout a landscape, it would not initially match the comprehensiveness of Alfred's front room. They found laying out a forest and rolling hills, through which a tunnel was dug, was not problematic but a new town would take some further thought. They had also decided that if Alfred were well enough, then after an inaugural trip to ensure everything worked just fine, they would bring him down to take a train ride with them.

They had by now made several trips to The Spinney, had emptied the front room and saw how this had saddened Alfred. Now an amalgam of the front room railway and what Matt and Ben added to the basement produced a growing and beautiful setting. They had retained the lake and much of the town but decided to make some changes in the countryside, they retained the mountains and ski centre and nursery slopes, as well as rolling undulating hills, with grazing sheep, alpacas and several stables for horse riding and equestrian competitions plus a training centre. They had added a river running from high in the hills down to the lake and half way down they established a campsite for the town's people. As for the town, now called Summer Town, there now existed a college of further education, with courses in animal husbandry, textile production and design and for beginners and one on computer programming.

Of course there was the need to construct a siding and shed and to store the six rails that were integral to the engine's trips further afield, this they sited deep in the forest. They had become accustomed to Loris's inquisitorial nature, which now focused on their frequent trips to the basement. Matt told him the story of his grandfather spending decades building a model railway and how he had inherited it and was now re-installing it in the basement. This explanation did not elicit any further enquiries.

For several weeks there was a lull in the need for them to intervene in any critical events and they made good progress in getting the basement ready for its first test run. However, before they had the chance to take that first ride, Loris called them to the radio room with more of a curiosity than an emergency. He told them whilst listening to the selected frequencies, he also picked up an interesting item on the terrestrial radio he had playing in the background. It appeared that there was international interest in a forthcoming meeting of the senior echelons of the International Crime fighting agencies, scheduled to take place in the near future. The meeting was not listed as secret, as the countries involved were happy for their respective electorate to learn of their serious intention to crack down on organized crime. What had peaked Loris's curiosity was the increased activity on the airwaves from New Scotland Yard, who were co-ordinating the transfer of a number of tactical response units to Cardiff, the location of the meeting. Of course, he added, it may just be a heightened sense of security or they may have information to suggest otherwise. It was what he said next that made both Matt and Ben consider carefully how they preceded with this intuitively bright fellow. He suggested that through their other channels they might be able to glean any further or more detailed information, regarding these activities. It was his emphasis on the words, 'other channels' that caught their attention. They thanked him for his attentiveness and said they would look into what he had told them and they left him to discuss further what course of action, if any, to take.

Matt suggested that it would be worth their while to visit the various law enforcement agencies and see what they could learn. They discussed the best sources of information, divided the workload and then went their separate ways, agreeing to meet at the end of the day.

They sat in the gazebo in the fading light of day and compared notes of their respective days' work. Ben said she had an interesting visit to the National Crimes Agency offices in South London where she discovered a closed meeting taking place with the heads of departments. Considering this worthy of some eavesdropping, she learned that Loris's intuition was correct and there was credible intelligence that forces, unknown at present, were intent on visiting Cardiff for nefarious means. The National Crime Agency (NCA) had picked up what they called increased 'chatter' via encrypted cell phones that the police had hacked. A very expensive phone system called Encrochat provided organised crime gangs with a smart phone with its GPS, camera and microphone physically removed. The unit comes with encrypted messaging apps and also a secure secondary operating system that could be wiped by entering a PIN thanks to self-destruct feature. The French had installed malware on units, which had many beneficial features but one in particular enabled the authorities to clone the phone's app data. A treasure trove of information had been collected, leading to massive drugs hauls and multiple arrests. In this case, it had alerted the NCA to the fact that organised crime gangs were talking about the meeting in Cardiff. Meanwhile,

Matt had been to Cardiff and checked in at the local CID offices and they too were involved in deciphering information received from London and their own local investigations. Whilst there was nothing tangible from either foray, Ben's intel did produce one nugget. Earlier in the year, the Dutch police, using the Encrochat hack, picked up chatter from the Hopi Boys, a notorious organized crime gang operating out of Amsterdam. They had learned that the gang had been in contact with other organised crime gangs (OCG's) in France, UK and Ireland, with a view to funding a large-scale action. There was no known target but an activity worth paying attention to. The two of them agreed that was sufficiently interesting enough to warrant a visit to Amsterdam to see if that could add to the Intel. They thanked Loris for his input and told him to remain vigilant and they would be investigating further. They began their search by a visit to the Dutch offices of Interpol; there they learned of various addresses for the Hopi gang but with little indication of which of them was currently in use. What they considered a better use of their time was to find Klass Holleeder, the erstwhile leader of the gang. The Dutch police appeared to have been active in tracking Mr. Holleeder recently and had made a note of his most recent known whereabouts. He was conveniently using a legitimate company as a cover which made tracking him that much easier.

Matt and Ben found a vantage point in the large boardroom of the Universal Tulip Company, a business where Mr Holleeder was the managing director. After a day of very little activity, a meeting was called which the duo thought well worth attending, especially as two armed security guards were posted outside the door to the board room. They listened with interest to the conversation between Klass and three unknown associates seated around the boardroom table. It would appear that there was indeed a plot by a group of gangs to undertake an action. It would make sense for them to want to remove the senior investigators visiting from Europe, who they considered were hampering their growing business interests. They did not specifically spell this out, despite the security, they referred to their targets as 'dying flowers' and the need to 'recycle them' Then one of those seated around the table let slip the word 'Wales' and this was the connection the two needed. They were gathering detailed intel that the security services would not be aware of and it was vital that Matt and Ben find out the whom, where and when before taking action. They continued to listen for some time, despite the confidence that the gang's deliberations were in private, Matt and Ben picked coded words and oblique references. There was some clarity when Klass turned to one of his associates with the instruction for the first instalment to be paid, at which point the somewhat studious looking individual he spoke to, opened a laptop and began typing. Matt quickly moved from his position to one where he could see the screen and take note of what was being entered. It appeared that €100,000 was being transferred to a bank account in Ireland and belonging to a Mrs P. Duggen.

Matt and Ben remained until they felt there was little more they could learn and agreed their next step was be discover why an organised crime gang would be paying a married woman in Ireland such a sum. Their first port of call was the Dublin Electoral Office in the hope that Mrs. Duggen would appear on the electoral register, she did not. Their next stop was the office of births, deaths and marriages and this time they had better luck. It appeared a Patricia Duggen of Ballyell married Shamus Gilligan of the 31st May 1987 and when they returned to the electoral register and searched for Patricia Gilligan her current address was conveniently noted. They accessed a nearby pc and searched Shamus Gilligan and were rewarded by reams of information regarding the head of one of Irelands most notorious crime families, commonly referred to as the Gilligan Gang. Armed with as much information as they needed about the gang, they concluded that it was more than likely it was the Gilligan Gang who were the ones planning to commit whatever action that had been spoken of. With the best part of ten days to go they reasoned it was premature to step in before any further tangible steps had been taken and they decided to attend to their respective workloads for the next couple of days. Matt took a trip to Swindon to take part in an outstanding interplanetary travel presentation. He had a growing desire to return to Philax 10, if at all possible and meet again with Yamnus to learn more of their galactic explorations which may in turn benefit planet earth's endeavours. Ben was being harangued by her publishers to send over a draft of her book, which she said was only just fifty per cent complete. She shut herself in her bedroom with a large pot of coffee and beavered away for two straight fourteen-hour days.

They gave Loris a broad outline of what they had learned with a strong word about the high degree of confidentiality that must be attached to anything he learned whilst in their employ. He struck them both as an individual with a high degree of integrity and they were comfortable with involving him in their affairs, at least with limitations, for the time being.

With eight days remaining until the Cardiff meeting, Matt and Ben transferred to Ireland, specifically to locate the Gilligan Gang. They headed for the address they had and arrived at the village of St Helens, just a few minutes' drive from the ferry terminal at Rosslare. It made the gang's location very handy for quick access to the mainland. They found a

well-fortified smallholding, securely distanced from any ot.
dwelling and they remained invisible whilst touring the
perimeter of the premises. The main house was a large single
storey brick built structure, with a gabled roof in need of repair,
witnessed by a number of cracked tiles and bird's nests were
well established in the gutters, all the windows were covered
with security grills. They were also able to detect several
CCTV cameras at various access points, as well as more
affixed to each corner of the main building. In addition there
were three out buildings, one quite large, in which a tractor, a
jeep and an unremarkable looking Japanese saloon, were
stored, along with sundry farming tools. The other two
buildings were securely padlocked and alarmed, neither of
which proved a barrier to Matt and Ben gaining entry. Inside
they discovered stacks of metal chests, in which they found a
considerable cache of arms and explosives with several RPG's
(rocket propelled grenade launchers) and numerous packs of
Semtex. They left to spend the night at home and to plan their
next moves, tomorrow would leave a week remaining until the
meeting and they would expect the gang to soon begin to move
into action. With the speed of their apportation, Loris assumed
Matt had been teaching and Ben shut in her room writing and
not flitting from one side of the country to the other, either
way, he did not ask and they enjoyed a dinner together. Loris

was very much at ease and appeared to be getting more proficient with the radio equipment, keeping copious voice notes of anything that caught his attention, which he thought they may be interested in.

The following morning, they returned to the Gilligan den and joined the family for a planning meeting. Sitting on a bench outside the front door was a large unshaven brute of a man, dressed more like a soldier for the Cosa Nostra, a loose fitting jacket, corduroy trousers and a flat cap pulled aslant low over his brow and with a shotgun resting across his lap, idly stroking a German Shepherd at his heel. They counted four further guards around the property, similarly armed. This was all a good indication that what was going on inside was not for outsiders to see or hear. With that, the outsiders entered the building and placed themselves next to a large grandfather clock, just inside the front door. Shamus and Patricia were seated on a coach together and three further associates, sat on upright chairs facing them. Between them was an empty chair on which stood a blue print, pinned to a board. Matt could focus on the print without changing his position and smiled as he read at the bottom of the print that the building was the Argarth Hotel, the site of the meeting. The gang obviously assumed that nobody would see the print they had copied and saw no need to mask the name. They were also to learn two pieces of critical information, the first, when Shamus mentioned their daughter Ciara. Whilst still very young, her parents had decided to register her at school using her mother's maiden name of Duggen, such was the unfortunate reputation of the Gilligan family they considered it would only hamper her education if she went by that name. He now smugly opined on what a shrewd move that was, having left university with a first in European Languages, she had moved to London and registered with a leading translation agency for freelance work. She was on a list of candidates being considered to work at the forthcoming International Security meeting. Shamus had assisted in her selection by administering some syrup of ipecac via take out coffee, to two of the selected translators, causing them to call in sick and Ciara became a last minute shoe in, to attend the meeting. Shamus added that with zero risk to herself, she had agreed to speed dial him as soon as all the delegates were seated and then cancel the call, the missed call was the signal he needed. The translators were situated in a sound proof room a short distance away from the meeting room, following the proceedings on CCTV and out of harm's way. He presently pointed to one of those seated opposite, a slightly built and athletic looking individual and told him to recite his role in the action. Greatly to the benefit of Matt and Ben, they learnt that he was to travel to the mainland the day before the meeting and

215

drive to Cardiff, not stopping anywhere for any reason. He was to find a secluded spot outside the city, leave his car and change into the uniform of a service engineer from an electrical contractor. He was to make his way to the office block adjacent to the hotel the day before and make his way to the roof. His face displayed an element of displeasure when reciting the part, which entailed him spending the next six hours on the roof of the building until darkness, as the interior was alarmed out of business hours. He would then lower by rope, a plank left on the roof two weeks prior, to bridge the eight foot ally way gap between the buildings, he was then to make his way across to the hotel roof. Next he would remove the steel cowl placed over a disused chimney and lower the explosive the exact distance as shown by a knot on the rope. Since the hotel had installed central heating many years ago, the owners had removed the internal fireplaces and bricked up the openings but chimney breasts and flues remained. With the aid of the plans, they were able to determine which flue serviced which floor and which room, plus the distance from the roof to the large second floor conference room, the only possible venue for the meeting. Once in place he could leave, the device being detonated by mobile phone. The resulting explosion would cause the floor to collapse with a high probability of a multiple loss of life and massive collateral damage. He would then

216

spend the remaining hours of the night on the roof and re-enter the office building in the morning when the alarms were switched off. Anybody seeing him would assume he had returned the following day and as there were numerous companies occupying the building, they would each assume he was visiting one of the other tenants.

Now that they had learned of the details of the plan, Matt and Ben felt it was time to consider how they could scupper it. It would appear that by way of an alibi, the Gilligan's had organized an outing for themselves and their crew to St Helen's Bay beach, where other beach goers could vouch for their whereabouts. They considered that whilst they were on route, all encased in two vehicles, it would be an ideal time to trap them, this they agreed, would fall to Matt to deal with. However, it was vital they first find out who would be responsible for detonating the bomb.

Matt was at the farm early enough to witness the cars being loaded with innocent picnic items. A Mercedes saloon had appeared earlier, carrying the remaining three gang members who were all dressed for the outing, in short sleeve shirts, shorts and loafers. The gang waited outside for Shamus and Patricia to appear and Matt immediately went into the building and was thankful for his timing. He found the Gilligans in the kitchen and Patricia was handing her husband a mobile phone, as she did so she reminded him of the code and he swore at her, telling her he was unlikely to forget it. He tucked the phone into the pocket of his jacket and as Patricia left the house, Shamus turned around to make a last minute call to the lavatory. Much to Matt's delight, Shamus removed his jacket and threw it over a chair in the kitchen, before entering the toilet and shutting the door. It took Matt less than a minute to access the phone, remove the sim card and replace the unit back into the jacket pocket. The entire crew were gathered outside as Shamus secured the house, it was obvious that despite being hardened criminals, this was a major operation and nerves were a little frayed. They stood around smoking and going over last minute details. Matt observed Shamus pat his pocket to feel the phone there and reassure himself, he then climbed into his car.

Ben would meanwhile incapacitate the member who she found on the roof of the hotel, as yet to lower the explosive device down the chimney. He lay sound asleep, as if without a care in the world and wrapped in a car rug.

The final part of the duo's plan was that shortly before they moved into action, they would deposit with the leading task force all the information they had which included the Dutch connection, the money transfer, a copy of the marked up hotel blue prints and details of the culprit on the hotel roof.

Finally, the outlined Ciara Duggen's involvement and where they could collect her and the gang itself.

The morning of the meeting saw the police out in force, road closures were enforced covering several blocks surrounding the hotel and armed escorts were provided for all the delegates. The police were keeping a close watch on the activities of all likely suspects but so far they had no concrete intelligence suggesting planned action.

Meanwhile, Ben sat watching a snoozing bomber who was quite unaware that whilst he slept, Ben had tied his legs and arms together. Matt made a quick visit to the Cardiff CID offices and caused a free-standing water dispenser to topple over. The startled receptionist rushed from her post and busily fussed about clearing up the spillage and whilst totally distracted, Matt entered and placed a large A4 envelope on the reception desk, marked for the urgent attention of Detective Chief Superintendent Andrew Carson. Earlier in their investigation, Matt had acquired the Chief Super's mobile number and to ensure he was alerted to the urgency of the situation placed a call when he had returned to monitoring the beach goer's progress. In addition to telling the Chief Super of the envelope awaiting his attention at reception, he also confirmed that the Gilligan's and their associates would shortly be found on the St Helen's Village Road, awaiting arrest, he added the location of the roof top bomber. The detailed information did not cause the seasoned policeman to treat the call as a hoax for one moment, quite the opposite. He quickly asked Matt who he was talking to but soon realized he would not find out as the line went dead. DCS Carson was already pouring over the contents of the envelope within a minute of ending his call with Matt. He was only too familiar with the Gilligan gang and before joining all the dots, grabbed his phone and barked orders to various subordinates, to round up the gang. Matt returned to the two vehicles, which were now in procession along the road towards the beach. They were suddenly brought to an abrupt stop by a freak whirlwind that had picked up and then dumped a large volume of sand, courtesy of Matt, on the windscreens of both vehicles. As the drivers frantically succeeded clearing their screens by the use of their wiper blades, they were then met with the sight of an impassable road, blocked by a six foot high pile of sand. Patricia and Shamus looked at each other, grappling to come to terms at what was a highly improbable situation, Shamus opened his door to survey the problem and as he did so his attention was drawn skyward by the deafening sound of a low flying helicopter, in fact a police helicopter, as was announced in large black letters on the underside. The noise of the whirling blades was joined by the piercing sound of sirens,

220

growing ever louder and ever nearer. By this time, the occupants of the two cars had clambered out and when assessing their predicament had been galvanized into taking to their heels across the adjacent field. Matt remained at the scene long enough to witness two lines of blue clad officers, approaching the fleeing gang members in a pincer movement. Shamus had grabbed the phone from his jacket pocket and was frantically stabbing at the screen and cursing, as the several burley police officers grabbed his arms and Patricia began yelling a string of obscenities at the offices who were placing her in handcuffs.

The door of the translators room quietly opened but the six translators remained undisturbed with head phones covering their ears, staring at the screens in front of them and talking into their mouth pieces. Ciara was startled when a WPC placed a firm hand on her shoulder and used the other hand to remove the translator's headphones so she could hear the officer telling her she was being arrested.

Likewise, Ben was in situ to see a startled sleeping gang member aroused by an officer and read his rights whilst still attempting to come to terms as how he had been hog tied. The show was over before lunchtime and Matt communicated to Ben to meet him at home. Loris was waiting by the door as they arrived, obviously in a state of excitement as he told them the airways were buzzing with the news of the surprise arrests in the UK, France and the Netherlands, foiling a plot the blow up the hotel where a meeting of senior international security personnel were gathered. Without pausing for breath, Loris told them it was a brilliant take down but wanted to know how they did it. He was stopped in his tracks by Matt telling him they had decided to disclose more of their operating methods which may also answer several of his more pressing questions. However, first they must visit their family. They gravitated to the study to listen and watch the continuing news streams, excitingly broadcasting the extraordinary apprehension of a notorious gang, some but not all, mentioned a bizarre stroke of luck when a freak sand storm waylaid the perpetrators. Matt smiled inwardly when DCS Carson appeared on screen, speaking into a bank of microphones, he was happy to take all the plaudits for the timely arrests and the prevention of a gross act of terrorism but was apologetic at not being able to share the undercover police work that had gone into such a well-executed police action. The international news led with the French and Dutch arrests but was more probing as to how the gang were apprehended. As they listened they could only hazard a guess at what the various security services were putting out to the press as to the circumstances that lead to the foiling of the terrorists plans, as well as detecting who the various perpetrators were.

Matt and Ben drove the ninety minutes to Halstead, enjoying the somewhat slower pace of a country drive to the somewhat maniacal pace of the last few days. They stopped at the gallery first and Kanika was genuinely delighted at seeing them, told an assistant to mind the shop and grabbing both of them by the arm and marched them along the road to a wine bar. They both felt as though they deserved a drink and did not object and even Kanika commented that they looked like cats that had found the cream. They fobbed this off with ease and happily settled down to listening to tales of the world of art and the latest local gossip. In short shift they had demolished a bottle of wine and Ben regretfully told her mother it was just a flying visit, as she had a deadline to meet with her publishers and they next made a stop at The Spinney. Alfred and Cynthia were surprised and delighted to see them, although Alfred was less surprised, knowing their abilities to move from place to place at a whim. Cynthia, as if expecting them, produced a fruitcake and insisted that they each take a slice. Matt thought his grandmother was in good spirits and physically was looking well and when she disappeared into the kitchen, Matt quickly asked his grandfather how she was. With hand gestures and a few brief words, he told his grandson that she was very well physically but no change as regards her mental faculties.

Matt was excited to tell him of their progress with the railway and that they expected to take a trial run in the next few days, plus their hope he could take a trip with them shortly afterwards. With a twinkle in his eye, Alfred said he could not think of anything he would like more. With the Summer House becoming more of a home, with the addition of more furniture and the odd bits of artwork and soft furnishings, they considered it high time to invite the family to visit and to meet Loris. They mentioned this to Alfred and Cynthia and they loved the idea, although Cynthia had seen the place when they first moved in, she was nevertheless keen to return. They also put the idea to Matt's parents when they stopped by and they too were keen to see where their son lived. Wendy was busy painting the front door when they arrived and Lans, now semi-retired, was banging about in the shed. On hearing their voices he emerged, holding out greasy hands by way of an apology for not hugging them. They happily accepted the offer to stay for tea but declined to partake of the apple pie cooling on the stove, saying that were full of Cynthia's fruit cake.

On returning to the Summer House, Loris told them the news was still continuing on their recent escapade but now interest was growing how such a successful police action was achieved and where such valuable intel had come from. A week later, a half page photograph appeared in the tabloids, taken by a beachgoer passing at the time, of a mysterious mountain of sand which appears less a sand storm and more to be a collapsed dune at St Helens Bay beach. The item was newsworthy as the dune, by unique good fortune, had collapsed across the road, trapping the gang of notorious criminals. Once again, the police made no notable comment but Loris nagged to learn the details of Matt and Ben's creative work.

Matt repeated what he had told him prior to going to Halstead and he would do as he said, if they could just take off their outer wear and have a moment's reflection, they would sit and talk. As always, he was amenable to whatever they proposed and returned to the comms room. Matt and Ben went upstairs and silently discussed their next move. They agreed that they would need, at the very least, to disclose that they possessed certain exceptional skills and why this must be kept secret. With that as the starting point, they called Loris into the sitting room and began a conversation of unrelated matters to begin with. They enquired if Loris were happy with his role at the Summer House, if his relative isolation was a problematic issue and if there was anything he would like to change in the current arrangements. He was happy to deal with the issues raised which they discussed further. Matt then broached the subject upper most on Loris's mind and certainly stopped him in his tracks by simply stating that he and Ben had certain unusual and exceptional skills, unique to them and no others. He paused to let those words sink in and then continued before Loris could interrupt, telling him that it must be appreciated that if anybody and he emphasized the word anybody, were to learn of this, their lives and those they hold near and dear, could be in jeopardy. An explanation as to how they came by these skills would, for the time being, remain unexplained but they appreciated that for them to work together, Loris should be aware what they were capable of. They could sense his brain working overtime and he stroked his chin as he contemplated a response. In answer to his unasked question, they would admit to their ability to travel long distances in a fraction of time but not the methodology plus their telekinetic powers. After Matt had finished speaking it was obvious that Loris had to be sceptical, at the very least, to accept fictional and comic book descriptions of super human powers. A quick silent exchange between Matt and Ben agreed on a demonstration, before which Matt warned Loris to expect the unexpected. Loris let out a muffled yelp, as he felt his chair lifted from the ground and carried out the front door to the gazebo. Once the look of total disbelief had left his face and he stamped his feet on solid ground, he burst of laughing, with his laughter interspersed with expletives. Ben added for good measure that if he still needed convincing then he should revisit the evidence from the several recent episodes involving their intervention, not least, his own sea rescue. After a lengthy pause, whilst he obviously was lost for words, he asked quite bluntly, if they were human, it was their turn to burst out laughing and he could do no less than join them, which served to dismiss the question. Matt told him that events in their lives would explain what had happened and how they were able to do what they do. For the time being, he must accept that such is the critical importance in possessing this knowledge, he must accept that they be allowed to choose the time and place at which to disclose all.

Loris finally found the words to express his amazement and his inability to fully rationalize what they had told him and of course, he would wait until they felt the time was right to take him into their full confidence. With that, life returned to their version of normal and work progressed in the basement. A control panel had been erected at the bottom of the stairs, the rail network was in place and the all-important siding was discretely in place. Matt told Ben that he felt that all was in place to decide on a time for an inaugural trip.

Matt sat at the control panel and thought long and hard if there was anything he had missed in setting up the railway. From where he sat it all looked good, the snow-capped mountains in the distance, beyond the sparkling lake and to the east the distant rolling hills with the town out of view to his right, the forest deep and impenetrable, stretched away to his left. Of course, what he was looking at was the product of his physical toil but he was eager to see the product of his imagination under the spell of the railway. After a respectable time he decided it was time to summon Ben for a train ride, she was in London but would be with him shortly and so he went upstairs to see Loris.

He was seated, as per usual on his office chair in the radio room, headphones on and impervious to any outside interference. He sensed Matt's appearance and removed his headphones, Matt asked if there was anything of any interest to report and Loris said there nothing of any consequence. He took the opportunity to reiterate his inability to fully absorb the staggering revelations that he and Ben had made, stressing that despite their demonstration, he felt it beyond his ability to compute something so far beyond the realms of accepted possibility. He stressed to Matt that on pain of death he would never disclose anything he learned but made no secret of his eagerness to learn more. At this, all that Matt would say was that he would learn more and the more he learned the more he would find it impossible to accept what he learned. Their chat was brought to a halt as he heard Ben at the front door. He told her to meet him in the basement when ready and returned there to await her arrival.

He had unpacked the engine a while ago and attended to the minor servicing required, placed it on the track below the console where he now sat and dimmed the lights. When he heard Ben open the basement door he turned the lights in the basement off, with just the lights of the operating console providing the only illumination. She joined him and they both sat on the antique couch he had bought especially for the basement. He took her hand and they instinctively closed their eyes, presently hearing the familiar faint sound of ethereal tones, growing in volume. They knew the precise moment to open their eyes to the joyous sight of the engine puffing steam, a short way along the track.

What came as a wonderful surprise was that by installing much of what was in the front room at The Spinney, also brought with it much of the life and soul that was so inimitable to the railway. This could not have been more wonderfully apparent to Matt than when he saw Sanjay lean out of the cab and wave at him, with a beaming smile on his face as the engine slowly approached and stopped, for them to board. They greeted each other like long lost friends and Ben was treated to a hug. He asked after Alfred and Matt told him he hoped to be visiting in the very near future.

Once aboard, in a matter of fact manner, Sanjay said he

assumed that Matt was on a tour of inspection and put the engine into gear. They took a detour to see the forest siding and shed and Matt checked that the six rails were neatly in place. Both he and Ben would always be amazed at the magical transformation of their handcrafted plans being converted into the mystical reality of the railway and surrounding landscape. At clearings in the forest Ben had suggested they put some lodges for people who enjoyed communing with nature and she pointed to several timber built lodges with smoke curling out from their wood burners and they heard the sound of children's laughter coming from beyond the trees. They witnessed an abundance of wild life, which was a particular wish of Matt's. They saw birds darting about in the trees above and a skittish muntjac, startled by the engine, dashing into the undergrowth. As they left the forest they slowed through a station where holidaymakers could disembark for the short trek to their accommodation. They soon began the climb to the lower slopes of the mountains and made the regular stop at the cable car station for skiers to get on and off the train. As they continued to climb Matt and Ben shivered and Sanjay with just a tee shirt under his boiler suit, laughed at them. The train puffed its way around the snow covered peaks where skiers were zigzagging their way down, they crossed a bridge and watched the skiers disappear under one side and reappear on the other. In the distance they could make out the dramatic change of colour as the white of snow gave way to the green of the foothills. They passed through a forest of pines and exited to see lush green pastures and they beamed with pride as they travelled through ploughed fields and those of golden corn and barley. There too was a shepherd, herding his flock and laughing as his dog barked and chased the passing train.

As they crossed a single span bridge that crossed the river, they looked down at a group of youngsters in the process of pitching tents by the river side and others building a camp fire. Ben turned to Matt and said she would love a holiday here and he replied he had the same thought. Ahead was the gaping black hole of a short tunnel through a rocky outcrop that Matt had planned and he turned to Ben with a smile, as the engine was swallowed into darkness. The dot of light ahead rushed to meet them and in no more than a minute they were once again in bright sunshine and upon another station to service the campers.

Their final stop was at Summer Town Station where they bade farewell to Sanjay. They had established that two trains operated, alternating two hours apart and they decided to catch the later one to return to their departure point. The first thing to strike Matt when alighting from the train was the increase in the number of people at the station and beyond. He guessed one of the reasons was his introduction of a college of further education. In any event, it gave the town an added vibrancy and the two of them were eager to explore further. They agreed to stop for a late lunch at one of the ethnic restaurants they had introduced and decided on an Indian meal. They located the restaurant, The Bombay Kitchen, one road back from the lakeside. They chatted constantly over lunch, realizing that in their busy lives they rarely spent any material time, just talking. Loris was the subject of much deliberation and they both became comfortably resigned to disclosing much more to him, if not everything. Matt touched on his desire to return to Philax 10 and to possibly meet with Yamnus again. He wondered if with their highly developed abilities, they were able in any way to help Loris to see, by giving him sight by natural means or by some technological intervention. Ben suggested this was not beyond the realms of possibility and they should at least investigate further. It was also agreed that with the delight of the land they had travelled and particularly meeting with Sanjay again, they would urge Alfred to take a trip as soon as they returned.

They had a little time left before they needed to catch the train and as they walked through the town, Matt spotted a dental surgery that sparked a memory and he pulled Ben down the side turning. At the end of the turning Matt stopped and was pleased to see at the top of the slope, was Woodland Cottage and he knew this would delight Alfred as well. The restful day had been a tonic for them both and with the knowledge that it took no time from their busy lives in the real world, they promised each other to repeat the exercise as often as they could.

Discarded food wrappings in the kitchen refuse told Ben that Loris was feeding himself and marvelled at his endless abilities for one without the benefit of sight. They told him of their plan to host a family dinner and he said he would be pleased to meet members of their family. His enthusiasm at meeting other people prompted Matt to mention his rather solitary existence again. He asked if there was anywhere they could take him to meet people. He thanked him for his concern and in reply said maybe they could get out now and again, maybe a visit to a local pub and even dine out occasionally. He didn't so much miss company as miss social intercourse of a general nature. Ben apologised for both of them, for being so inconsiderate and of course they would amend their behaviour accordingly. In addition, he admitted they had been seriously remiss in not addressing the question of money and that now he was a permanent member of the team, it was only fit and proper that he were paid accordingly. Ben and he had exchanged thoughts on the question of amounts and Matt made the offer to

Loris, asking him if it was acceptable. For his part, he said that with his food and lodgings provided, he wanted for little but the independence that a salary would give him was most welcome and he was more than happy to accept their offer.

The change of routine was therapeutic for all of them, they found a lovely inn, just over a mile away in Alderton that became their local and Matt visited the small marina opposite their home and found the owner of a small cabin cruiser that they could hire for the day.

When the forecast suggested a run of good days they planned a river trip and travelled sedately inland up the River Deben until they reached Woodbridge where Matt had booked a table for lunch at a hotel. Loris would accept no argument when the bill was presented and he insisted on paying, he laughed and said he had spent nothing since moving in with them. The relationship between the three became more solid as the weeks past and built upon their mutual respect and trust.

When they invited Alfred to take a train ride, they suggested that the time was right to take Loris along. Alfred had agreed to stay over and that allowed him time to get to know Loris and he warmed to him immediately. Loris was a good people person and as soon as Alfred mentioned he life on the railways, Loris listened enthusiastically to all his anecdotes from his days with British Rail. Alfred was sitting by the riverside when Matt and Ben joined Loris in the comms room. He removed his headphones and even without seeing their faces, he sensed a slight tension in the air and suspected they were about to talk about something important. Matt told him that what he was about to be told and to shortly experience, would be beyond his wildest imagination and he would find it difficult to attach this forthcoming experience to reality. Matt then began to recount the story of Yuri, the engine, the front room railway and their own trans dimensional travels. He told Loris that he would not be surprised if he treated what he was just told as something straight from the pages of a science fiction novel. However, he urged Loris not to ask any questions but to wait until they had entered the basement and he had experienced all that they had outlined to him as proof of the veracity of what he had been told. Maybe their own experiences had allowed them to convey, in more convincing terms, the truth in what they had told him but he remained calm and merely said he would digest all that they had told him and take things as they came.

They called Alfred in and the four made their way to the basement with Matt holding Loris's arm as they descended the stairs. It was a tight squeeze for four of them on the couch but with Loris wedged between Ben and Matt, it served to calm his beating heart. With the light extinguished, Matt instructed all to close eyes and relax and told Loris to listen out for some heavenly harmonic tones. As they jointly exhaled, calmness descended and the faint sounds could be heard. Loris's hands gripped the arms of Ben and Matt as the warm air brushed his hair and countryside sounds assailed his ears. Despite Matt's attempts to prepare him, nothing in the human experience could ever truly prepare anybody for something quite so supernatural. Matt could only hazard a guess at how amplified the shock of the experience must be to somebody devoid of vision. Ben was whispering to him, telling him they had experienced this transfer from one reality to another, on many occasions and it was nothing short of wonderful. They dwelled longer than normal, although Alfred had stood and was walking towards the engine that was slowly approaching; he turned to Matt and Ben and nodded approval at their work that he could so far see. Finally, Loris said he wanted to stand and producing his cane they walked along the edge of the track. He smiled and said he wasn't imagining the sound of a steam train, was he? The engine drew alongside and Sanjay literally jumped down from the cab, shouting with excitement, at seeing his old friend. Loris was still repeating terms of wonderment and disbelief as they encouraged and aided him up the steps to the cab. They introduced him to Sanjay and asked if he would rather sit in one of the carriages or remain in the cab, he chose the former and they left Alfred to catch up with Sanjay as they moved through the first carriage to find a window seat. There were a handful of passengers with whom they exchanged polite greetings and took their seats with Loris. He stuck his head out of the window and started to yell with delight as the train gathered speed, all the while Matt, yelling over the sound of the engine, described the scenery they were passing. Ben was prompted to tell Loris in a joking way that if he didn't stop shaking his head it would fall off. However, they knew full well what Loris was feeling and only sorry he could not see what they had created. He was able to tell them that they were passing through a forest and with his head still out of the window and literally smelling the air, guessing at the names of the trees they passed. His sublime pleasure at the experience was now peppered with thanks to Matt and Ben for allowing him to share with them this out of world experience and they replied they were happy to share his enjoyment.

Alfred had joined them and complemented them on their countryside work, approving the location of the siding and as they climbed the hills, said he particularly liked the addition of crop fields and the lower green foothills, especially remarking on seeing sheep herding and the busy camp site. He took Matt aside and told him that he had spoken to Sanjay and informed him that he was passing control of the railway to him

237

and he said that he would happily work with him. They had stopped at the nearby station and Matt asked Loris if he would like to get off here for a walk through the campsite and along the river. They arranged to meet Alfred back at the cottage later in the day and assisted Loris off the train. They said their goodbyes and Sanjay climbed down to shake Lori's hand.

Loris rested his hand on Matt's arm as they walked between the tents and stopped to admire some of the family sized tents in the process of being erected, describing for Loris's benefit the size and accommodation of these canvas homes. They found a flat area of grass, close to the river edge and sat. Loris began his questioning and Ben and Matt answered as best they could. He accepted their honesty and told them he believed they were telling him all that they were able to. He was prompted to discuss their activities back in the real world and asked if they felt that the best use of their extraordinary powers was to be intervening in random, one off, cases. They prompted him to expand on his thoughts and he suggested that there were large scale human issues affecting hundreds of thousands, if not millions, of people, such as earth quakes, floods or even wars, that could benefit from their powerful intervention. Whilst both Matt and Ben had thought about world issues, such was the magnitude of the intervention required, they were not sure their experiences thus far would be up to what was required in such an enlarged arena. However, they agreed that perhaps now was the time to consider a seismic shift in their endeavours going forward.

They spent a leisurely time along the riverbank and then made their way back to the station to wait for the next train back to town. As the train approached Summer Town, Matt began describing the layout of the town and the makeup of business and residential properties. As they disembarked, Loris wanted to know about the people he could hear moving about and chatting nearby. Matt admitted that he was mystified as to the very nature of the people, only saying that from the years when Alfred ran the railway, these people were a manifestation of his imagination and had spawned more as he added his creation. Ben added that her take on the subject was that the citizens of Summer Town appeared to be exceptionally contented, more so than people from their own reality. They wanted for nothing and provided all that they needed for a healthy and fulfilled life. As they reached the dental surgery, they told Loris of Alfred's cottage and took the short walk up the slop. Alfred was sitting on the veranda drinking a mug of tea and waved as he saw them approaching.

Before he suggested it, Matt told his grandfather not to bother to cook dinner for all of them and that they would eat later. They wanted to get back home and with the hour plus drive ahead, suggested they leave shortly. Loris enthused about the whole experience and said, almost matter of fact, how extraordinary it was that of the almost eight billion people that lived on planet earth, just the four of them were so privileged as to know of and enjoy this supernatural reality. Alfred checked on the time of the last train and they made their way back to the station in time to board.

CHAPTER 11

WORLD CHANGING EVENTS

Once back home Matt and Ben deliberated long and hard on their next steps and finally arrived at a decision on which they both agreed. Whilst it had undeniable inherent risks, the rewards were great enough to justify the action. They would disclose to Loris the details of their trip to Philax 10 and how they obtained their powers but as important for Loris, was the possibility that this highly intelligent and advanced civilization could take a new look at the question of his lack of sight. Additionally, they had determined that if they were to take the quantum leap, of interfering in world affairs, it would aid them to learn if there were further powers to be gained which would be more effective on a global stage.

With the plan in place it only remained to choose the time and they decided this would be after the family get together at their home. Whilst the idea for the event was spontaneous, to ensure its success involved considerable organization by Matt, Ben and Loris. They needed more chairs, more crockery and cutlery, more glasses and a lot of food and beverages. Despite the lengthy preparation they enjoyed the distraction, although Loris would continuously rush to the comms room when he thought he heard something of concern and it took considerable will power not to disappear and attend to every emergency. They had invited Alfred and Cynthia, as well as Kanika, to stay overnight and were pleased that they had now pretty well fully furnished the place and that included the two spare bedrooms for the overnight guests.

The folks up at Bawdsey Manor had given them the name of a good local caterer and they provided a fine menu of hot and cold foods to suit any discerning palate. Rather than a sit down meal, the large kitchen table was laid out with a wide choice of cold meats, an assortment of fish with plenty of salads and artisanal bread, for people to help themselves and find a place to sit, either inside or outside. Matt and Ben were pleased how everything looked and all was prepared in good time, the family arrived on the appointed day with both Cynthia and Wendy bringing home baked desserts. Loris was warmly welcomed into the family, making friends with his amenable manner and intelligent conversation. Despite increasing frailty displayed by his grandparents, they played their part in lively debates and the late night discussions of the duo's success and notoriety.

His mother, father and Kanika had also come laden with gifts and home warming presents, from a coffee making machine and electric wine cooler, to a beautiful painting, commissioned by Kanika, of The Spinney on a summer's evening which brought nostalgic memories to both Matt and Ben. Lans told his son that he was buying a solid hull boat for river trips and he would bring down the inflatable for them to use on the Deben. The time came for their parents to leave, endlessly glowing at the impressive home their children had made and thanking them for the lovely spread they had laid on. Alfred, Cynthia and Kanika climbed the stairs to bed, as the caterers cleared up and Ben suggested the three of them adjourn to the study. Ben began by telling Loris that he was now fully aware of their unique abilities and the awesome magic of the railway but that there was yet more to tell. Matt delved into the history of the engine and the belief that its origin was a probe from a dying planet. He told him of the advanced technology of the probe, incorporated into the engine that took them on their first trans dimensional trip to the planet of Philax 10 and of the Philadrons, adding that their civilization was eons older than their own. As the story unfolded, both Matt and Ben could see they were reaching the limits of Loris's acceptance the out of world stories they continued to tell him. There were, he continued, ten dimensions and none are replicas of our own. Whilst aboard the train, the occupants create energies about themselves, which allow them to move from one frequential state to another. These energies are a geometric construct of ourselves and will ensure our return because as we move from one dimension to another, the construct may change but our presence will always remain extraneous to these different dimensional surroundings, which will guarantee our return. He told Loris that he found it difficult to fully comprehend all that he spoke of and accepted that he too would indeed struggle but there was a reason he told him all this and engendering his words with as much caution as he could, he told him that it was possible that with the highly advanced abilities of the Philadrons, their investigations could result in the possibility of him gaining the ability to see. However, the decision and choice as to whether or not to embark on this quest, was entirely his.

For his part, Loris told them that he was beginning to become accustomed to the fantasy world of his benefactors and that being blind his entire life was the only view of the world he knew. If it were to continue that way, he would know no difference but if what Matt had told him could offer him something he had never thought possible and still didn't, then he would be a fool not to welcome the chance and at the very least, to learn more. He added that if he remained sightless, he would always be grateful to them for trying and in any event, the prospect of a trip, the likes of which they described, was in itself more than enough to contemplate.

They suggested that in the morning they would drive Ben's mother and the grandparents' home and on returning they would make the trip with Loris. Matt added that they had considered further the comments Loris had made about expanding the best use of their powers and this would entail moving onto the world stage. In this regard he suggested they had best upgrade their communications and that Loris should look into installing additional screens in the study, which would stream real time news from around the world.

They were up bright and early the next morning and Ben fixed a light breakfast. They gathered around the kitchen table, reminiscing on days gone by and all that had happened in their respective lives. They drove to the Spinney and then the gallery and were back at the Summer House by midday, telling Loris if he was prepared then they should head for the basement. Once seated in front of the console, Matt explained to Loris that they had not made a return trans dimensional trip and he was still a little unsure that he could perform the mental gymnastics required, to make the precise journey. With that said, the lights were extinguished and they sat and relaxed.

Sanjay was his normal cheery self and when Matt explained he would like to take over the engine and Sanjay should wait for the alternate locomotive, he happily accepted this and climbed down from the cab, whished them a lovely day and walked a short distance back along the track to find a convenient spot to wait. The journey to the wooded siding took little time and Matt slowly positioned the engine at the end of the line. Retrieving the small remote from his pocket, he uncovered the six rails and activated the remote, waiting until he saw them slowly moving into place. Climbing aboard and closing the doors and windows to the cab, he heard the familiar grinding of metal and a clank, as the rails connected and he put the motor into gear. He explained to Loris what was expected to happen next and what he and Ben needed to do. Matt suggested Loris hold on to a guard rail with both hands and he and Ben joined hands and entered a state of intense concentration aiming to direct the engine through the portal and to the correct destination. They braced themselves for the remembered moment when the noise of metal wheels on a metal track abruptly stopped and the moment the siding wall disappeared. They crossed into the abyss and the light show began with Loris sensing he was in a completely alien environment. He called to them to tell him what was happening, as the sensations he felt were unlike anything he could relate to and Ben described the silent flight and the amazing coloured light streams, shooting stars, supernovas, space clouds and so much more. They stopped in that remembered blackness but something was different, Matt was more than a little concerned. He was very cold and the blackness was more a swirling maelstrom of vapours. With growing alarm, Ben asked if he knew where they were, he said he didn't but just knew it was not where they wanted to be. He suggested they leave and try again, explaining to Loris the problem. They took a few moments to calm their nerves and once again concentrated on the dimensional transfer to Philax 10. The sensitivity of the engine was comforting, as they instantly began to silently move. This leg of the journey appeared to be at lightning speed, which dazed all three of them but when the engine next stopped, a matter of moments later, Matt was comforted by the feeling that the solid blackness was that which they had encountered on their previous visit.

Tentatively, he stretched his arms out of the cab and drew them apart, letting in bright light and he declared success. They disembarked and as they slowly proceeded, the blackness totally gave way to bright light. They described to Loris the familiar experience of what they were seeing and the weightlessness he would feel. They stood on the same spot as before, this time however, they remained where they were as Ben pointed to a globe moving rapidly in their direction. It stopped abruptly when a short distance from where they stood and hovered twelve feet from the ground. They could make out an occupant and were delighted to see it was Yamnus observing them. The globe settled close to the ground and Yamnus appeared through an opening, greeting them with friendly salutations. He told them that he had been alerted to their arrival and was eager to know how they had prospered during their absence. Loris appeared a little agitated, as no words had been spoken and he had no idea what was happening. They described to him the appearance of Yamnus who was now communicating directly with them and he visibly relaxed, nodding his head and smiling. He extended his arms until he felt both Ben and Matt and clasped them as a sign of affection; by his touch they also detected his excitement. They boarded the globe with Matt explaining to Loris the details of their mode of transport whilst they returned to the hub. Ben began to recount for Yamnus all that had transpired in their lives since they last met. Yamnus was intrigued at the primitive criminality that existed on planet Earth but was intelligent enough to appreciate that early evolution was rife with such behaviour. She then went on to tell him the prime reasons for their visit, beginning first with their desire to learn if they could help Loris to see, explaining that he was born without sight and adding their wish to investigate if it were possible to add to their powers. Yamnus promised he would summon their finest minds to examine their friend and see if by what means they may be able to assist. With that in hand, Yamnus wanted to know exactly how they had utilized the skills they had obtained when last on Philax 10 and how they would use enhanced powers. In answer they explained the small matters they had been involved in but had come to believe such powers could and should be utilized in solving far greater problems and injustices, for the benefit of far more humans. Yamnus explained that, on their first visit they had considered that the relative limitations on their mental development were such that they did not want to overload them. He suggested they subject themselves to examination first, after which they will discuss if and how their wishes can be fulfilled. Whilst preparations were made he led them once again to the largest of the globes where they were shown to wicker style, shell shaped seats that floated above the ground. The scene that they had greeted on their last visit was now very different and they found themselves in a replica of an English country garden. As they stood and stared, telling Loris what they were looking at, a tall female being appeared, dressed in a long white smock, with billowed sleeves. She had an ivory white complexion and the green eyes, favoured by Philadrons and gossamer white hair. By way of greeting, she placed her open hands together and said her name was Torossa and she would bring them some refreshments. With good reason, Loris remained surprised and somewhat unnerved, at the use and his acceptance of mental telepathy and

249

was constantly shaking his head from side to side. Matt smiled and said he would soon become accustomed to it. They sat on their floating chairs and Ben told Loris that Yamnus was consulting their finest minds to ascertain what help they could give, if any, regarding giving him the ability to see. Meanwhile Torossa had returned with a tray floating in front of her, on which there was a jug of clear liquid and several plates of what they discerned to be fruit. Both Ben and Matt assured Loris that he should not be concerned about the texture nor smell of any of the food or drink, as they appeared to have reproduced, with uncanny accuracy, the taste of all that they were accustomed to eating and drinking on Earth. They educated Loris as to the strange but captivating aspects of life on Philax 10 and Yamnus silently appeared and patiently waited until they had stopped talking. He communicated to them all simultaneously that they had studied the many working parts of the human eye and that if Loris were willing, they would study initially his optic nerve, lens, cornea, pupil and retina and if there appeared no problems in these functions, they would look at his ora serrata, rectus and vitreous body. Yamnus then looked at them, as if waiting for a response and they looked at each other embarrassed that their limited knowledge of their own eyes prevented them from making any meaningful response. Of course, Yamnus could detect their dilemma and assured them that they were both confident and competent to undertake the investigation he had suggested. No procedures would be undertaken until they had the results of such an investigation and had consulted with them further. Loris suggested that all that Yamnus had said sounded eminently reasonable and he signified his agreement. Yamnus then summoned an assistant who led Loris away. Yamnus remained and suggested that he discuss what additional abilities the two wished to be endowed with. He continued by saying that with little problem, he could give them the ability to understand every language spoken on planet Earth. Likewise, significantly enhanced hearing and vision could be attached to those current operating faculties. The hearing enhancement would enable them to target a particular sound, be it a spoken word or artificial, such as a radio signal, from a great distance and amplify it to a level of audibility. The visual enhancement skill required some degree of practice, as concentrated viewing would breakdown the molecular structure of different substances to become transparent, the skill was to not reduce everything to that state and thereby see nothing. Of a more complex nature is the facility to produce fire from the energy that every sentient creature produces. However, he cautioned, the most effective degree of fire creation devolves from the venting of raging anger which can be taxing on the weak human form, this we shall term purple fire. Red, blue or

251

green fire, being less fierce can be used effectively and well within a human's physical capability. All forms are emitted by the mental channelling of the force through the palms of your hands.

Perhaps the most useful skill we can give you, Yamnus continued, is our long practiced molecular moulding ability. With practice you would learn to mould the molecular structure of one object into a completely different one. The scale to which this can be achieved will depend on the individual species and he suggested this again would be limited by humans but nevertheless, where none other possess such a skill, it would be viewed as a wondrous ability and at this, for the first time, he attempted a laugh.

There was little need for Matt and Ben to talk over what Yamnus had told them, they had used the powers they already had been given to great effect and with no adverse effects to themselves. They told Yamnus that they would rely on his judgment to continue the process to make them more effective and invulnerable in their pursuits.

He led them to a familiar chamber and once seated they were connected, as before, to multiple tendrils that appeared from above. By whatever means they drifted off into the familiar state of unconscious bliss and with a far more receptive brain, the sensation was markedly different and felt like a gentle river of data flowing into their heads. They did not know how long they were comatose but regained consciousness with a somewhat euphoric feeling. They were eager to try out their newly acquired skills and Yamnus, who was waiting nearby, suggested they exit the globe and experiment. Their first discovery was that molecular moulding could only be achieved on an object of a similar molecular construct, in this way they managed to change a small tree into a chair but not a glass bowl. Ben managed to set the chair alight, with a small flame from her outstretched hand and Matt quickly mastered his enhanced vision, seeing every item Yamnus had announced he was concealing under his robe. Little by little they were becoming more proficient but Matt had a pressing matter he wished to discuss with Yamnus and asked if he could spare some time. As always he was most obliging and Matt asked if he was familiar with the Milky Way galaxy and planet earth's solar system. Yamnus replied that whilst he could not say he was familiar, he was aware in general terms of the scope and content of both, having visited a number of the constellations and planets within the galaxy. If Matt had any detailed matters in mind, he would happily consult with one of their librarians. With that, Matt mentioned a planet in the constellation of Volans in what Earth had named the Goldilocks zone, where scientists on earth had discovered signs of an atmosphere that could allow life for humans. Yamnus was silent for a while but in deep contemplation, he then advised Matt that whilst he had not travelled within that particular zone, he was familiar with it from his research. He could not comment on its suitability for humans, however and he had momentarily communicated with several keepers of the tomes containing the detailed information that he sought. He added that such was the volume of data they had on the subject it may take a little while to determine if they could help. Matt thanked Yamnus and said he would happily wait for a response and next asked for any progress with his friend.

They returned to the globe where presently they were surprised to see four individuals appear before them, with Loris by their side. He assured them he was fine and that his experience at the hands of their elders, as he referred to them as, was yet one more wonder to behold. For the examination he was placed in an induced sleep without feeling any physical contact and from that moment reported that he felt as though he were floating on a cloud but with ever changing lights in the sky around him.

Yamnus and the assembled group silently conversed until presently they departed and Yamnus turned to impart their findings to Loris, Matt and Ben. It would appear from the time of his birth, the retina and blood vessels to the eye had not developed and not connected, preventing the vital transfer of information from his eyes to his brain. Yamnus told them that the enlightened ones had said there were two options available that would greatly assist Loris. The first was the production of a communicator that would be attached across his eyes. It would 'see' what seeing eyes would see and transfer these images by miniscule connectors to the optic nerves at the back of the eye. The brain would adapt and accept these images as if they were being transmitted by the eyes. He added that the communicator would need to be permanently connected for the adaptation to become secure. Loris did not appear to be over enamoured by this option but thanked Yamnus and waited to learn of the second. Yamnus reminded Matt and Ben of the lake they had visited on their last trip and that deep on the bed of the lake there lived a hybrid animal plant called an Imerin, its uniqueness extended to the fact that it possessed two pair of eyes, which they had assessed were a 98.7519% match to a humans eye. With this degree of compatibility they were of the opinion that they could bridge the inadequate connectors in Loris's eyes by grafting parts from the Imerin's eyes and expect a successful outcome. The three sat there and not for the first time, they were aghast at what they were hearing. Loris did not hesitate in telling Yamnus of his desire to take up the second option but first wished to know of any risks involved.

At first Yamnus appeared confused by his question but quickly realised why it was being asked, replying that there were no risks. A reply that shocked Loris until Yamnus added that they never undertake any procedures that involve Philadrons that could in any way endanger their wellbeing and this would apply to humans. Loris sat there quite stunned and for the first time they saw what looked like tears welling up in his blind eyes. They went to him and placed their arms around him and Yamnus watched with mild curiosity at what appeared a strange custom.

A male appeared, who had the features and countenance of somebody of great age and he was dressed in a white tunic and white trousers. His closely cropped white hair matched a short beard and his green eyes sparkled, he placed a wrinkled hand on Loris's arm and the two departed. Matt told Yamnus they were deeply grateful for all he had done for them and Loris and could never repay his gifts. In response Yamnus told them that throughout the many millennia of their development, they had discovered that bestowing their knowledge onto others had reaped its own rewards and they had no memories of periods of neither strife nor conflict. He suggested they return to practicing their newly adopted skills whilst waiting for their friend. They were surprised at the length of time that lapsed but were distracted with honing their growing arsenal of powers.

Finally they were summoned inside and watched as Loris approached them accompanied by Yamnus and the elder who had left earlier with him. He had a covering over his eyes, which concerned his friends but they were assured that the procedure met all their pre set criteria but that they were concerned that his brain may go into shock at the sudden arrival of light and images, when none had been there before. They suggested that when they return to their reality, they remove the covering in darkness and gradually introduce light of greater intensity over a period; the period would be determined by Loris's comfort level. On being asked, Loris told them he had suffered no pain or discomfort during the lengthy procedure but admitted now to be experiencing a bit of a headache but more than a little excited on what he may or may not see.

They told Loris that now would not be the best occasion to tour the planet but that they hoped to return again when such a trip would be possible. Yamnus suggested they rest a while as they had all undergone changes, which their bodies may require a passage of time to accept, in the meantime he would check if the librarians could assist with Matt's enquiry. They returned to the beauty of the garden and happily rested with more food and drinks being offered. They

257

lost track of time but when they all agreed to feeling fit and well to travel they called to Yamnus. He returned with the news that the librarians had been successful in retrieving some data containing information on the Volans constellation. As they had no use for physical means of transcribing information, he invited Matt to spend a short while with the scholars who now held the information he required and they would make the necessary transfer direct to his hippocampus. Matt conveyed his thanks, told his associates what was happening and left with Yamnus. As they moved towards the globe transport bays, Matt was prompted to ask where they were going. Yamnus explained that all the serious institutions learning on Philax 10 were in different locations, chosen for the suitability of their functions. They boarded a small globe and sped off in a direction unfamiliar to Matt and the geography rapidly changed. Without gaining height, they began to manoeuvre around a gigantic range of granite rock towers, some Matt assessed, to be several hundred feet high. Eventually they slowed and dropped towards what appeared to be a manufactured platform. On alighting Yamnus approached a solid face wall, which dissolved as he approached, he turned and beckoned Matt to follow. He found himself walking along a gently sloping marble smooth passageway, illuminated in a way he could not fathom but bright enough to see that ahead were a number of figures, Philadrons he assumed, busily floating up and down sheer faced walls and stopping at one of a myriad of shelves. They appeared to be variously taking form and then disappearing from his sight, a most confusing vision. At his distance, Matt was unable to see what the shelves contained and exactly what he was seeing and asked Yamnus. Yamnus explained this was indeed one of the libraries and the Philadrons he could see had no need to maintain a physical appearance, which he did in the presence of visitors from another planet. They conserved energy, only materializing when they needed to handle a data module. He went on to explain that this was but one of several libraries which dealt solely with the multiverse. Each level, he said, contained around a million data modules and there were one hundred and twenty five levels. They arrived at the centre of a huge cavern and Matt craned his neck looking upwards, using his enhanced sight to see the humongous amounts of information stored. They were presently joined by a Philandron who to all intents and purposes, looked like Yamnus and who, thankfully Matt thought, maintained a permanent physical appearance. Yamnus introduced Matt to Dengor, who was introduced as the librarian who had researched the Volans constellation and after a polite greeting, turned and they followed him through a small archway under one of the lower shelves. He found himself in a small room with several of the shell shaped seats, which gently moved several feet above the floor. Dengor moved towards one wall and appearing not to touch anything, there appeared an array of small screens in front of Matt on which reams of data flowed at speed.

Yamnus pointed to a seat and Matt sat, instantly feeling the seat mould to his body shape and at the same time the familiar sight of tendrils appeared from above and attached themselves to various points of his skull. Similarly, he felt the sensation of drifting away and yet remained in a state of receptive consciousness whilst data flowed into his head. As total consciousness returned he was amazed at the detail they had stored on several of the planets in the constellation and in particular one on which they had found organisms. They went as far to suggest that by their calculations these organisms could, over many millennia, advance to a level of reasoning and sapience. However, what this suggested to Matt was that this particular planet had the overwhelming ingredients necessary to sustain human existence. He further scrolled though the trove of information they had given him and found the location of this planet and now had to determine how he could disclose this unbelievable discovery to his Space Agency colleagues with any hope of being believed.

He gave grateful thanks to Dengor and Yamnus and

asked, as he now had more knowledge than he could possibly have imagined, if they could now return, which they duly did. Once reunited with Ben and Loris, he told them what he had learned and they were both equally taken aback, Ben simply saying that to planet earth this would be the greatest discovery since electricity.

Once again, more thanks were given to Yamnus and he responded that he was always happy to impart their learning to others. He delivered them back to their departure spot and with a final farewell, the three stepped back into darkness where their engine awaited. With each experiencing such immeasurable physical and mental changes, they were anxious to return to the Summer House and familiar territory, to gather stock and relax whilst contemplating a dramatically different future.

Matt and Ben continued many hours of testing their skills, paranoid at being spotted by passing boats or unannounced visitors but that fortunately did not happen and they reached a point when they were eager to go into the field and right some wrongs and bring some criminals to justice.

Loris was impatient to remove his eye covering and early in the evening on the third day since returning, whilst they sat in the gazebo watching the setting sun, he reached up and slightly raised the covering over his left eye. Matt saw what he was doing and rushed inside to fetch a pair of sunglasses which he handed to Loris. He put the glasses on and reached underneath them to continue lifting up the covering a little further, his eye was firmly closed and he sat for several moments, as if building up the courage to take the final step. The sun had set and in the dusk, he began to slowly open the eye, the discomfort was evident and he whimpered a little but he persisted. He did the same with the other eye, making repeated attempts at lifting the covering and replacing it. He finally admitted that his eagerness was premature as he felt a burning sensation in his eyes and the beginning of a headache; he also thought it best to wait until the following day before making another attempt. They all adjourned to their respective bedrooms, Ben to work on her book and Matt to dwell on the stunning discovery of a habitable planet within reach of Earth at some time in the future and Loris to rest his eyes.

The following day Loris appeared at the kitchen door as the other two were having their breakfast, he stood in the doorway, wearing sunglasses. They could see he had removed the coverings and he turned his head from left to right and up and down, a broad grin covered his face and he yelled that he could see, over and over again. He removed the glasses as tears gushed down his face and it was evident he could see. He walked to Ben, kissing her on both cheeks and then to Matt, who stood and they hugged. It was a wonderfully momentous and highly emotionally charged occasion and Matt, not knowing what to say, asked if they looked like what he expected. This made them all laugh and Loris told them they are the most beautiful people he had ever seen, then correcting himself by saying they are the only people he had ever seen.

They sat and talked, delirious with joy and happiness, ignoring the continuing chatter that came from the comms room. As the excitement of the occasion waned they formulated plans for the next week or so, with Ben being harassed by her publishers to finish her book and Matt having to decide whether or not to accept a further teaching assignment but also needing to return to Swindon where he had alerted Richard McAllister that he had made a shattering discovery. He decided to draft a brief paper outlining the revelation that one of the known planets in the Volans constellation contained all the necessary precursors for human life to exist. He included enough verifiable data but also an introduction to some of the data he had been given on Philax 10. Whilst it may well be dismissed as unverifiable and even fanciful, it was also well within the realms of reason. He had concluded it was best to reveal the entirety of what he knew, knowing his findings would be dismissed out of hand but let them disprove a single word of his findings and then an intelligent discussion could be had.

Whilst they were distracted, Loris would have time to become accustomed to his gift of sight and spend time reading the many technical books and magazines that had been beyond his reach thus far. He had become prone to taking a nap in the afternoons, to rest his overworked eyes. It was agreed he would widen his search to look for more meaningful and impactful events that may be of interest. Meanwhile Matt headed back to Swindon to have a pre presentation meeting with Richard McAllister. The minute they met in the Agency restaurant, Richard wanted to know what this shattering discovery was but Matt would not be rushed. He placed before Richard documents evidencing the numerous advances made in space travel and exploration that he had been a party and main contributor to and at no point has he ever been found to be wrong on any theory or discovery. In addition to developing these advances with the Agency, he had played a pivotal part in developing fuels and lightweight alloys that could significantly accelerate the journey time to the far reaches of space. He withdrew another file from a briefcase and placed it before Richard but holding his hand on the cover to prevent him from opening it. He told him that before he read it he should bear in mind what Matt had just said because he was about to learn what could be one of the greatest discoveries man has ever made in its journeys into outer space. He removed his hand and Richard opened the folder and began to read the document, expelling air and shaking his head as he read more. Matt took the opportunity to fetch more coffee and by the time he returned Richard sat there looking incredulously at him, with his mouth agape. He told Matt that he was compelled to believe implicitly, every word of this historic document because of his past performance but he pleaded how he was going to convince the other members of the team but more importantly, the decision makers in Whitehall. Matt was at pains to explain that his assertions about life sustaining properties on at least one planet in the constellation were, to his mind irrefutable, however he understood that his learned associates would continue to push back on yet another of his ground breaking papers. However, he asserted again that he defies any of them to provide any shred of evidence that refutes his findings. Richard could not deny that every fact, theory or assertion he had presented prior to this paper, could not be shown to be anything other than one hundred per cent solid but this was something different, way different. He suggested that he distribute the paper and set a meeting for the following week but he would send the papers under a red notice, meaning top security and not a word to a living soul. It gave everyone a little time to contemplate the enormity of what they read and if remotely possible attempt to validate what Matt had postulated. At the meeting Richard started the proceedings with exactly what Matt had just said, listing his accomplishments and solid track record and hope it sets the stage for Matt to add the finer detail to his paper. Matt was happy with Richard's proposal and said he should urge them to take whatever steps they wished to validate or refute the information he was presenting. However, Richard cautioned that even if the Agency was on-board, to actually take any steps to physically verify what he had said would not only take convincing central government to part with hundreds of millions, if not billions, of pounds but the need to accelerate current technology to make a trip of thirty five light years in our life time.

Before he took the podium, Matt took Richard aside and instantly regretted what he said, he told Richard that such was the importance of his revelations not just to the UK Space Agency but to the entirety of mankind that should this revelation not prompt an accelerated effort to explore the Volans constellation, he would be forced to find support elsewhere. Richard was suitably shocked at this and told Matt that if he was considering talking to the Americans or anybody else, who had no experience of him and his work to date, he would find it an impossible task to convince them to fund a venture to travel thirty five light years on his unproven testimony. Matt was sufficiently chastened by Richard and apologised, saying he was so totally convinced by what he was saying that perhaps he was blinded to the fact that others might not be quite so taken.

CHAPTER 12

ONTO THE WORLD STAGE

It was not long in an ever changing and developing world, coupled with their decision to widen the search to find global matters of interest that Loris contacted Matt and Ben, suggesting they return for a review of his current findings, at their earliest convenience. He had noted several large-scale events that were worth discussing, the first was a rise in armed right wing militia in North America that the US government were extremely nervous about. They discussed the issue but decided the National Security Agency and other domestic intelligence agencies were well able enough and democratically inclined, to be able to deal with the problem themselves. They went through insurrection in the Balkans and uprisings in the Middle East, which in all circumstances were either the growing pains of nascent democracies or the burgeoning power of the people wanting to change or overthrow despotic and dictatorial regimes.

They suggested that Loris maintained a watching brief over as many as he was able to and make timely reports, at which point they would review and act accordingly. The event he left to the end to present was a most curious one, which began with his interest being piqued when hearing of an oligarch by the name of Lennox Dubachov. He added that he had an interest in uber wealthy people whose riches stemmed from questionable origins. He did some research on the man and discovered he had amassed a personal fortune of almost $30 billion from Kalingorsk, a Russian company that was the world's largest iron ore producer, smelter and exporter, he co owned the company with three high ranking members of the KGB. Rarely a week went by when he did not feature in the media for one reason or another, be it a social extravaganza or a mega acquisition. He had bought a twelve million dollar chalet in Klosters, the most exclusive resort in Switzerland and then more than double that buying the chalets either side if his. And then it all stopped, without apparent rhyme or reason, he suddenly fell off the grid. Some investigative journalist had discovered that he had liquidated all his major assets, his homes in France, Switzerland, UK as well as his personal Boeing 747 and had purchased Koristan Island in the East Siberian Sea and nothing more was written about him. Such behaviour had made Loris all the more curious and he began by looking at the island. He could not fathom why somebody with his immense wealth, would buy an island in a place where the climate is characterized by frigid winters and where the coldest inhabited places in the world are found. With his new found sight, he had checked detailed shipping data and discovered that there is zero commercial shipping activity in the East Siberian Sea, it neither being on the way to or from anywhere of commercial interest. However, since Dubachov purchased his island there had been increased traffic to and from the island. On a global map covering several thousand shipping movements a day such non-commercial activity had not been registered. Closer investigation, captured by US surveillance satellites, revealed the traffic to be small feeder vessels but too many to be simply a supply service for a virtually uninhabited island.

With no reason to investigate further, Loris put the matter to one side that was until he read that a certain Igor Leitzman had been arrested in the US for channelling funds to several fundamentalist organizations. Reading the article further his attention was caught by the mention that Leitzman, also a billionaire, was a board director and shareholder of Kalingorsk and reputedly Dubachov's right hand man. Further research uncovered these organizations to be funders and supporters of the New World Order, a conspiracy group which promotes the idea that there would come to pass the emergence of a totalitarian world government. The one element puzzling Loris was the huge sums of money involved were beyond Leitzman's means, which lead Loris to think again of Dubachov. He postulated that maybe Dubachov was involved in this conspiracy and his island purchase was part of the plan. He was quick to assert that it may be a farfetched idea but that if checking it out was not too problematic, it may be worthwhile. Both Matt and Ben agreed that Loris's investigations merited a further and closer look and decided to spend a bit of time along the Siberian coast, complimenting on is astute take on Dubachov. However, before embarking on a world trip, they suggested finding out if any of the world's security agencies were interested in Dubachov.

Their first port of call was the Bureau of Counter Terrorism in Washington DC and the use of their power of enhanced vision was richly rewarded. Within a short time they discovered on the fifth floor was room marked as 'Of Interest', which contained a multitude of cases with varying degrees of interest to the agency. The room held files on more than three hundred active investigations. Speed reading through them they landed on one which detailed the Bureau's interest in an organization going by the name of the Peoples Liberation Front but what made this find all the more interesting was the conjecture that the Front had received substantial funds from a shell company called Petrov Mining, once owned by Kalingorsk, Dubachov's iron ore business. They next visited the National Counter Terrorism Security Office in the UK and found other thin strands of information which connected the movement of funds from Dubachov or Leitzman to extremist entities in various countries, all were current but none appeared to be live actions. With many foreign security agencies sensitive to sharing their intel, getting a full picture is often missed. With their ability to piece together additional information gleaned from counter terrorism divisions in several countries, they became more convinced there was a plot in the making.

They returned to the Summer House to brief Loris on what they had found and he agreed that it was certainly worth pursuing. They formulated a plan as to what they hoped to achieve on a visit to Koristan Island and rested for the night, departing early next day. They were surprised to learn the island was in fact a defunct volcano and a view from above revealed a harbour and a few nearby domestic as well as commercial buildings. Moored up in the harbour was what looked like a less than sea worthy container vessel, being worked on, with welding sparks appearing from inside the vessel and grinders working on deck. Further back from the harbour was a substantial fortress looking building, which they guessed from spotting a swimming pool, was where Dubachov lived. Closer inspection of the volcano crater revealed that a tunnel had been blasted from the outside into the lower part of the crater and only by using their enhanced vision could they detect light emitting from inside the crater. They moved into the crater where they were astonished to see a two-story building had been erected but the exterior was disguised to resemble hardened lava and only the smallest escape of light gave its true identity away. The tunnel lead into the rear of the building and on entering, their first impression was of a storage facility, as the ground floor the surface was roughly hewn and with locked cages containing metal cases, which they would inspect later. The first floor contained sparse living quarters and a large open plan office wherein fifteen workers sat hunched over terminals, typing furiously.

On closer inspection, it appeared that each operative was entering figures, adding to reams of financial data, which was currently meaningless to both Matt and Ben. Just before moving on, Matt stopped and returned for a further look. Ben asked him if he had made any sense as to what they were processing and he said maybe he had. Each terminal was dealing with a different foreign currency, which told Matt which country it represented. He also reasoned that they could usefully employ copying the data stored on each terminal and told Ben they should be present when the operatives logged on, to copy the passwords doubtlessly used. He stored that information and they moved up to the second floor on which there was just one room, guarded by two heavily armed men, brandishing hand held machine guns. Entering through a fortified chamber they were confronted by who they can only assume, was Lennox Dubachov himself, seated on a throne like chair at the head of a marble top table. Despite being invisible, they both felt intimidated by his ferocious demeanour. This huge barrel of a man was dressed in a shiny silver grey suit with an open collarless white shirt, with the top three buttons open and a healthy bush of curly silver hair protruded, he had a short fat neck topped with a shiny bald head. He had small but intense eyes which bore down on the three other occupants seated around the table, with a look of both anger and contempt. Once again they were grateful for the newfound linguistic abilities and could understand the Russian dialect being spoken. The conversation covered the operation of this nerve centre but not exactly its purpose. He was issuing demands to one quaking individual to find more men to work on the vessel but saying they must have experience, he didn't want just more muscle. They decided that the vessel in the harbour required a closer inspection. This individual was dismissed and rushed from the room and the next in line began to read information from an electronic note pad. Matt hovered behind him and saw a list of code names on the screen but with country designations alongside, he immediately realized and told Ben, these countries were the same as those listed on the terminals on the floor below. He scrolled to the next page and Matt was treated to list of the same countries but with numbers attributed to them, which it became clear were numbers of recruits who were termed combat ready. On hearing the numbers, Dubachov angrily demanded that he expected the number of recruits to be far higher, considering the fortune he had invested. Ben was next to the third man, who had not said anything but now produced his own note pad. The numbers man was dismissed with orders to accelerate recruitment and the last remaining individual waited until the door had closed before he spoke. He appeared to be in charge of security and intelligence, his first report disclosed weaknesses of security of the units operating out of three territories and Dubachov ordered him to deal with it with extreme urgency, a leak, he added with portentous tones, could jeopardize the entire operation. It appeared that every unit acted autonomously and as they learned more they realized Dubachov had been stringent in ensuring they could not be traced back to him, he wanted them surgically removed, if there were any signs of exposure. Finally, he asked how near completion the vessel was and was told the final fitting out would be completed by the end of the following month. They were unable to learn what the vessel was to be used for but felt it was integral to their plans. When Dubachov was left alone they returned to the first floor for another detailed reconnaissance. They now saw various operatives initiating investment buy or sell orders and when doing so a company name was logged, different for each operator. They made a note of the territories and company names for further analysis. Dubachov had obviously invested vast sums in nominee names and doubtless covered by the secrecy of tax shelters.

Their last port of call was the ground floor cages and the metal chests, which on closer inspection were found to contain a veritable arsenal of weapons. There was everything from small arms to heat seeking missiles and grenade launchers and everything in between. They decided they had best return to base and begin to disseminate all the information they had seen and heard.

When they arrived home, Loris was, as per normal, in the comms room but now surrounded by a mountain of books. He had been online and had purchased a large number of books, covering a multitude of subjects, ranging from global politics to black holes. He laughed when seeing their astonished faces at the pile of reading matter and told them he had many years of catching up to do. They gave him a brief outline of their trip and suggested after they rest and clean up, they get something to eat and discuss the next steps. Loris smiled at the less than subtle hint and told them chicken stir fry will be about thirty minutes. As they sat and ate, they agreed that the subject they had not discussed was why a highly successful businessman, with no prior involvement in politics, should embark on an all or nothing attempt, to take over fifteen sovereign territories. Ben suggested that perhaps, with the territories representing in excess of nine hundred and thirty million people, more than ten per cent of the world's population, maybe Dubachov viewed this escapade as a stepping stone to world domination. Matt and Loris thought about this extraordinary idea and it was Loris who postulated that mad men are prone to doing the most inexplicable things.

Another wonderful surprise for Matt and Ben when they returned and a delight for Loris was he was now experimenting in the kitchen. He apologised and said this was the first time he had ever cooked anything but both Matt and Ben agreed that his chicken stir fry was first class, the vegetables where crunchy and the chicken tender with just the right amount of garlic and ginger in the sauce.

Matt said that before they start discussing the trip, Loris should consider taking driving lessons and he could then shop for household provisions, rather than relying online for everything and it would also provide an excuse to get out of the house. On to business and Loris sat silently as between them they appraised him of everything they had learned. It was agreed, as with all of their endeavours, that it was necessary to obtain a significant amount of tangible evidence, prior to contacting the relevant authorities. In this case, whilst they were developing a general picture of what Dubachov was up to, they were woefully short of establishing finite details of what the plan was. They all agreed that a further in depth visit was required but this time perhaps they could copy some files from the computers they saw, to build the evidence pack they needed.

Before retiring for the night Matt and Ben sat and chatted, the subject on both their minds was how they were coping with the constant apportations, instantly moving from one continent to another, in almost the blink of an eye. They were feeling fatigued and were concerned it may be placing an excessive strain on their bodies. Considering the time line they had garnered from their last trip, they believed that if they rested for two or three days, the project would not suffer unduly. In any event, they could easily find any number of domestic matters to deal with; they had been neglecting the house or more specifically attending to those matters that make a house a home. The study still remained an unused and unfurnished room and Matt suggested they install some exercise and fitness equipment to which both Ben and Loris wholeheartedly agreed. From both online stores and a trip to

Ipswich they selected a cross trainer, a spinning bike, a rowing machine, a running track and some free weights. In fact such was the volume of items on their shopping list that two trips to town were required. The three of them had the first day out to Ipswich and came home late in the day, laden with a host of items ranging from cooking utensils and a collection of electrical items from the small to the large. The largest was an enormous top of the range television, which Matt set up the minute they were home. The next day Matt returned to town on his own and ordered for delivery the kit he had not sourced online, plus exercise mats and medicine balls.

At the end of the third day they both felt rejuvenated and were ready to get back to work. Before they did so, Matt had the dubious prospect of presenting his paper on the facts of an alternate habitable planet for mankind, to what was destined to be a highly sceptical audience. He travelled to Swindon with a heavy heart but determined to give it his best shot. On entering the meeting room he was not able to gauge what his associates were thinking. Richard was his normal professional self and without stepping on to the podium, he took the microphone and presented Matt's case as well as he could. He also added that in the short period he had worked with Matthew Henrick he had been nothing short of amazed at the incredible intelligence, insight and encyclopaedic knowledge of the man.

His personal sentiments aside, as intelligent and rational people, we cannot let ourselves be swayed by our prejudiced mistrust of the unknown.

It was then Matt's turn to speak and he marshalled all his resources natural and otherwise and began his uphill climb. At the end of thirty minutes, it appeared that an astrophysicist by the name of Bartholomew Fernsby had been appointed spokesman for the others. He began by heaping great praise on Matt and the contribution he had made to the advancement of their learning on all matters concerning the cosmos and space travel. The nub of what the learned Mr Fernsby was saying, was that he had no compunction in accepting the general veracity of what Matt had said but most regrettably and echoing others, he said Central Government was not in the position to divert several billion pounds that they do not have anyway. Painful as it was for Matt to hear, he had to accept that it was an expected and reasonable response. He thanked them for their thoughtful and considered opinion and made a hasty exit.

He took the long drive home and told Ben of the disappointing outcome but she too expressed the opinion that it was unlikely to have been a workable project. It was Ben's turn to cook and she made a worthy attempt at a Thai prawn curry which Loris and Matt enjoyed, although it required much iced water to quell the fire in their mouths.

The following day, after breakfast they took off for Koristan Island and made straight for the vessel in the harbour. Once inside they were able to make an educated guess as to the purpose of the work being undertaken. There were two decks, on the upper deck there were numerous cabins fitted out for single occupancy, however, the fixtures and fittings suggested that the intended occupants were not lowly crew members. Each cabin, apart from a bed not a bunk, came with silk sheets and a billowing duvet cover, plus a small bathroom with toilet, wash basin and shower. Also there was a state of the art steering and communications room with a bank of screens, which included radar and sonar monitors. What was of more interest was on the lower deck where a large conference room had been set up, inside a submersible. The submarine had been set on a slipway with its nose facing the rear of the vessel. Warranting closer inspection, they found that the aft of the vessel had been modified to provide a huge hatchway, which was set to raise giving access to the open sea, an effective escape hatch for the submarine. Matt and Ben silently conferred and agreed that an at sea conference was being planned, coupled with an escape facility.

With all the computer terminals in use, they decided to visit Dubachov's fortress office and see if there was anything of interest occurring, returning to the computer deck at night when the operatives may well have left. Dubachov was not in his office and they decided to see if he was in his fortress home. Indeed he was and a fortress it certainly was, at each of the sea facing windows was mounted a heavy duty assault machine gun but more sinister was a number of rocket propelled grenade launchers, mounted on the flat roof where several armed guards, dressed in military fatigues moved around the perimeter, looking through binoculars either out to sea or inland. They reasoned that either Dubachov was expecting uninvited visitors or was just well prepared in case any should decide to come.

The man himself was in a lavishly appointed lounge area where one wall was covered with a dozen screens, all of which were on and showing either financial indices or news channels from across the globe. Various individuals, male and female, of various ethnicities, ferried in an out of the room. One or two appeared to be tending his creature comforts and came in carrying food or drinks, whilst others came in with documents for him to sign or what looked like reports for him to read. Looking at the documents, Matt and Ben deduced many covered his requirements for the sea going summit. Whilst they were perusing the paperwork he was attending to a ringing phone in his pocket and removed a small golden cell phone. He was talking to his security and intelligence man, asking him if everybody had confirmed their attendance. Their acute hearing picked up the reply to the question which was that thirteen had confirmed and only two were outstanding. A further exchange ascertained that private planes had been chartered to ferry the delegates but Matt and Ben were perplexed at to where they were being ferried to. They reasoned that the only place a plane could land would be on the mainland, which was just four miles from the island. There were thousands of square miles of isolated land in eastern Siberia, where any activity would go undiscovered and unobserved. Further reconnaissance revealed that close to the water's edge, on the mainland, a rudimentary landing strip had been laid out, complete with cleverly disguised landing lights.

They reckoned that if they could gather the data, which charted the funding of the various groups and the groups identities, they would be a long way towards building their case. Conserving their energy, Matt and Ben found an empty cottage, doubtless belonging to one of the workers, close by the harbour and rested up, keeping a watching eye to ensure they were not disturbed by a returning resident. As darkness fell, they revisited the floor of terminals and saw that many of the operators had left but a small number remained. They waited patiently and when finally they were alone, they retrieved the passwords they had previously noted and stealthily moved along the row of terminals, inserting memory sticks and copying large troves of data. Their enhanced mental abilities allowed them to scan the information and ensure that only what they considered of value was copied. Such was the volume of data, it was late into the night when they had finished their work and stored the drives, returning home. Both being exhausted, they took to their beds and left it until the following day before downloading the information they had.

At breakfast they briefed Loris on the previous day's exploits and he became quite animated with enthusiasm at the prospect of what was being uncovered. They had set the downloads in progress whilst they ate their poached eggs and complimented Loris on his rapidly improving culinary skills. They had set up a terminal on a desk in the lounge and sat around the screen waiting for the downloads to complete. When finally complete, they all silently read and Matt slowly scrolled from document to document and page to page. They now had comprehensive details of the fifteen countries and tried to find a link between them. Covering diverse parts of the globe, the fifteen were the United States, Brazil, Bolivia, Argentina, Belarus, Romania, Ukraine, Libya, Niger, Kazakhstan, Uzbekistan, Mozambique, Angola, Myanmar and Vietnam. To say they were aghast would be an understatement, although what they read was reinforcing what they had suspected. The evidence they now possessed proved that Dubachov was funding, via shell companies, fifteen individual organizations, in fifteen territories across North and South America, Europe, Middle East, Asia and Africa, sufficient to equip and train large groups of militias, for a co-ordinated day of insurrection in the name of a new world order. Many of the documents were headed with the name of The Peoples Liberation Front. They sat in silence, contemplating the enormity of what they had discovered.

Loris suggested a fresh pot of coffee and they once again poured over the detail of the plans they had before them. They logged the bank accounts and stock portfolios, showing the combined wealth of the enterprise, which ran to several billion dollars. Surprisingly, Dubachov had committed to record the details of the arms stores by territory, believing that on an isolated, heavily armed island in the East Siberian Sea, their secrets were safe. At that point Loris sat back in his chair and put into words what the others had been thinking, Dubachov had invested in preparation for an all-out global wide insurrection.

Importantly, they had surmised that the delegates to the summit each represented the fifteen countries and their travel arrangements had been planned with a great deal of subterfuge, to ensure that anybody with an unhealthy interest in their movements would be thrown off the trail. They read that that for each delegate, a holiday destination had been arranged or an overseas business trip. Either way, no delegate would board their final flight to Siberia, from their home country and when they did travel, their individual arrivals would span a fortnight. It would also be the first time that the delegates had met each other although they knew the movement was worldwide they did not know the names or identities of the other players. It became apparent as they read and re-read the data, the crucial piece of missing information was the day the plan of action was to take place. However, they did discover that the vessel was to be named New Horizon and to fly a flag of convenience, designating Libya as its registered home. It would be registered as a cargo vessel and would set sail on the 23rd of October, which was six weeks hence. They were unable to discover what course the vessel was to take but decided they would be on board when it sailed.

They considered they were getting closer to having sufficient information and evidence, to place it in the hands of those able to stop the plan going live. However, such was the enormity of the enterprise and the number of participants, they were concerned that the governments involved may not be galvanized into action in time. They deliberated how they may guarantee that all their work would ensure a just result. It was Ben who stunned the other two with a radical proposal when she suggested that they produce a comprehensive dossier for distribution to the fifteen leaders of the countries involved but in order to convince them of the genuine emergency they faced, she and Matt should appear before them, from invisibility to visibility. Before Loris and Matt could speak, she added that they would need to ensure their identities were secure and would need to adopt perfect disguises and suggested becoming Philadrons.

After due consideration Matt and Loris warmed to the idea with Matt saying immediately that if he was pushed to give a name, he would call himself Yamnus and Ben responded, she would call herself Ukvul.

CHAPTER 13

THE WORLD IS STUNNED

Once the three had digested the magnitude of what they intended to do, they agreed it would need a lot of very careful planning. If they were to continue to intervene in large-scale criminal and nefarious activities, the unfathomable consequences of their presence would become harder for all concerned to deal with. In addition, in order to get slow or recalcitrant governments to act, they would have to be confronted with a very compelling argument and a visit by beings from another planet could just do the trick. They set about discussing how to ensure this earth-shattering event was executed with the utmost care and attention. In this regard they needed to create the persona they would use. Whatever items they would use for their disguise must be acquired with zero chance of traceability. Ben sourced two long brown wigs of a perfect texture of silkiness and by the application of her newly acquired skill of molecular moulding turned them into pure white. Matt applied the same skill when purchasing from an opticians, two pair of coloured contact lenses, which he morphed into the startling green of the Philadrons.

Their skills with latex needed practice, which also

required blending a white dye with the latex to arrive at the perfect Philadron complexion. After several attempts they had produced the masks to completely hide their humanoid features and identities. They purchased rolls of suitable cloth in a local haberdashers, to cut and make the tunics and robes they had seen on Philax 10 and Ben set about, changing the colour, cutting patterns and making up the garments. They reasoned that even if there was the merest perception of a disguise, their appearing out of thin air would so disarm their target that any such doubts in this direction would be completely deflected.

They auditioned for Loris in character, hoping that he was able to detect the smallest error in appearance which they could correct. After painstakingly getting into character they stood in the lounge and called for Loris. He appeared at the doorway to the comms room and stopped dead in his tracks. From his look of total astonishment they realized their disguise worked perfectly. When they made their final appearance they would communicate telepathically and so no voice recognition investigations could unmask them.

The plan of action was to obtain the personal phone numbers of the individuals they would be visiting. Their first contact would be a telephone call but with the use of a voice synthesizer. The call itself would cause various degrees of total disbelief, shock and alarm and the words used must be carefully crafted for maximum effect. Firstly, they must locate their target, without a visible presence, check the details of their movements and current location and study their personal effects. They must also convey that they mean no harm but at the same time assert that they bring information of great importance and should be listened to. All this must be achieved whilst dealing with the mindboggling fact that these targets were being confronted by an alien from a planet many light years distant. By disclosing some of the very personal information they had collected it would further demonstrate their abilities. They realized that each situation would require a tailor made performance but in each case the closing comment, during that initial phone call, would be to announce their imminent appearance before their target. The conversation would be brief but initiated by a warning that if anybody were summoned, their alien visitor would instantly disappear. They would produce a memory stick and pass it kinetically to the target, telling them what it contained, that they should immediately study the contents and contact the other leaders, whose names are listed.

They had devoted quite some time in an attempt to arrive at a compelling reason why these particular countries had been chosen and not knowing this, they felt, was a weakness on their part. Typing out two lists, they sat with an atlas each and put up various explanations, none of which filled them with confidence. The only theory that gained some traction was that there was a positive geopolitical dimension to each choice. The chosen governments and leaders were easily malleable with financial inducements or the offer of securing their continued hold on power.

They both realized that only a certain amount of planning could be put in place and that depending on how they were received would determine how they acted and what was said. They had calculated that between the two of them they could visit all fifteen territories and submit their evidence in the space of a day. However, that would depend on everybody being where they hoped and alone, a remote likelihood and quite possibly a longer time frame would need to be considered. In addition there were some territories where they suspected there were less than honourable office bearers. Such individuals would hardly be willing to comply and serious persuasive measures may be required. The speed and nature of their visits would leave no doubt that visitors from another world had arrived. The world would be electrified by the news which would doubtless be announced to the world's media, this in turn would set the world abuzz with speculation and global leaders would be conferring like never before. In turn, this would mean that Dubachov would learn the possibility that his master plan had been unearthed and so secrecy and speed of action, was of paramount importance.

The following day they ran through the whole procedure again, making some very minor changes until they believed they had arrived at a perfect set up. Matt and Ben had looked at each other, when in full alien mode and admitted they were happy they could pass off as visitors from Philax 10. Both wore ivory white, silk wigs of real hair and with the facial adjustments of ear and nose reductions and enlarged forehead, coupled with the startling green eyes, they felt this part of the plan was in place. As well as having researched the identities of the individuals they needed to meet, they had added the heads of Interpol and the UN to the list, knowing they would immediately contact the leading terrorist agencies around the world. Loris was able to collate the names and approximate locations of the target heads of government. Obviously, Matt and Ben would need to find the precise location of their respective individuals when the moment arose. They played and replayed every scenario they could think of and then more and considered their powers more than adequate to deal with any eventuality. It was now time to return to the island and see how the plans for the summit at sea were progressing.

The first thing they noticed when they arrived was that there were many more workers on the vessel, the hull was being cleaned and painted and an array of satellite dishes and aerials covered the roof of the bridge. At the nerve centre, inside the cone of the volcano, the number of guards had increased; Matt and Ben assumed that Dubachov was getting nervous as the climax to his plan drew closer. With barely three weeks remaining until the tanker was launched, they assumed that all the delegates would be arriving a couple of days prior. They were still totally in the dark as to when the dogs of war would be called to action and it may be that this summit would reveal the missing details they sort.

They next visited the first floor data entry centre, where the operatives were once again busy at their terminals, only this time the nature of their work appeared to have changed. There was no longer a ream of financial data filling the screens but instructions were being sent out to effect payments to all recruits with immediate effect. The names on the receiving end of the instructions would be the heads of the fifteen units and doubtless the delegates who would soon be arriving.

Dubachov was alone in his fortified office, yelling into a mobile phone but not in his native tongue, they were surprised that he was now speaking fluent English. They picked up that he was speaking to an American who was complaining that his men were angry at not being paid. The two watchers gleaned from the conversation that there were in excess of five thousand militiamen in North America and were quite surprised at the number and could only wonder at what the final worldwide tally of fighting men would amount to. Dubachov voiced strong assurances that as they spoke, the transfers were being made and would be received before they met.

Matt and Ben left and reappeared on the landward side of the island, where no dwellings or activity was based. Matt suggested to Ben that now would be good time to check up on the level of activity in each territory. They had the details of the main protagonists and would be able to locate them and discover the finer details to add to their evidence files. These files would enable each government to pinpoint the full extent of what their relevant authorities would be up against. To make best use of the time available they decided to split the countries between them, Matt would take those based in North and South America and part of some of Eastern Europe and Ben the Middle East, Asia, Africa and the remainder of the eastern European collection. With the next steps agreed they returned home and told Loris of their final plans. He was concerned with the amount of work they had given themselves but they argued it was vitally important and the workload was manageable.

Within a fortnight, exhausted but with the job done, they sat and collated the information they had collected. They had noted the extent of the various bases of operations and the major participants for each territory and calculated that all told there were in excess of thirty five thousand armed mercenaries scattered across the territories, all in an advanced state of readiness for an insurrection and turning a new world order conspiracy into a reality. In addition they had located the vast majority of the stockpiles of armaments and they began the task of collating the wealth of information they had gathered and asked Loris to data entry it all and then download the information onto memory sticks. Despite being exhausted Matt and Ben appeared buoyed up from their travels and swopped stories of the most challenging encounters, Loris listened, completely captivated. Starting in Texas, Matt found the US contingent in a massive cattle ranch twenty miles west of San Antonio; he recounted being initially mystified at arriving and just seeing a vast head of cattle being herded and a busy farm in operation. It was an excellent cover, many of the farm hands were nothing of the sort and only on checking the barns did he find many of them had been converted into living quarters and storage dumps but no way were there five thousand men in situ and he ended up visiting three other states and eight different locations to track most of them, three days' work in all.

The most interesting, was his trip to Brazil and the Mato Grosso, there was a fully equipped military base in the middle of some impenetrable jungle, accessed only by air and housing upwards of two thousand men. The smaller destinations, such as Belarus or Uzbekistan, were a breeze but he was suspicious by the encampments, which were not exactly situated out of sight. This led him to believe they operated with the tacit approval of highly placed government operatives.

For Ben's part, she chose Libya worthy of note, located a hundred miles inland from Benghazi, there were a thousand heavily armed militiamen being rigorously trained in searing temperatures and with state of art weaponry on display. She also mentioned how impressed she was at the discipline and training she witnessed in Vietnam, at a camp in the southeast and approximately seventy miles inland from the coastal town of Nha Trang. With several thousand square kilometres of rugged and unpopulated land, it was easy to hide a well-camouflaged encampment. Ben had toured the camp and took stock of three Russian built Hokum attack helicopters, a large tarpaulin covered area under which there were no less than fifty assorted jeeps and armoured personnel carriers, a stock of armaments sufficient to take over a small country, including a large number of hand held surface to air missiles and too numerous to count, stocks of grenades and launchers and machine guns. The militiamen, numbering in excess of two thousand, were vigorously training from dawn until dusk, at which point they appeared to enjoy an abundance of appetizing looking food, cooked over open fires.

Both had the presence of mind to return with a large number of photographs, adding further compelling evidence as to the strength of the movement. They now were happy to conclude that following their ultimate visit to East Siberia and the summit at sea, they would produce the memory sticks to be given to the designated country leaders. Matt mentioned to Loris the need to wipe the memory sticks clean of fingerprints.

With several days remaining before the need to return to the island, Matt and Ben attended to outstanding personal affairs and both welcomed the refreshing feeling of normality. They brought their individual workloads up to date and after three days were ready to continue with the urgent matter of Lennox Dubachov. With the 26th just four days hence, they decided to go to the Island to be there when the delegates arrived, there would doubtless be additional data they could add to the files.

They had located one of the small dwellings near to the harbour that was in a bad state of repair and was not currently occupied, however, it suited them as a resting place where they could assume their physical form whilst waiting. Their heightened hearing picked up the sound of the first jet arriving and they moved quickly to see it touchdown and to witness a small welcoming party escorting two delegates to a launch moored at the water's edge. The weather in eastern Siberia fluctuates between frigidly cold winters to blisteringly hot summers and whilst late October was not the dead of winter, it was seriously cold at a bone chilling minus four degrees centigrade. The new arrivals hurriedly disappeared into the small cabin on the launch, for the choppy trip to the island. Over the ensuing days they watched as the other delegates arrived, to be currently housed in Dubachov's citadel home. He acted as the consummate host, with copious amounts to eat and drink. He missed no opportunity in gathering them around and holding court, telling them their names would go down in history as the creators of a new and more just world which would overthrow the corrupt and tyrannical rulers who had so subjugated their people. Matt and Ben listened attentively to his spouting rhetoric but were unsure how much his audience truly took to heart. When alone, they suggested, they were just as likely to be joining the insurrection as a means of achieving greater personal positions of power and wealth.

A final dinner was held at which Dubachov announced that tomorrow being the 26th they would board the New Horizon for its maiden voyage. As Matt and Ben looked on at the feast, they realized they had not eaten for a while and decided to raid the kitchen when everybody was in bed. Early the next morning, in driving rain, the delegates were led in a line to the New Horizon, which Dubachov pointed out that for security reasons would be their home for the next two days. They would sail around the East Siberian Sea where no other shipping ventures and only communication satellites pass overhead. Matt and Ben agreed that in the time it took, Dubachov had done a good job in turning the rusty vessel they had first seen, into a rather good looking leisure tanker. There were nods of approval from the delegates as they were shown to the cabins but Dubachov was eager to show them his most impressive modification, the submersible conference room. On being presented with the strange sight, more than one of the delegates voiced concern. At this Dubachov's short fuse was lit and he angrily told them he had spent a fortune to ensure they were safe and protected. In the most unlikely event that their gathering was interrupted, despite all the precautions he had taken, it was remotely possible that a three hundred and fifty meter long vessel may well be spotted from the sky. He bellowed that the holds were full of agricultural machinery and the crew had manifests to show they were on legitimate business and were circling whilst carrying out repairs. In the remote possibility that they discover on their radar unwelcome vessels, the submarine will launch from the aft of the New Horizon and can be out of sight, under water within ten minutes. There are sufficient provisions to last for a short submerged journey around the coast to a secluded place of safety. He laughed at their discomfort and told them their concerns were ill founded. He led them to the side of the sub where a set of steps had been placed next to the conning tower. The hatch was open and he squeezed his huge bulk through the opening and climbed down. There were a collection of grunts and groans as several of the larger delegates struggled with the reverse access through the hatch and down the narrow ladder inside. The meeting room was comfortably appointed, with leather padded conference chairs and a well-stocked drinks trolley close by. When everybody was seated, with Dubachov at the head of the table, he pressed a button on a small control pad at his fingertips and a smartly dressed man of Asian appearance entered. He introduced Hassan, who was armed with an order pad, he told his guests that they could chose from a wide variety of tea and coffee or numerous wines and spirits. Hassan moved around the table and took orders and departed, the armed guard who had been posted outside, secured the door.

Dubachov produced a stack of folders that he had retrieved from the floor by his chair and slid them individually across the table. The personal files would be handed back to him when they disembarked and were not to leave the New

Horizon, however, they were at liberty to take them to their cabins for closer study when they adjourned. Each file, he continued, contained the full picture of the strength of the Peoples Liberation Front. They were all aware of the forces within their own country or territory but up to this point had no idea, in global terms, what the Front amounted to. There was silence as Dubachov spelt out the global reach of the Front and allowed them to digest the extent of what had been achieved. Proceedings were interrupted by a knock on the door and Hassan entered with the drinks order. Matt and Ben could see by the looks on the faces around the table that none of them had any idea the scale of what Dubachov had planned and each had a looks ranging from disbelief to fear. As discontented individuals, without the ability to make the political or economic changes they wanted, it was no surprise that when approached by somebody who showed great sympathy at their frustrations and offered large sums of money to build up the support to make the changes they wanted, they were only too willing to go along. He told them to save their bedtime reading as he wished to speak to them about other matters not contained within the files. The room was once again secured and the two eavesdroppers were extremely interested to learn of Dubachov's plans to co-ordinate the calls to action they had been developing as individuals. He asked each delegate in turn to give a brief assessment as to strengths and battle readiness of their individual forces. Matt and Ben listened and despite having witnessed first-hand the extent of the forces being gathered, they found what they heard quite chilling. After the last of them spoke, Dubachov suggested that when the world was in a festive mood and collective minds had turned to peace and good will, then Christmas Day would be the perfect time to take back control and ring in the changes they wanted. As he wandered off topic and began moralizing on the justness of their cause, Matt and Ben began looking through the files, which lay on the table top, making careful mental notes of relevant facts and figures. What neither of them expected to see and what Dubachov wanted them to discover in the solitude of their cabins, was contained at the back of each file. The last pages contained a summary of the all the money that each of them had received from the movement, together with details of meetings they had attended over a period of three years and with people whose names would be well known to the authorities of their respective countries. Finally, was the stock list of the armaments and where the items were stored which in several cases were in premises that could be traced back to each respective delegate. Dubachov had no need to spell out exactly why he had brought these personal details to their attention but by doing so, their loyalty and obedience to the cause was assured. Matt told Ben that at the first opportunity they should attempt to obtain copies of those files.

They decided to return to the island and talk over the full ramifications of what they now knew and what should be added to the evidence pack. They appeared in Dubachov's secure office, knowing it was locked tight and nobody dare enter without his presence. They helped themselves to a drink from his drinks cabinet and sat in silence to gather their thoughts. Matt summarised the tangible evidence they now had. It amounted to details of every cell of the People's Liberation Army, who was in charge, the names of every mercenary or militiaman on their payroll and the extent and location of the armaments plus crucially, a clear path for the flow of hundreds of millions of dollars. This was all supplemented by the paper trail, through emails, bank details and account numbers plus signatories, which connected the dots back to Dubachov. They now had the call to action on Christmas Day when they believed the world's attention would be focused elsewhere.

Exhausted and in need of rest and some creature comforts they decided to head back home and update the files they were to hand over, with the latest information they most recently gathered. They had paid no attention to the time difference between Siberia and Suffolk but realized instantly that it was the middle of the night and the house was in total darkness. They whispered goodnight to each other and both collapsed into bed with barely enough time to get undressed before both were sound asleep.

Matt heard, before he was totally conscious, a light tapping on his door. Loris poked his head in and placed a steaming cup of coffee on his bedside table. Matt croaked his thanks and Loris laughed, saying he knew it was not a night on the town that had brought Matt home in such a condition. He said he had left a cup outside Ben's room, not wanting to go into her room and Matt said he would take it into her. It was a slow start for the duo and mid-morning before they appeared washed and dressed. Loris was busy in the comms room and Matt prepared them a light breakfast. They suggested to Loris that when he had some time that they get together and they would update him with all the additional intel they had collected and he could add it to the files they were to present. Whilst the action was two months hence, Matt suggested that some of the countries did not have the most efficient law enforcement departments, not to mention the added problem of corrupt Law enforcement departments and Matt stressed that they would need as much time as possible. Loris added that in the case of the three South American countries involved, it would be well advised to inform the international community of all the relevant facts so that they may put additional external pressure on those areas of weakness. Loris suggested that would be Interpol and the United Nations. With the large sums of money that Dubachov had spread around, they were sure corrupt ministers would be on his payroll and doubtless some involved in law enforcement.

Loris busied himself preparing files and transferring information onto memory sticks, meanwhile Matt suggested to Ben an interesting alteration to their attire. If they could be lengthened by maybe a meter plus, when they both appeared they could levitate a meter off the ground and give the appearance of being up to three meters tall, an impressive sight, providing the robes were long enough to settle on the ground, the illusion would work. If they moved it would appear that they floated and they both enjoyed the idea of the spectacle.

Whilst they could get away with producing their evidence pack in six languages to cover the fifteen territories, it still took Loris three long days to produce the finished article. The relative speed with which Matt and Ben could make their presentations would ensure that each candidate believed it was a simultaneous release but when they inevitably compared notes, they would be totally mystified as to how they each saw the same identical beings at more or less the same time.

They divided the list between them and considered that there was no more they could do. After calculating the time differences, allowing for delays due to not being able to comfortably confront an individual, who may be indisposed for any one of a number of reasons, they reconsidered how long the operation would take and felt that they should be able to reach the most important people within two or maybe three days. They suggested one more good night's rest and they would set out on the final leg of their mission.

The two were up early the next day and were in character when Loris came downstairs, he stopped on the bottom step and stared. With all seriousness, he said that despite seeing them adopt their alien persona previously, right now they would leave anybody they confronted utterly speechless. Without speaking they thanked him, he wished them good luck and told them he would mount the radio to listen for any breaking news, once they had launched this final phase.

Matt's last words to Ben was to call him if she needed help and with that he disappeared, heading for The White House in Washington to meet with President Henry Logan whilst Ben decided her first port of call would be Tuan Ngo the President of Vietnam. Matt found President Logan finishing his breakfast and about to go to his office. He watched as he kissed his wife and young daughter, put on his jacket and told the secret service man waiting outside his door that he was going to the Oval office. As he took the short walk downstairs his phone rang and he reached inside his jacket to take a call that would remain with him for the rest of his life. Ensuring the President was alone, Matt launched into his rehearsed speech, which appeared to do the trick, synthesized to sound suitably off worldly, the President appeared both momentarily shocked but also understandably apprehensive, as he listened to the detailed personal information Matt possessed. As he reached the Oval office, he met his head of security waiting to see him and Matt decided to leave him in no doubt as to the seriousness of his intentions. Before the President opened his mouth, his phone rang again and Matt watched as he looked at his phone and for one second hesitated but decided to accept the call. Matt cautioned him not to talk to the security man and that he should enter his office where they would meet. The President looked furtively around knowing he was being watched and his security man questioned the President's alarm. He fobbed off the man and rushed into his office, once again looking around before closing the door and at that precise moment, Matt appeared, standing in front of the fireplace, peering down at the President of the United States. There was an audible intake of breath as the President stared at the giant of a being with long white silken hair and startling green eyes. Matt made an attempt, as best he could, to put the man at ease, which was no easy matter, as he spoke to him telepathically. The President shakily found a seat not taking his eyes off Matt and momentarily found his voice. Barely able to speak, he managed to strain out the obvious questions at Matt, who he was and where was he from. Calmly Matt explained he was from a distant planet many light years from Earth and they had studied his planet. His visit had been prompted by the discovery of a troubling situation which he described as being an armed rebellion about to be unleashed, the likes of which his planet had not seen for many decades. Matt smiled as a jumble of panicked words once again flowed from the President and he suggested that the President just listens. He proceeded to outline the advancing danger from the Peoples Liberation Front and the enemy within. As if from thin air a memory stick appeared and floated from where he stood onto the President's desk, he was urged to look at the contents immediately and to act accordingly. He told the president they would meet again and his final words were that they would be contacting the other world leaders and urged him to do likewise. With that he bade him farewell and he vanished but remained in the office long enough to see the President remain behind his desk, staring at the spot where Matt had been standing. He breathed a huge sigh of relief before opening a lower desk drawer and removing a bottle of bourbon and a glass, after downing a large measure he then took a lap top from a top drawer and inserted the memory stick and scanned the contents. Now somewhat more composed, he began hitting the keys on his phone, demanding to see his chief of staff plus the head of the Army, Marine Corp, Navy, Air Force and Space Force. Such a summoning caused uproar at the White House but the President kept tight lipped. Satisfied by what he had heard, Matt left.

Ben's activities were no less dramatic; her arrival in Hanoi found President Ngo in a limousine on his way to meet the British Ambassador. He was alarmed when his mobile rang as very few people outside his family had the number. Beth followed their preprepared script, speaking in synthesized English which she knew he spoke fluently and divulging detailed information about his personal effects down to the amount of money in his wallet. The President was aghast and readily listened to what she said. He was told that when he arrived at the British Embassy, he should ask for a private room to attend to some extremely urgent business. In watching his demeanour, she believed he was more curious than anything, having been given information that should have been impossible for anybody to know. Once in the room he had requested, his phone rang again and Ben spoke a few calming words of peace and goodwill, including the fact that she would appear imminently. When she did appear, towering over the diminutive Vietnamese, his curiosity rapidly turned to a mixture of shock, fear and disbelief. He began jabbering in Cham, his local dialect and Ben instantly stopped his talking by transferring the memory stick from her hand across the room into his. With placid obedience, he withdrew a tablet from his briefcase and inserted the memory stick. She assumed the contents would set in motion the necessary response and it did. She explained that they would meet again and once again that her presence on earth was to aid mankind. The President stood wide eyed as Ben vanished and he rushed from the room, yelling into his phone that an emergency meeting of the heads of all the security services, including the army and air force, be called.

Within moments she arrived at her next port of call, which was Myanmar and located President Thint Myant-U who was shut in his presidential office taking an urgent call from his Vietnamese counterpart. This struck Ben as perfect opportunity and she waited until the disbelieving president had completed his call and she called him on his cell phone. She followed the generally scripted introduction but adding what she had just seen, telling him of the conversation he had moments ago made his jaw drop and so it remained as she appeared in front of him. He needed little convincing as to the veracity of her words and was quickly calmed and galvanized into action, summoning his generals and making international calls.

Without little trauma she was able to shock and stun the heads of state in Angola, Mozambique, Niger and Libya.

Matt was equally as successful in speeding on from the US to Brazil, Bolivia, Argentina and across the globe to Belarus, Romania, Kazakhstan, Uzbekistan and vitally to Lyon to visit Interpol, specifically to meet Secretary General Pierre Arnaut the current head. He was seated in a grand office on the top floor of a modern building overlooking the river Rhone which dissected the city. A serious man in his sixties with a full head of silver hair, he had on receiving Matt's call, immediately grabbed a red phone on his desk, which Matt had disconnected. Matt counselled him to remain calm and not to call for assistance, it would be greatly disadvantageous to many. The remainder of the brief conversation prepared him for Matt's appearance. Whilst it could never be said than any of the people he confronted had readily accepted what he told them, his appearing and disappearing, telepathic communication and telekinetic skills, left them in no doubt that they were in the presence of something inexplicable. However, in the case of monsieur Arnaut, Matt detected an almost ready acceptance and a hint of excitement, at the encounter. He made the point of informing the Secretary General that when whatever forces take the Horizon, they should locate and pass to him, fifteen files containing pivotal information about each of the head insurrectionists

His last visit was to New York and the offices of the United Nations and he arrived at the New York headquarters in time to hear Secretary General Samir issuing urgent demands to the nine members on the list of fifteen, to meet for a critical closed session meeting but told them to, by whatever means, bring to the meeting the Ambassadors from the remaining six countries. Matt was impressed by what he heard. The fact that he made the calls personally convinced those he called of the import of the matter. Matt could see he was ticking off the Members as he made the calls and had reached the last of them when Matt decided to call the Secretary on his personal cell phone. Startled to be receiving a call on this device, he hurriedly answered, thinking it was perhaps a personal matter and was visibly perplexed to be listening to a strange voice reciting the details of the phone calls he had just made moments ago. Having gained his attention, Matt then gave brief but intimate clues of the Dubachov plot and finally dropped the bombshell as to who he was. Despite all that Matt had said, it was obvious the Secretary General of the UN was not about to accept that he was speaking to a being from another planet. Although he told Matt he had been forewarned by several members of the UN that they had been visited. Matt noted his reticence but told the Secretary that they would meet imminently and described the office plus the exact point where he would appear, in less than five seconds. The line went dead and the Secretary General was about to make an internal call when Matt appeared, looming over his target but not in any menacing way but merely placing his hands together in a greeting. He telepathically continued to assure the Secretary General that he would likely have been informed that his mission was one of peace and that he must now urgently deal with potentially the most violent acts, which are planned to occur in fifteen nations of his world. As the he listened, too stunned to speak, a memory stick glided across the space between them and landed in front of him. Matt told him that he knew he had been informed by several members as to the details of the planned insurrection but he now had a most comprehensive evidential package from which to mount a combined action to ensure the plot was foiled.

A seasoned politician of several decades Secretary General Samir gathered enough of his senses to inquire who Matt was and where he was from, as he inserted the stick into his computer. He was told that the being in front of him was Yamnus from a distant planet unknown to those from Earth but he had become familiar with humankind over several millennia. Before leaving, Matt said they would meet again and he disappeared, remaining invisible and watching as he made an internal call to find out how many Members and Ambassadors had arrived, whilst staring at his screen with a look of alarm. He was told all but two had arrived and they had called ahead to announce they were minutes away. Matt decided his work was completed and headed home to find Ben and Loris in excited conversation as momentous acts were unfolding in the seats of power across the world. Loris said that from the start of their worldwide action, every screen had lit up but as no public sighting had occurred there was scant speculation. Fortunately, thus far the Governments involved had remained tight lipped as to what they had learned. Either that or believing if they said anything, they would be ridiculed. Loris told them from what he had learned, the reaction had differed between countries. Whereas in the more developed countries there was virtually nothing to report, other than frenetic activity amongst the armed forces and intelligence networks. In other parts of the world, the leaders had not been as circumspect as to the fall out that may arise from the general populous learning leaked information, about a possible visit from aliens from another planet. In such countries variable amounts of people, from hundreds to many thousands, gathered outside Government offices demanding information but were told it was nothing more than propaganda.

When Loris had brought them up to speed, Matt and Ben compared notes to confirm how their individual visits had fared. Matt told them of his impromptu appearance at the UN and Interpol and hoped that it would be filtered in the best light possible. Loris went to the kitchen to make some coffee as Matt and Ben sat and watched the endless loop of news from across the globe. The marshalling of significant armed forces was bound to generate speculation, the mainstream media postulating on aggressive action from any one of the several more left wings states who had amassed considerable fire power. The more fringe media not wanting to be left out where developing bizarre theories ranging from a storm of meteorites heading to earth to a coronal mass injection or solar flare which threatens to interrupt or destroy every countries electronics. They admitted to not really having thought about their closed encounters creating such ramifications. They discussed if it would aid or aggravate the situation if they made an appearance.

In the meantime Matt told Ben they would need to get to the New Horizon as soon as possible. Although he was reasonably confident that in the short term, the information they had delivered would not be leaked to the media, their worry was that in the case of the less stable regimes, information would find its way to Dubachov very quickly if he didn't already know. And so after removing their outfits and taking a shower, they ate a quick meal and sort the whereabouts of the tanker.

CHAPTER 14

A FITTING END

They located the vessel to the north of Wrangle Island and heading eastwards. The delegates were either in their cabins or those who maybe were a little claustrophobic, braved the arctic temperature and wandered around the decks, all with thick coats, gloves and traditional Ushanka fur hats covering their ears and cheeks.

Although they had not yet formulated a plan on how to prevent the launch of the escape submarine, they reasoned it would be easier to trap them on-board than to do so under water. They took physical form deep in one of the holds and discussed the best was forward. Matt suggested they cripple the aft hatch, preventing the sub from transferring from the ship to the sea. They kept that suggestion in abeyance and considered further. There was a certain amount of weaponry on board, which could cause whichever force was to apprehend the group, a certain amount of trouble. Ben suggested that they first disable the larger weapons, seal all the metal boxes containing explosive devices and then look at the question of the aft opening.

317

Apart from the guards outside the sub, there were no other mercenaries below decks, allowing the two to work unhindered. Removing firing pins, blocking barrels and sealing cartridges together could be done without raising initial suspicion. As for the opening, they could see a network of cables attached to the top corners, which would hydraulically lift the aft section along a rail mounted on the roof of the deck. Following the cables lead to a motor, which they disabled by fusing all the working parts together.

At several locations around the upper deck they found armed men peering through binoculars and with Ak-47 assault rifles slung over their shoulders. To, all intents and purposes the perpetrators appeared calm and in control. They decided during a lull in proceedings, to check on some key leaders to ascertain how their plans of action against the Peoples Liberation Army were progressing.

Matt found President Logan in his shirtsleeves, with his tie loosened and shirt unbuttoned, he was speaking in one phone and held another against his chest. He was issuing instructions to the head of counter terrorism to move on all the cells they had located in the various States with immediate effect. In the other phone he listened to the Chief of Naval Operations telling him they would arrive in the East Siberian waters in five hours' time. All this was good news for Matt and he called the President to thank him for his swift action and to tell him that the prime suspects, plus Lennox Dubachov would be contained aboard the New Horizon. In addition he decided it was good politics that he visits the Russian premier to apprise him of the US actions and assure him action was being taken under an International arrest warrant and that in the interests of détente, the Russian government should give its blessing for the swift termination of the most atrocious planned act of terrorism. He was sure he could convince the President to act accordingly. Finally, he gave him the current location and heading of the ship. The President was calmer with this encounter and wanted to know if they could meet again when this matter was concluded, so that they may become better acquainted and for the first time he asked the name of his alien visitor. Matt told him Yamnus and that he was sure they would meet again. In rapid succession he looked in on the leadership in the South American territories of interest and those of Eastern Europe. None matched the level of retaliatory action of the US but all had been contacted by Interpol and the UN and were left in no doubt that any signs of complicity or inaction would not be tolerated. With those two powerful international bodies actively involved, a high degree of positive action was taking place. He next visited President Gusin Pavlovich in Moscow and arrived with inches of pristine white snow covering Red Square. It took no time to locate the President; he was at Government House, overlooking the Moskva River and about to enter a meeting of Federal ministers. Matt dispensed with the usual introduction and made a call, the President calmly said he was aware of the rumours of visitors to Earth but had dismissed them as Western propaganda. Matt realized he was about to meet a total sceptic and with time being of the essence, he had best rapidly convince him of his misconception. President Pavlovich was striding towards the door of his office, about to leave, when Matt appeared looming over him and blocking his exit. The president leaped backwards with his mouth agape but Matt calmed him and instructed him to sit. He rapidly appraised the President of the situation unfolding on a small Siberian island and following the revelation of Matt's intimate knowledge of the Presidents most secretive business affairs plus his ability to disclose as much to the world at large, it was a painless task to extract an agreement for the Government to acquiesce to the united action against Dubachov and his cohorts and remain at arm's length.

Matt and Ben got together again at the Summer House, she was less optimistic than him and she told Matt that she was forced to intervene in Angola, Mozambique and Niger to galvanize them into more aggressive and immediate action. She at first became angry at their less than urgent attendance and decided to investigate the reasons for this attitude. She visited various leaders' homes and eavesdropped on private telephone conversations. Her snooping paid off when she tracked one national leader to a remote location and discovered him in deep conversation with a suspicious looking individual. Listening in on their conversation, she quickly ascertained that the pressure being exerted by Interpol was causing concern and that this particular leader was urging a warning be given to their compatriots. It was as they had suspected that Dubachov's money had turned less morally upright politicians and that the news of counter measures under way would soon reach the New Horizon. She decided the risk of forewarning Dubachov was too grave and intervened by effectively kidnapping the two collaborators she had witnessed. Without them having any idea what happened, she waited until they had both got into their respective motors and using her skills caused the tires of both cars to be punctured, simply by sending some nearby shards of glass to do the job, plus she sealed the doors. She left two panicked and terrified men screaming to nobody in particular.

After a brief respite they returned to the tanker and sure enough Dubachov was in a state of panic. He was at the bridge, demanding of anybody who would listen, if their position had been compromised and if the radar were picking up anything in the vicinity or in the air. He had received several calls, from a number of the territories, alerting him of heightened activity by various serious law enforcement entities. They assured him that their constant sweeps were not picking up anything but he was still not placated. He had installed a communication network throughout the vessel and he called all delegates to the conference sub together with their personal effects. Visibly disturbed at Dubachov's current state of angst and probably, Matt and Ben assumed, from his less than subtle reminder of how much under his control they must remain, they stood agitated as he told them he had unsubstantiated information that their activities may well have been compromised. As a precaution he suggested they board the submarine and he would prepare their escape launch should it prove necessary. With no dire warnings from the bridge nor any other worrying communications received, Dubachov and his co-conspirators sat and drank and nervously spoke of the forthcoming day of reckoning.

Matt and Ben were delighted to see all the perpetrators now cosseted inside the submersible and they next turned their attention to the armed guards. As the US naval forces would be in range of radar very shortly, they decided they had best attend to disarming them and waited patiently for the appropriate signal. Some fifteen minutes later they picked up that appropriate signal when the vigilant ex-Russian navy officer, who sat glued to the radar, screamed to say he had picked up a large vessel heading in their direction. They decided the most expedient manner was to use their powers of molecular reconstruction to turn the crews' weaponry into harmless implements. Accordingly, Matt started on the port side and Ben the starboard side and within a few minutes a dozen or so terrified mercenaries were seen staring at the pitchforks and garden rakes, instead of assault weapons which they threw to the deck and were seen running to the bridge. At almost the same moment, the Russian grabbed an internal radio unit, used to communicate with the submarine and reported in few words what he had seen and Dubachov asked for an estimated time of contact. The reply did not please him and he told his partners in crime, who were watching him intently, as he listened to the radio that an unidentified vessel was approaching and they should prepare to take a trip under the sea just as soon as the vessel was identified. He summoned the crew who would operate the sub to immediately prepare the vessel for launch and screamed to the bridge to open the aft hatchway. No sooner had the order been given than the bridge reported that the rear hatch motor had seized. Dubachov was incandescent with rage, telling whoever would listen that he would personally execute whoever was responsible for this failure. As an additional measure, Matt suggested they cripple the track on which the sub sat, just in case Dubachov had the maniacal idea of ramming the aft opening. This they achieved by up-ending the track to form a buffer, just as they heard the diesel motors fire into life. This was shortly followed by the engaging of the propulsion motor, the hold was instantly filled with acrid diesel fumes and the vessel shook with the vibration of the submersible motor. The mercenary guards had fled at the first signs of the sub preparing to move and Matt and Ben, effecting one final containment measure, raised a large metal container, doubtless full of arms and placed it squarely over the conning tower hatch. They looked through the hull of the sub and saw what could only be described as pure panic, there was screaming threats made in a multitude of languages and Dubachov was man handling terrified men off the ladder leading to the exit hatch and was attempting to open it, with no success. The duo now moved to the bridge and although none of the crew wore uniforms, a large man with full beard and tattooed arms, wearing a naval hat, had the bearing of seniority. He had heard the noise from below and attempted to get sense from the terrified guards who had come from below decks but he failed to understand what they were saying and ordered some men to investigate. All around was chaos, with the disarmed guards gulping vodka from bottles and talking deliriously, the crew in the bridge were ignoring them, looking

324

intently through binoculars. It was the burly Russian who swore as he realized he was looking at the USS George H.W. Bush, a Nimitz-class supercarrier destroyer, noting that it was dispatching numerous fighter jets. He turned to the others on the bridge, who had seen what he had seen, calmly telling them the game was up and not to be stupid enough to put up any resistance, he then radioed Dubachov. He moved the receiver away from his ear as Dubachov heard the grim news, screaming at the Russian to get as many men below decks to get them out of the sub.

Matt suggested Ben keep her eyes on Dubachov, as there was no telling what a trapped man may do and he would remain on the bridge to ensure the destroyer was unhindered in its approach. Within the span of the next ten minutes, Ben communicated with Matt to tell him that Dubachov was in the process of waving a pistol about and the occupants of the sub were running from the conference area trying to find hiding places. Whilst there were a number men crawling over the sub there was nothing they could do. With the conning tower jammed with an immovable object on top of the hatch and no physical means of removing it, they radioed the bridge reporting the problem. Matt told Ben that the destroyer was no more than ten minutes away and she joined him on the bridge where they clearly saw the Stars and Stripes on the huge vessel.

Approaching at full speed, with its full complement of guns all trained on the New Horizon, a loud message was broadcast advising the New Horizon prepare to be boarded. At the same time a rigid hull inflatable came powering from the concealed starboard side of the destroyer, on board sat a dozen heavily armed Navy Seals in black combat gear.

On board the New Horizon it was panic stations, all those in the bridge and the upper deck, who between them possessed nothing more than side arms, had already calculated the odds and came to the side rails with their arms aloft. As the marines began to board, Matt and Ben went below to witness a thick rope had been placed around the metal box and a half-dozen men were straining to pull it off the coming tower. It was wedged tight and they were never going to move it but feared Dubachov's ire if they didn't make an attempt. Looking through the hull, Matt noted with satisfaction that Dubachov had been overpowered by several of the others on board the sub and was tied to a chair with a gun pointed at his head; he also saw one of the delegates with a bloodied shirt and being tendered by another. He was likely as not shot by Dubachov, which caused the others to take charge. At that point Matt and Ben heard the sound of heavy footsteps descending to the lower deck. With rifles and side arms pointed, six men lead by a heavily decorated marine, approached the submarine and they quickly restrained the crew below decks and they were unceremoniously escorted onto the destroyer. They had been notified who the occupants of the submarine were and posted guards until a company of engineers could board and extricate the occupants. Without a shot being fired the New Horizon had been taken in less than thirty minutes and Matt and Ben were pleased to see before they left the scene, that one marine was seen to be carrying a stack of buff files, the very ones Dubachov had handed to his co-conspirators with their work but before they headed home Ben said she had another thought.

Ben mentioned that she had had a last minute thought and Matt was curious, asking what was on her mind. She suggested they return to Dubachov's fortress and she would explain. There was similar panic at the fortress as there was on board the New Horizon. Those ashore had obviously witnessed the arrival of the destroyer and were making hasty preparation to leave. Witnessing this activity, Ben suggested that she wait to tell him what she was about to and they just ensure nobody leaves the Island, including the workers in the offices and docks.

There were a number of craft moored in the small harbour and it was a simple task to sink them. Those who had worked swiftly to make good their escape and those about to, were horrified as one boat after another began to inexplicably take on water. The destroyer had dispatched a helicopter which was about to land near the harbour and would obviously take care of all those on land. Matt and Ben returned to the fortress and Ben began to explain that Dubachov, whilst holding vast wealth in clandestine investments, probably had reserve funds close by as an emergency stash. She imagined the State would take over the island and all other tangible assets they could find but knowing Dubachov, she felt sure he would have a safe and who knows what riches it would contain. She suggested that when the authorities eventually came to the island, there would be many corrupt individuals from the lowly foot soldiers, all the way up to government ministers, who would not hesitate in requisitioning the contents of the safe for themselves. Ben said they should prevent anything of value falling into the wrong hands and remove whatever they found of value and pass it over to Interpol. They arrived at his unoccupied private quarters and searched for a safe; their enhanced vision enabled them to locate a large combination safe behind an oil painting of the Winter Palace in St Petersburg. They both looked into the safe and together with a stack of documents that may be of interest, they also saw four large satin bags full of gems and several stacks of bank notes in various currencies plus fifteen large bars of gold. Matt told his accomplice what a sterling idea it was and they set to work opening the safe and investigating in detail the contents.

The bags contained a mixture of blue and pink diamonds, rubies, emeralds and black opals, which between them they guessed to be worth several million pounds. They didn't stop to count the cash, which consisted of a foot high stack of US hundred dollar bills, and an equal stack of hundred rouble notes. The documents appeared to be a mix of title deeds to various properties and other sundry documents, which they also decided to pass to Interpol. They were unable to transport the gold, being too heavy plus apportation only allowed them to transport items they were carrying or attached to their body. They scouted the Island and found a suitable rock and carved a small hole in it, placing the gold bars inside. Next they jointly moved a huge boulder in front of the entrance, making a note of the location.

Exhausted but pleased with their achievements, they headed for the tranquillity of home. Loris was waiting for their arrival with the latest revelations to come across the airwaves and via broadcast media. They showed him the riches they had returned with and he was stunned at the beauty of the gems and mountain of cash that they emptied on to the kitchen table. He told them there had been little let up on the continued agitation in many countries, anxious to discover more about the aliens, as the various leaks had referred to them as. There was much talk about the timely intervention of these newly arrived visitors and the headline that grabbed their attention from the newsreels and newsfeeds was 'Alien Angels Prevent Armageddon' which had taken hold in various languages around the globe. There was a constant stream of clips showing security forces and army raids across North and South America, Europe, the Middle East, Asia and Africa and shots of arms caches which the news casters estimated was sufficient to mount not just an insurrection but a global war.

Several hours after returning home, Matt had showered and was dressing, Ben was washing her hair and Loris was glued to the television but with one ear on the radio. He yelled to the other two that they may want to watch a broadcast that had been announced, from the Secretary General of the United Nations. They gathered on the couch as Secretary General Samir appeared in front of a microphone. He announced to the world that he had been in conversation with the leaders of the majority of the nations of the free world and was asked to broadcast a message they had all agreed upon. He officially declared the arrival of visitors from another planet and he spoke indirectly to Matt and Ben by thanking them deeply and sincerely for the aid and assistance they had given to the world. He went on to say that they had dispelled generations of baseless fears that if ever the day came when intelligent life should arrive, it could bring with it the end of mankind. They have shown that the world can sleep peacefully in the knowledge that they have assisted in averting an evil plot, which could have led to the deaths of tens of thousands of people. No longer would millions of people need to harbour fears and misgivings from things they did not understand and for that the world is grateful beyond words. Matt turned to Ben and could see she had tears in her eyes and he leaned over and took her hand. The broadcast ended and was once again replaced with a continuous broadcast of how the thwarting of the uprising was unfolding. Shortly after this broadcast it appeared that in every developed nation on earth, tens of millions of people took to the streets and looked to the skies. It would take some time to determine if the majority saw off-world interference in the affairs of mankind as a force for good or not

After they have watched much of what the media had to show and say, Matt suggested they deserved a holiday and he knew just the place, an idyllic timber lodge in a secluded forest, a suggestion that both Ben and Loris whole heartedly agreed to. He added it would be a suitable time to plan where next they could exercise interference in the misdeeds of others.

THE END

Published by

www.publishandprint.co.uk